In a land of fortune and fear, only love dares to hope.

South of Warrior Reef

Robert Haywood

Ark House Press
arkhousepress.com

Cataloguing in Publication Data:
Title: South of Warrior Reef
ISBN: 978-1-7645620-8-9 (pbk)
Subjects: FIC042030 FICTION / Christian / Historical;

Design by initiateagency.com

Author's Note

One of my most cherished memories is of waking up at 5.30 am in November 1960 and going up to the promenade deck of the liner *Fairsky* to catch my first view of Australia. I made my way to a spot just below the navigating bridge from where I could look out over the bow, and there it was – a long stretch of coastline emerging from the darkened horizon, and the twinkling lights of Fremantle, welcoming me to the corner of the world I'd been dreaming about.

I was 16 years old, the product of a working-class home in the industrial West Midlands of England, which still bore the scars of World War II. But for years, as in the words of a popular hit song of the 1950s, I'd been dreaming about '*faraway places with strange-sounding names*'. Consequently, when my parents decided to migrate to Australia, I was filled with excitement. Standing there on *Fairsky's* deck, watching the Australian coastline emerge from under a vast open sky lit by brilliant colours of red and gold, I could see my dreams coming true.

However, life in sunny Sydney – our final destination - pleasant though it was, wasn't quite the stuff of my teenage fantasies, fed, as they were, by the likes of Robert Louis Stevenson and Jean Paul Gaugin. Those *faraway places* had for me crystalized into two spots: the remote far-north of the continent and the nearby islands of the South Seas. They seemed so exotic and different from the gloom and grime of the West Midlands.

It was 14 years before I got my chance to go there. I was a young clergyman, completing my first appointment in a large public housing development on the outskirts of Sydney. I badly needed a break and managed to get myself a job as honorary chaplain on a couple of cruise ships (one of which was the *Fairsky*) bound for the islands of Melanesia. Sailing into Noumea one morning, I felt the same elation as when I first saw the coast of Western Australia. Since then, I've travelled extensively throughout those regions, including periods of service as an outback minister and an army chaplain. And though the feeling of romance has faded, my love for that region has not.

Forty years of exposure to its culture and history has confronted me with a different reality than the rosy picture of colonization that I learned at school. In the last quarter of the 19th century, northern Australia and Melanesia were the furthest outposts of British civilization. It was a wild and adventurous era that saw the worst of European imperialism in the brutal oppression and exploitation of natives, and the best of it in the spiritual and humanitarian endeavours of people who devoted their lives to bringing what they saw as Christian civilization to the indigenous people. Many of the latter were women, like Florence Young, a courageous young missionary who helped lead the fight against the brutal *Blackbirders,* like the notorious Captain *Bully* Hayes, who is the model for my character *Bulldog* Homer.

It also witnessed some larger-than-life characters like Frank Jardine, who helped pioneer white settlement in far north Queensland and brought law and order to that remote corner of empire, and Sana Solio, niece of Malietoa, supreme chief of Samoa. Frank met Sana when her mission schooner called at Cape York while en-route to islands where she was to work as a missionary. He fell in love with her and pursued her into the Arafura Sea, boarded the mission schooner and, much to the disapproval of her missionary companions, persuaded her to return with him to Cape York, where they reigned as uncrowned king and queen for the next 50 years. Their story provided inspiration for the characters of Michael Burns and the beautiful Sele Saena, the real hero of this story.

Port Benson, Refuge Bay and the islands of Vitu and Mabi are all fictional places, but Warrior Reef and the other places that form the stage on which this story unfolds are as they were in the late 19th Century. Viewed from the mores of the 21st Century with its disdain of European imperialism and sensitivity towards indigenous cultures, the characters that dominate *South of Warrior Reef* may sometimes seem paternalistic and racist in their attitudes. Yet to be authentic, a story must reflect the reality of the era it describes. Sele, Michael, Amelia and Geoffrey were all products of their generation. Time alone will judge them fairly, as it will us.

Robert Haywood
Wollongong, NSW, 2025

Prologue

Fifty nautical miles northeast of Cape York, Australia's most northerly point, lies an extensive area of coral known as *Warrior Reef*. It is part of the Torres Strait, a shallow stretch of water separating Australia from Papua New Guinea and linking the Coral Sea to the Arafura Sea. Prior to the advent of accurate charts, sailing those waters was fraught with danger because of the numerous reefs, sandbanks and islands, and during the latter part of the nineteenth century many ships, venturing into those uncharted waters, simply disappeared.

It is commonly believed that many of them fell into the hands of the people who inhabited those islands. Though related to the Melanesian natives of New Guinea, these people were, nevertheless, quite different ethnically and had their own unique indigenous culture. They were seafaring people with a proud warrior tradition that kept them constantly at war with each other.

But by the second half of the nineteenth century their islands – especially those around Warrior Reef - suffered an infestation by some of the dregs of European and Asian civilization - escaped convicts, former Yankee whalers, Chinese and Japanese beche-de-mer fishers, Malay slavers and other villainous cutthroats who brought untold misery to the native population. The *pearl-fever* that swept those hazardous waters in the final quarter of the nineteenth century exacerbated their misery until public opinion, often aroused by the reports of the first Christian missionaries, brought about change.

The Torres Strait islanders still celebrate those missionaries in their annual Coming of the Light Festival.

PART ONE

3 June 1878 – The Southern Ocean

They called it 'threading the eye of the needle' - navigating a ship that hadn't seen land for weeks safely through the narrow stretch of water between Cape Otway and King Island. It was the final and sometimes most perilous challenge for the masters of vessels carrying gold seekers to Melbourne - the world's latest boom town. To make this landfall successfully after weeks traversing the vast Southern Ocean required an ability to navigate by dead reckoning that took years to acquire. It was a skill that Captain Arthur Travis had developed over forty years of sailing the world's oceans but was now compromised by his inability to limit himself to one glass of rum as the sun dropped below the horizon.

The barquentine *Nancy* was ninety-seven days out of Liverpool when she made her final approach to Cape Otway, and Geoffrey Glaston was looking forward to seeing land again. He and his wife Amelia were the only passengers aboard the sturdy, three masted vessel, except for an uncouth businessman named Mundine, whose stock of rum, including eighty barrels of Jamaica's finest, occupied much of the *Nancy's* hold. Had Geoffrey known that such a cargo was to be loaded when they called in to Kingston, before heading south to catch the *Roaring Forties,* he would probably have chosen another vessel. Had he foreseen that the master of the *Nancy* would develop a boozy companionship with their fellow passenger, he would most certainly have done so. Spending evenings at sea in the company of rough men drinking themselves into insensibility was not what a young clergyman wanted his new wife to be exposed to on their long voyage to Australia.

Geoffrey climbed the steep companionway from the tiny cabin he and Amelia shared onto the *Nancy's* main deck. The last light of the winter afternoon was fading, and the first stars were already visible behind the scudding clouds. The ship was making good speed, surfing down the waves that lifted her stern before sweeping under her keel, then wallowing slightly in the following trough before the next wave repeated the action. The westerly wind that had powered them along ever since they'd entered the latitudes below forty degrees south seemed to be strengthening, evidenced by the numerous whitecaps on the waves.

'Good evening, Reverend. Mrs. Glaston not feeling well?'

Geoffrey recognized the voice and turned to see Henry White, the ship's 27-year-old first mate.

'No,' he replied. 'She's seasick again. It's this corkscrewing motion.'

'It'll ease when we pass Cape Otway and turn northeast. We'll be under the lee of the mainland then and the ship will ride much easier.'

'How long will it be before we reach Cape Otway, do you think?'

'Cap'n Travis thinks we should pass the cape early tomorrow morning. We should be 'threading the eye of the needle' tonight.'

'Isn't that dangerous at night?'

'Well, if we really are where the skipper reckons, we should sight the Cape Otway light after dark, and that will give us a bearing.'

'And if his calculations are wrong?'

'Best not to worry about that. Cap'n Travis is an experienced navigator, and he's determined to get to Melbourne the day after next.'

'But why? What difference is an extra day or two going to make?'

'Our friend Mundine has offered the captain a nice little bonus if we get to Melbourne before the *Hoylake* does.'

'The *Hoylake*?'

'She's a barquentine about the same size as *Nancy*. She was in Kingston when we were there and taking on the same sort of cargo.'

'Rum, you mean.'

'Yes; and destined for the same market - the Victorian goldfields. There's so much money being made up there that the diggers will pay almost anything for good liquor.'

'But surely there will be enough business for both shiploads.'

White shook his head. 'The problem is getting the stuff to the goldfields. Mundine will need to hire several bullock wagons to transport all those barrels, and there aren't enough teams to go round. Mundine has a rival on the *Hoylake* who is as determined as he is to get there first and relieve the miners of their gold.'

'But isn't he putting us all at risk?'

White shrugged his shoulders. 'The skipper doesn't think so. It's not the first time he's done it at night.'

'But with all this sail set and the wind freshening?'

White nodded uneasily. 'He reckons we'll pass Cape Otway before the wind gets strong enough to cause us any trouble, and by that time we should be well ahead of the *Hoylake*.'

'And what do you think?'

'I'm just the mate, Reverend. The captain gives the orders and I carry them out.'

'Well, Captain Travis might listen to me. I shall go and plead with him.'

'I wouldn't advise it. The two of them have been hard at it for at least the past hour. They won't be in a frame of mind to respect a man of the cloth.'

'I don't think I have a choice. I've got my wife's safety to think about – as well as my own.'

'Be careful, sir. He can be quite nasty when he's drunk.'

Geoffrey could hear Amelia's groans as he passed their tiny cabin. He thought about going in to tell her what was happening but decided against it, realizing it would only increase her anxiety. The captain's suite was at the far end of the passage and extended across the ship's stern. The sound of laughter coming from behind its solid oak door rose above the howl of the wind. Geoffrey knocked firmly and was gratified to hear the laughter stop.

A voice called out 'Who is it?'

'It's me, Captain Travis, Geoffrey Glaston. May I come in?'

'It's the God-botherer come for a drink.' Geoffrey recognized Mundine's voice.

A moment later the door opened and Captain Travis stood glaring at Geoffrey. 'What can I do for you, Mr. Glaston?'

'Forgive me if I sound presumptuous, Captain, but I wonder if it's wise for us to be proceeding under full sail when we're so close to land and the wind is so strong.'

'You have nothing to fear, Reverend. I've made this trip many times. I advise you to go to your cabin and get some sleep. When you wake tomorrow, we'll be in sight of land and the day after be in Port Melbourne.'

'But Captain, the wind is increasing even as we speak.

A stream of curses exploded from Travis. 'I am the master of this ship,' he shouted, and if I say we will sail on that's what we will do. Now go back to your cabin before I forget you're a clergyman.'

Geoffrey refused to be intimidated and stood his ground. 'Captain Travis, I must respectfully advise you that you are currently in no fit state to make such decisions.'

'Are you questioning my ability, sir?' Travis roared.

'I do not question your ability, Captain. But I am concerned about your capacity to make wise decisions when you've been drinking heavily.'

Mundine guffawed loudly from inside the cabin. 'He thinks you're pissed, Captain. You ought to clap him in irons for inciting mutiny.'

Travis grabbed the front of Geoffrey's coat, pulling him forward so that their faces almost touched. 'You are seriously trying my patience, Reverend Glaston. Now, return to your cabin before I take Mr. Mundine's advice.'

Geoffrey felt a surge of panic. He abhorred physical violence. But concern for his young wife overcame his fear.

'If you do not take your hands off me, Captain Travis, when we get to Melbourne, I shall personally see to it that you never command another vessel again.'

Travis bellowed with rage as Mundine staggered to his side and added to the abuse. Geoffrey flinched, waiting for the blow he was sure would come. Then he felt a hand on his shoulder and turned to see Amelia standing behind him, her face grey with nausea and her eyes wide with anxiety.

'Please, Geoffrey. Come away.'

'That's right, Mrs. Glaston. Take him back to your cabin before he causes any more trouble.' Travis released his grip.

Relief washed over Geoffrey as he turned to follow her back to their cabin, but he'd never felt so impotent. 'Forgive me for making a scene, my love, but I feel a great sense of unease about all this.'

Amelia squeezed his hand. 'God hasn't brought us this far to abandon us now, dear.'

'That's right, darlin', take him back to yer cabin. What he needs is somethin' nice and soft to take his mind off the weather.' Mundine laughed.

Travis thrust him roughly back into the cabin. 'Keep your mouth shut. I'll have none of that talk in the presence of women.'

He kicked the door shut and the two of them staggered back to their rum, leaving Geoffrey and Amelia to return to their cabin, comforting themselves that their ordeal was nearly ended.

2

4 June 1878 – Cape Otway

The sound of the ship's bell ringing continuously woke Geoffrey with a start. It was followed by a man's voice – he recognized it as Henry White, the first mate - calling all hands on deck. From up ahead he could hear the commotion caused by the rest of the crew tumbling out of their foc'sle berths and the heavy tread of someone rushing past his own cabin door.

By now Amelia was also awake. 'What is it, Geoffrey, what's going on?'

'It's nothing to worry about, my love. I suspect the captain has decided to shorten sail because of the rising wind.'

'It sounds more serious than that. Do you think we should get dressed and get up on deck?'

'You wait here, darling. Let me go up and see first.' Geoffrey pulled his overcoat over his nightshirt and stuffed his feet into his boots. 'I'll be back in a jiffy.'

As he made his way to the hatch, he heard the unmistakable voice of Captain Travis roaring out above the shriek of the wind: 'Stand-by to wear ship.'

Geoffrey poked his head through the hatchway. Through the darkness he could see men scurrying to positions, ready to man the sheets and braces that would allow the vessel to turn before the wind. He looked aft to where Travis stood staring up at the rigging and saw White grabbing his arm.

'There's too much sail up, skipper. We could lose the boom if we gybe her now.'

Travis shook his hand off. 'We don't have time to shorten sail. We're too close to a lee shore. We'll be on the rocks in minutes if we don't do it now.'

He cupped his hands to his mouth and bellowed: 'Let go the sheets and braces.' Then he nodded to the helmsman: 'Gybe-oh.'

The helmsman began to spin the wheel to bring the ship round on a new course. Travis watched the sails anxiously as they began to shimmer and then fill again as the wind swung across the ship's stern. The sailors manning the large mizzen began to ease the boom out over the port side rail, carefully taking the strain against the mounting pressure of the wind. As the long boom swung further, the pressure of the wind grew stronger, and the men began to lose their footing.

The seaman in charge yelled: 'We can't hold it, skipper. The wind's too strong.'

Travis and White ran to assist, but they were too late. The boom hurtled round as far as it could go then splintered against the mizzen mast, falling over the ship's side and tearing the huge sail.

'Get an axe and cut that boom away before it smashes a hole in the side,' Travis roared.

The coxswain was already on his way, racing to the carpenter's store. He returned with a large axe and began to swing it against the bits of rigging still connecting the shattered boom to the vessel. He leaned over the rail to get a better angle of attack when suddenly the ship gave a lurch and slewed violently to starboard. The unfortunate man lost his balance and with a scream fell over the side, vanishing into the blackness before anyone could throw him a line.

'Leave him go.' Travis shouted. 'There's nothing you can do for him.'

He turned and began to curse the helmsman for not holding a steady course.

'It wasn't me, skipper. I reckon the keel hit the bottom and pulled her around.'

Travis uttered more expletives then turned to White. 'Get up for'ard with the lead line. If the sea is shoaling, we're in real trouble.'

White ran forward calling for a crewman to join him with the lead line. They positioned themselves on the starboard bow and the sailor swung the lead weight forward into the heaving waves, letting the line out until he felt it touch bottom. Then he hauled it back in again. White looked at the markers and shouted back to the captain, 'Three fathoms, sir.'

'God help us!' Travis said quietly. 'That means there's hardly any water under our keel.'

The seaman swung the line again and hauled it in after it had struck bottom. 'Three fathoms and shoaling,' White called out.

'We must be over a sandbar,' Travis muttered. 'Put your helm hard a starboard,' he shouted to the helmsman. 'Let's hope there's deeper water there.'

The ship struck just as White called two fathoms. The force of the wind pushed her bow deeper into the sand until she was well and truly stuck, heeling steeply to port and presenting her stern to the full fury of wind and waves.

Still standing in the shelter of the aft hatch, Geoffrey felt a hand grip his arm. 'Have we run aground, Geoffrey?' Amelia's voice seemed calm enough, but her face betrayed her anxiety.

'I fear so, my love. We'd better go back to our cabin and get dressed in warm clothes.'

'Why?'

He tried to keep his voice calm so as not to increase her alarm. 'We may have to abandon ship.'

'Oh dear God!' She held on to his arm even tighter.

'We have to trust the captain's judgment, my love, and God's mercy.' He hasn't brought us this far to abandon us now.'

Amelia nodded. 'I'll try,' she said.

But Geoffrey's thoughts were less convincing than his words.

* * *

As the first grey streaks of dawn appeared, the raging wind had driven the *Nancy* so firmly onto the submerged sandbar that nothing less than a full tide was likely to float her free. The immediate problem confronting Travis was that the tide was falling, and it would be another seven hours before the next high tide. But his greatest fear was that the huge waves sweeping over the deck would soon begin to smash the ship's exposed stern. Had they been facing the other direction the ship might have survived the force of wind and sea, taking it all on her strongest point - her bow. But stuck as she was, she risked breaking up under the relentless pounding.

'She won't be able to take much more of this, skipper,' White said.

Travis nodded grimly. 'We've got to abandon ship, Mr. White. Have the crew swing the boats out on the leeward side ready to launch as soon as there's a drop in the wind.'

'Aye aye, sir.' White began to below orders to the crew, while Travis returned to his cabin to collect the ship's log and a few personal items that he stuffed into his pockets. As he passed the Glastons' cabin he banged on the door. Geoffrey opened it, his face betraying his anxiety.

'You and Mrs. Glaston need to get up on deck right away. We're going to take to the boats as soon as the wind drops enough to launch them.'

'Are we close to land, Captain?' Amelia asked.

'It's too dark to see, but we can't be too far from Cape Otway. God willing we'll get a lull soon before the whole ship breaks up.'

Geoffrey wanted to scream at him: I tried to warn you of this, you stupid man! Instead, he asked: 'Has Mr. Mundine been told?'

'Not yet. He should be in his cabin. I'd be obliged if you would wake him and tell him to get ready to take to the boats.'

'Very well, Captain.'

Geoffrey ran to Mundine's cabin and pounded on the door, but there was no response. His first thought was that Mundine had already gone up on deck, but decided to look inside, just in case. The cabin was in total darkness. He stepped inside and nearly fell over Mundine's body, sprawled across the cabin deck. Thinking that he must have been injured, Geoffrey turned him over gently and checked to see if he was breathing. Mundine's bloodshot eyes opened but failed to focus.

'Wassamarra?' he slurred.

Geoffrey realized he was hopelessly drunk. He tried to lift him up into a sitting position, but Mundine pushed him away and lay flat again.

Geoffrey shook him awake. 'Mr. Mundine, you have to wake up. Captain Travis is about to abandon ship.'

Mundine opened his eyes again. 'Waddya say?'

'We're going to take to the boats. The ship is breaking up.'

Mundine tried to focus his eyes as Geoffrey's words began to sink in. 'She's breakin' up?'

'Yes. Now please get up. We haven't much time.'

Mundine struggled to his feet only to fall on his bed again. Geoffrey took hold of him and tried to pull him up, but he was like a dead weight.

'Orright, I can manage.' He pushed Geoffrey's hands away. 'Just gimme a minute to get me head together.'

'All right, but please be quick.' Geoffrey left him to sort himself out and returned to his cabin where Amelia, pallid faced, was ready to go.

They got to the open deck just as Travis ordered the ship's boats lowered into the water. As he'd hoped, the wind had dropped momentarily, and the waves on the sheltered side of the ship had fallen enough for the crew to launch the boats and scramble aboard.

Travis saw the Glastons and beckoned them over to the larger of the two boats. White and several sailors were already in the smaller one.

'Where's Mundine?' Travis shouted.

'He's coming,' Geoffrey replied. 'But he's still drunk.'

'Get in the boat, the two of you. We can't wait any longer. The wind will be up again at any moment.'

'We can't leave him, Captain. I'll go and get him.' Geoffrey ran back to the hatchway.

Travis let out a string of profanities then ordered Amelia into the boat. 'Your husband and Mundine can get into the other one, but you're coming with me. Mr. White,' he called out to the mate. 'Wait a couple of minutes for the reverend and Mundine then cast off.'

White signaled his acknowledgement, but Amelia refused to enter the boat without her husband. She ran back to help him get Mundine. Travis began to curse again but White pacified him by telling him he would wait for both Glastons and Mundine. So, Travis gave the order to cast off, and the sailors bent their backs to the oars and began to pull away from their stricken ship.

Within minutes the darkness had swallowed them up, but there was still no sign of the three passengers. Henry White looked anxiously at what bits of sail and rigging still remained on the *Nancy's* spars and noted that the wind seemed to be picking up again. He was about to give the order to cast off when he saw Amelia emerge from the hatchway, tugging at what appeared to be a large black sack, but which turned out to be Mundine's helpless bulk, shoved from behind by her husband.

'Get him over here quickly,' White yelled. 'We have to cast off. The wind's getting up again.'

He pulled the boat hard under the *Nancy's* port rail, ready for the Glastons to roll Mundine's dead weight down, when a sudden gust of wind roared through the rigging, sending them sprawling against the mainmast. Above the shriek of the wind, they heard a cracking sound above their heads and looked up to see the long, wooden gaff begin to snap from where it straddled the mast. They hardly had time to call out a warning before the whole thing came crashing down onto the boat, crushing White and another man and spilling the others into the waves. The Glastons watched in horror before rushing to the rail, only to see a few white planks bobbing madly up and down in the swirling maelstrom. Of White and the others there was no trace.

Amelia buried her face in Geoffrey's chest; her body wracked with sobs. Geoffrey held her tightly as he looked over his shoulder to see if Mundine was all right. As the wind grew in intensity and shrieked through what remained of the rigging, Mundine lay crumpled on the deck, snoring.

4 June 1878 – Cape Otway

It was the sound of galloping hooves that woke Michael Burns from sleep. He pulled himself wearily from the rough cot that occupied one corner of the slab hut he had called home for the past year, wrapped a blanket around his shoulders and stumbled across to the window. His head ached from the aftereffects of the cheap rum that was his main cosolation these long, lonely nights. Moments later the door burst open and Billy, his Aboriginal head stockman, rushed inside.

'Boss, you come quick. Big ship on rocks.'

'A big ship? Where?'

'Lizard Head, boss.'

'Get the horses and wagon harnessed,' he ordered. 'And throw plenty of rope in the back, and some blankets. There may be survivors.'

He dressed quickly and ran outside as Billy was backing the two draft horses into the traces. Then, with Billy trotting ahead on his stock horse, they set off to cover the three miles to Lizard Head.

The tide had turned by the time they got there, and Geoffrey Glaston could feel the deck under his feet lifting slightly as the rolling waves surged under the ship's stern and turned to foam in the shallow water around it.

'What's happening, Geoffrey?' Amelia called out from inside the hatchway where she'd been sheltering.

'I think the tide has turned, my love. There seems to be more water passing under the ship.'

'Will we float off?'

'Perhaps. But where will we end up then? We don't know if the hull has been holed. At least we won't drown here on this sandbank.'

'We will if this ship continues to break up.'

Geoffrey turned to look at Mundine, who was now fully awake, and clear-headed enough to be very frightened.

'God hasn't brought us this far to abandon us now, Mr. Mundine.'

'Jesus, I hope you're right,' he muttered.

Amelia stepped out onto the deck. 'Perhaps you ought to be praying to our Lord, Mr. Mundine, rather than taking his name in vain.'

'I don't think he'd listen to me, but I hope he's listening to you two,' Mundine replied.

An extra-large wave suddenly swept under them, and they felt the whole ship shudder before settling back on the sandy bottom. It was followed by an even bigger wave that lifted the stern violently and caused it to slew around to the right, exposing the vessel's port beam to the violence of the wind. Amelia screamed as what was left of the main mast snapped off its base and fell over the side.

'She's breaking up,' Mundine shouted, his voice betraying his panic. 'We're done for.'

Geoffrey ran to Amelia and enfolded her in his arms. 'Be brave, darling,' he whispered.

Three more huge waves bore down on them, crashing into the ship's exposed side and smashing the flimsy gunwales before pouring across the open deck, sweeping the three survivors off their feet. Terrified, they each clung to whatever pieces of the ship still seemed secure and waited for the next wave big enough to complete its destruction. But then the *Nancy* began to twist slowly in an anticlockwise motion, pivoting on that part of her keel that was stuck in the sand, propelled by the force of wind and waves. By the time the next big wave arrived the ship had slewed around far enough to be presenting her port bow to the oncoming sea, which lifted her clear of the sand bank and began to push her into deeper water beyond.

'Are we going to drown, Geoffrey?' Amelia's voice seemed to betray no panic, only resignation.

'I don't think so, my love. Look!' He pointed away from the direction of the wind to where the black mass of Lizard Head could now be seen in the early morning light. On top of it, silhouetted against the lightening sky, he could see horses and men.

Michael and Billy had arrived at Lizard Head just in time to see the drama unfold. Michael took a small, brass telescope from his jacket pocket and trained it on the stricken ship as she began to slide off the sandbank.

'I can see people aboard her. Not many though.'

They continued to watch the ship drifting helplessly. 'You know about the currents here, Billy. Where will she fetch up?'

'There, boss. *Walauwaru.*'

'*Walauwaru,* the wedge-tailed eagle.' Michael followed Billy's outstretched arm to where a rocky shelf emerged from the foam, close to the head of a narrow inlet that was sheltered by Lizard Head. Michael could see how the current swirled around the headland and into the inlet, fetching up on the curiously shaped black basalt rock shelf that, with a little imagination, could be interpreted as a wedge-tailed eagle diving into the waves.

They continued to watch the *Nancy's* slow progress round the headland, rolling giddily from side to side as the waves pushed her in one direction and the cross current swung her in another. But it soon became clear that Billy's prediction was correct. As she passed under the lee of Lizard Head and into the sheltered waters of the inlet, *Nancy* spun round again, presenting her stern to the waves which pushed her irrevocably closer to the rocky shelf.

Michael heard the sound of her keel crunching onto the black basalt and immediately sprang into action. He threw a rope to Billy and grabbed a lighter one with a small piece of lead attached. 'Come on. Let's get down there.'

He mounted the stock horse and Billy jumped up behind him. Together they galloped down a rutted track that led to the beach. By the time they got there the ship was well and truly aground, leaning precariously on its starboard side. He could see figures waving to him from the deck.

'We haven't got much time, Billy. The tide's rising and she'll float off the rock into deeper water pretty soon. We need to get those people off. Give me the end of that rope.'

He connected the light rope to the heavy one and began to swing the weighted end round and round until he was satisfied it had enough momentum. Then, letting go with his right hand, the weighted line soared up and ahead in a long, curving trajectory, finally falling onto the *Nancy's* deck, where Geoffrey grabbed it before it fell back overboard.

Michael cupped his hands to his mouth and shouted for them to haul the line in. Gradually the light line began to slide across the face of the slippery rock until its final coil opened to where the heavy line was attached.

'Keep hauling,' Michael shouted. 'When the thick line reaches you, tie it firmly to something solid.'

He saw the figures on the ship signal their acknowledgement and then looked round for a place to secure his end of the rope. There was a spindly tree growing out of the bank just above his head. He secured his end of the rope to it, then sprinted back to the water's edge where he saw that the survivors now had the heavy line aboard.

It was Mundine who snatched the rope from Geoffrey's fumbling hands as he tried to tie a knot that would hold it secure.

'You do the praying, Reverend. I know how to tie a bowline.' He made the line fast to the capstan and bellowed back to Michael that all was now ready.

'You'll have to slide hand over fist down the rope,' Michael bellowed. 'Do you think you can do that?'

Amelia turned to her husband and said, 'I don't think I'll be able to climb down that rope, Geoffrey.'

'Me neither,' mumbled Mundine.

Geoffrey leaned over the rail and called out. 'There are only three of us left aboard. I think I'd be able to swing myself along the rope, but it would be impossible for my wife and Mr. Mundine.'

'Do you have any lengths of canvas?' Michael called back. 'Or anything else you can tie over the top of the rope and then sit in to slide down?'

Amelia tugged at Geoffrey's sleeve. 'I've seen something like that. I saw the sailors use it to paint the top of the mast.'

'Of course; the bosun's chair. It's in that locker next to the focs'l.' Geoffrey ran to the locker and was relieved to find it unlocked. The bosun's chair – a canvas seat attached to stout supporting lines that could be shackled to a halyard and pulley – was hanging from a hook next to the very pulley wheel they needed to run along the line. They soon had it rigged with the bosun's chair beneath it and signaled that they were ready for the first person to go.

'Make sure you tie that light line to the chair,' Michael shouted. 'Then the next person to go can pull it back.'

They waved their acknowledgement, and Michael saw Amelia step onto the ship's rail and settle herself in the canvas seat.

'Hold tight, darling,' Geoffrey said as he launched her into space.

She covered the distance between ship and shore in less than ten seconds. Michael helped her down onto the sand and signaled for the chair to be pulled back aboard the ship. Mundine followed, his huge bulk straining to fit into the canvas seat and his weight dragging the lifeline down to where it barely skimmed the surface of the water. Geoffrey then completed the final run ashore without mishap.

As Geoffrey's feet touched the sand, Amelia threw her arms around his neck, tears streaming from her eyes. 'Oh Geoffrey, I thought we were going to drown.'

Geoffrey hugged her to him. 'There, there, my love. We're safe now. It's just as you said: God hasn't brought us this far to abandon us now. And he sent this good man to help us.'

He turned to Michael and took his hand, pumping it furiously. 'I don't know your name, sir, but I thank God for you and for your foresight in being here and bringing those ropes.'

Michael smiled. 'My name is Michael Burns. But it's my stockman, Billy, you should thank. He's the one who told me your ship had gone aground.'

Geoffrey and Amelia walked over to Billy and took his hands in theirs.

'My dear chap,' said Geoffrey. 'How can we ever thank you. We owe you our lives.'

Billy looked down and quietly mumbled, 'S'orright, boss.'

Amelia shivered slightly as the wind blowing off the sea chilled her damp clothing. 'Oh, what a desolate place this is,' she said.

Geoffrey hugged her himself. 'I was thinking how beautiful it is – wild and beautiful; so different from England.'

'Do you think so?' she said.

She turned back to Michael. 'And what do you think of this place, Mr. Burns? Do you find it beautiful?'

'It's a hard land, ma'am; but it is beautiful in its own way - not like the gentleness of the English countryside. But it's a damn side – sorry, pardon my language – it's far better than the place I came from.'

'Is that a Midland accent I detect, Mr. Burns?'

Michael smiled. 'It is, indeed, ma'am.'

'But there's also a touch of Irish brogue,' she added.

'I was born in Ireland, but my parents left during the great potato famine and settled in Staffordshire - the *Black Country*, they call it.'

'Yes, I've been there. Not the nicest part of England - all those slag heaps and blast furnaces.'

He nodded. 'I couldn't wait to get away from it. I ran away to sea when I was fourteen. But now I look after a sheep station behind these cliffs.'

'Well, the two of you were sent by God, that's all I can say!'

'Me, sent by God! Dunno about that,' he mumbled sheepishly.

It was Mundine who broke the silence that followed. He took Michael aside and whispered in his ear, 'I don't want the reverend to hear this, but there's a small fortune in rum, including eighty barrels of Jamaica's finest, in the hold of that ship. If you can help me to get it ashore, half of it's yours.'

Michael looked at him quizzically. 'Who does it belong to?'

'It's mine.' Mundine answered. 'Or should I say that it's mine after I pay back the loan I got from the Australasia Bank.'

'Then you aren't in a position to give me half, even if we were able to get it ashore.'

'Listen,' Mundine whispered. 'As long as you say nothing to the good reverend and his lady, all the bank will know is that the ship and its cargo was lost.' He broke off his explanation as he saw Geoffrey Glaston walking towards them.

'There may be other survivors somewhere along the coast. Are there other people around here you could get to search the coastline?'

'It's twenty miles to the nearest town,' Michael replied. 'But Billy's people are nearby. No white man knows this coastline like they do. I'll have Billy get them searching. How many people got off the ship?'

'Captain Travis, the master, and ten others got away in the larger of the ship's boats. We were about to get into the other boat with the ship's mate and four sailors when it got smashed and they were all drowned.'

'I see,' Michael said. 'Well, we'd better get you all back to my hut. Then we'll start the search.'

* * *

Two hours later, as Geoffrey and Amelia sat before a roaring fire with mugs of hot tea in their hands, Michael announced he was about to leave with Billy to organise a search for survivors.

'Mr. Mundine has kindly offered to help,' he said. 'So, he'll bring the wagon while Billy and I ride on ahead.'

'Then I'll come, too,' Geoffrey said.

Mundine was about to object, but Michael got in first. 'Thanks, Reverend. But we may need all the extra space we can get in the wagon. I think it is best if you and your good lady stay here until we return. Your prayers for those poor souls will probably do them more good. Ginny will look after you.' He nodded towards the Aboriginal woman who was stirring a pot of hot stew over the fire.

Geoffrey nodded his assent. 'I suppose you're right. But shouldn't we try to notify the authorities and have them organize a search, too?'

'Yes. I'm going to send one of the native stockmen with a message to the police in Port Benson. It's not much of a place but it's the nearest thing we've got to civilization in these parts. The police will be able to round up a few of the locals to help search the coastline. But it'll be hours before they can get here. We can't afford to wait for them.'

'God go with you, then. We shall hope and pray for Captain Travis' safety.'

'You can, but I certainly won't,' Mundine muttered to himself as he followed Michael outside. 'Well, Mr. Burns. What do we need to get those barrels ashore?'

'A good bit of luck, I imagine. And a tide that's not too high to float her off those rocks.'

4 June 1878 – Cape Otway

'She's still there,' Mundine shouted excitedly as they reached the crest overlooking the inlet.

He was right. High tide had been and gone but the *Nancy* was still aground. However, the constant battering by the waves had smashed the stern windows and water was surging through the captain's cabin and lower deck. The main deck was still dry but was strewn with pieces of shattered mast and rigging, and the hull was lying at a precarious angle.

Michael examined the wreck through his telescope. 'Her hull still seems to be intact, but it's hard to know if the water's gettin' into the hold.'

'Well as long as the barrels ain't smashed, the rum will be OK,' Mundine said. 'How long do you think we've got to get 'em off?'

'We have about two hours of the ebb tide to run. Then another six hours before high tide. But the next high might be bigger than the last one and could float her off the rocks. We'd better not waste any time.'

They left the wagon at the top of the track and scrambled down to the beach. The rope they'd used to get the survivors ashore was still in place.

Michael and Billy used it to haul themselves aboard the ship and then pulled Mundine, wedged into the bosun's chair, up after them. They removed the hatch above the ship's hold and looked down into the darkness.

'Lotta water down there, boss,' Billy said.

Michael nodded. 'We need a light to see what we're doing.'

'There are lamps in the passenger cabins,' Mundine said. He hurried aft and soon returned with an oil lamp. 'You got a match?'

They lit the wick and settled the glass cover over it. Then, with Michael leading, they climbed down into the ship's hold.

The water was almost to their knees, and many of the lighter items of cargo had come adrift and were floating back and forth.

'Where's the rum?' Michael asked.

'It must be back here,' Mundine answered. 'I remember Cap'n Travis telling the mate that the barrels were to be secured amidships because of their weight.'

They sloshed their way further into the bowels of the stricken vessel, past packing cases and sacks of grain and found the barrels of rum, still securely lashed together in stacks around the base of what had been the mainmast. Michael opened his jack knife and cut through the ropes holding them in place. Then he climbed up onto the top of the stack and rolled one of the barrels down to where Mundine was standing to catch it. Its weight knocked him back into Billy's arms and the barrel crashed to the deck below.

Michael jumped down and helped Billy pick it up. 'It's heavy. How're we going to get all these on deck in the few hours left to us?'

'We've gotta do something,' Mundine grunted. 'There's a small fortune here.'

Billy took Michael's arm and pointed to the opposite side of the ship. 'Look, boss. Water, 'e come there.'

Michael held the oil lamp high and scrambled across the canting deck to where Billy was pointing. Some of the planks along the starboard side had sprung, and a large hole had opened up.

'You're right Billy. This is where the water's been getting in. It's not too bad at the moment because the tide's low, but it will soon start to flood.'

'Then we'd better get moving.' Mundine started to drag the heavy barrel that had knocked him over along the sloping deck towards the ladder. 'Gimme a hand,' he grunted.

It took all three of them to manhandle the barrel up the ladder and onto the open deck and, by the time they'd done it, Mundine was already exhausted. He collapsed against the capstan, breathing heavily.

'I can't do any more lifting like that. You two will have to lift the barrels up and I'll roll 'em over against the rail, ready to get them ashore.'

Michael swore under his breath. He could see that Mundine was going to be of no use. 'It's not going to work, Mundine. Billy and I can't do this on our own. And how are we then going to get them ashore?'

'Float 'em, boss,' Billy said.

Michael stared at him for a moment questioningly and then slapped him on the back. 'You may be right, Billy. Things float easier in salt water than fresh. Let's see what happens. Give me a hand here.'

They raised the barrel onto the ship's rail and then let it drop into the surging foam. At first it disappeared, and they thought it had sunk. But then its top reappeared and, with just a fraction of its bulk showing above the water, it began to float slowly with the rising tide towards the beach.

'But we've still got to get the other barrels up on deck,' Mundine said.

'We don't need to.' Michael replied. 'We'll roll 'em through the hole in the side of the ship.'

'But it's the wrong side.'

'Don't worry, Mundine. The way the current runs, they'll still wash up on the far side of the inlet. But we need to make that hole bigger before the waves start washing in. Are there any tools aboard?'

Mundine staggered to the carpenter's store and returned with two large axes. Michael took one and Billy the other. They made their way back into the hold, slipping and sliding across the tilted deck to the spot where the planks had sprung. With a few well-aimed blows, they smashed the timbers until the hole was wide enough for the barrels to pass through. Then they returned to the stack and began to roll the barrels, one by one, towards the opening. The slope of the deck worked in their favour. As each barrel fetched up against the side, Mundine would guide it through the broken planks and propel it with his foot into the waves below.

By the time they had the stack down to its lowest level, the tide had risen sufficiently for the waves to be sweeping through the hole, making their task more difficult, and they could hear the ship's timbers groaning as the rising tide began to lift it higher.

'We haven't got much longer,' Michael said. 'Let's put our backs into it.'

Soaked to the skin and nearly exhausted, they manhandled the remaining barrels across the deck and into the rising water that was now coming through the hole.

'Right, let's get out of here while we still can,' Michael ordered.

With Mundine in the lead, the three of them struggled to the ladder and scrambled up onto the open deck. Michael hustled Mundine across to the bosun's chair and forced him into it.

'Go,' he said and pushed him across the ship's rail.

The rope above his head sagged under Mundine's weight and his legs temporarily disappeared below the waves until his momentum carried him across the rocks and onto the beach beyond. He slammed into the small tree at the far end of the rope and collapsed, cursing but unhurt, onto the sand below.

Michael tapped Billy on the shoulder. 'Right, Billy. You go now. Same way we came aboard.'

Billy grinned and, with both hands gripping the rope, swung his legs up and around it, making his way to safety hand over fist. Michael watched him go, willing him to move faster. He kept glancing nervously at the waves, some of which were now breaking over the shattered stern. Then a thought suddenly crossed his mind.

Sprinting back to the hatchway, he dropped down into the knee-deep water below deck and struggled into the stern cabin. Daylight streamed through the smashed windows as he looked around and spotted what he'd been hoping to see. Fixed to the bulkhead was an iron safe, its door swinging open. He ran his hands around its interior hoping to find something that the captain, in his hurry to get off the ship, might have missed. But the only thing he found was a small oilskin package, stuck right at the back of the bottom shelf. It was clearly nothing of any great value, otherwise the captain would have taken it. But Michael grabbed it anyway and stuffed inside his shirt.

The ship suddenly gave a lurch, throwing him off his feet. He felt the stern lift momentarily and then settle again on the rock face. But this time she didn't stay there. He heard a grinding sound coming from below and realized she was beginning to slide back into deeper water.

He struggled to his feet and was about to drag himself back along the passageway when something else caught his eye. The sudden lurching motion of the ship had sprung the door of a long cabinet, and its contents fell to the deck. Among them were a rifle and a bandolier of cartridges. Michael grabbed the rifle and swung the bandolier across his shoulder. Then he scrambled back to the hatchway and onto the deck. He could see

Billy standing at the water's edge and calling for him to get off the ship. He wrapped the rifle sling across his chest, swung himself onto the rope and began to pull himself along it as fast as he could, burning his skin as he slid along.

Suddenly, there was a loud screeching sound as the ship lifted high enough to slide fully off the rock face into deep water. The rope connecting her to the shore suddenly went taut, tearing the small tree it was attached to out by its roots. Michael let go of the rope and fell into the waves below, disappearing below the surface. He rose for a moment and gasped for air before another wave rolled him over and forced him below the foam again. He struggled to get to the surface but the weight of his sodden jacket and heavy boots pulled him down. He managed to get his head up for a moment and gasped for air, but another wave broke over him, causing him to swallow a mouthful of water. Coughing and choking he found himself being pulled beneath the waves again. Panic gave him new strength as he fought desperately to get to the surface. He felt his lungs about to burst as again he surfaced and gasped for air.

Somewhere in the distance he could hear a voice shouting to him. 'Behind you, boss; behind you.'

He turned his head in time to see another wave bearing down on him with a wooden grating riding its crest. With his last bit of strength, he reached up and grabbed its edge before it smashed into him. Once again, he found himself being rolled over by the force of the breaking surf, but he hung on to the grating until the wave had passed. He managed to haul himself onto it before the next wave lifted him up again and hurled him towards the rock shelf. Aware of the danger of being smashed against the jagged rocks, he began to kick with his feet in an attempt to steer his tiny raft towards the beach.

Once again, he heard Billy's voice above the roar of the surf. 'Grab rope, boss. Grab rope.'

The rope came spinning through the air towards him. He could see Billy, up to his waist in the surf, holding on to it as the coils unwound and it splashed into the sea, less than six feet away. He kicked his feet furiously in his attempt to reach it, but another wave caught him and washed him closer to the rocks. He made one last lunge for it as the next wave bore down.

Billy felt the line go tight in his hand and began to haul it in as fast as he could. He saw the wooden grating lift up onto the crest of the wave and smash onto the rocks. But the tension on the rope was still there as he pulled it in with every bit of strength he could muster.

He shouted to Mundine, 'Come quick, boss. 'Elp me pull 'im in.'

Mundine, who had been watching the looming disaster from the safety of the beach, quickly sprang into action. Wading out into the surf he took hold of the rope and began to heave in time with Billy's weakening efforts. The additional muscle power worked. Michael's head appeared out of the roiling surf, spluttering and gasping for breath. The next wave did the rest, lifting him up onto its crest and dumping him unceremoniously onto the shingle.

'I thought you were a goner,' Mundine said.

'So did I,' Michael gasped. 'And I would have been if it hadn't been for Billy.' He pulled himself to his feet and staggered over to where the Aborigine was coiling the soaking line. He held out his right hand and Billy, somewhat self-consciously, took hold of it in his.

'Thanks, Billy. If it hadn't been for you, I'd be bait for the sharks now.'

Billy looked down at his feet. 'No worries, boss. I'd even do it for a blackfella.'

Michael threw his head back and laughed. Then, to Billy's embarrassment and Mundine's disgust, he pulled the stockman to him and hugged him. 'Blackfellas like you are as good as any whitefella, mate, and a darn sight better than most.'

Mundine spat on the ground. 'What the hell were you doing running back into the cabin like that?'

'I wanted to see if there was anything of value left in the captain's cabin.'

'And was there?'

'Only a rifle and this.' He withdrew the brown envelope from where he had stuffed it inside his shirt.

Mundine took it from Michael's hand. 'Hell! I'd forgotten about this.'

'What is it?'

'It's my share certificate. I bought five hundred shares in a company that plans to operate horse drawn buses in Melbourne.' He opened the envelope and showed them its contents. 'Bad luck that this is all that was there. These shares ain't worth much more than the paper they're written on. But no matter, we've still got the barrels of rum – if we can find them.'

'Them over there, boss.' Billy pointed to the far side of the inlet where a small shingle beach, sheltered from the full force of the waves by a headland, was already littered with barrels they had thrown overboard. Others were still bobbing around in the water.

'OK Billy, you see if you can get the wagon down onto that beach. Mundine, you come with me.'

'You plan to keep that rifle?' Mundine asked.

'Only if we fail to find the captain,' Michael answered. He unslung it from his shoulder and looked at it. 'It's a Winchester repeating rifle.'

'Yankee guns, ain't they?'

'Yes. They are very fine rifles; much better than the old single shot Remington back at the homestead.'

'You know a bit about guns, then?'

Michael nodded. 'I know a bit. We used to shoot at sharks when I was at sea. It turned out that I was the best shot out of all the crew, so I got the job of watching for sharks when the crew got a chance to take a swim.'

Mundine shrugged his shoulders. 'Very impressive! Now, show me the way to where those barrels are washing up.'

Michael led the way to the far side of the inlet where the barrels had floated. Mundine, cursing as he slipped on wet rocks, staggered behind him.

'You roll the ones on the beach up above the high-water line.' Michael told him. 'I'll get the others ashore.'

He waded out to where the barrels were floating and, one by one, pushed them up onto the shingle, where Mundine, sweating and still cursing, rolled them up above the waterline. He stopped for a moment to wipe his brow and saw Billy carefully guiding the horses down a defile that ended on a grassy flat just a few feet above the beach.

'Get a move on, you lazy, black bastard.'

Michael waded out of the water and grabbed him by the collar. 'You watch your mouth, Mundine.'

'Don't tell me you're a nigger lover!' Mundine sneered.

Michael grabbed him by the front of his shirt and pulled him forward. 'It's because of Billy that we've got these barrels ashore, and I'm still alive. So, like I said, watch your mouth.'

'Take it easy, mate. He's only an Abo!'

Michael felt his blood begin to boil. 'That's how people used to talk about me and my family. "Bog Irish" is what they'd call us – as if they were something better.'

Mundine was about to make a sarcastic reply, but the look in Michael's eye persuaded him not to. 'All right, all right! Keep ya shirt on.'

Michael let go of him and went back to retrieving the remaining barrels. An hour later they had them stacked, ready to load onto the wagon.

'Those barrels marked with the letter P are the ones we really want. The letter P means they're premium quality. There should be eighty of them. The other eighty are just cheap stuff. But the miners will still pay good money for what's in them.'

'We'll need several trips to get this lot back to the homestead,' Michael said. 'We'd better start now.'

'Wait on,' Mundine interjected. 'What happens if someone sees 'em there? We want people to think they all went down with the ship.'

'You're right. We've got to hide them somewhere. The authorities in Port Benson will mount a search party as soon as word gets to them, and people will be scouring this whole area looking for survivors. Billy, what do you think? Is there somewhere we can stash these barrels; somewhere the whitefellas don't know about?'

'Yeah, boss. Place my people go when big fire 'e go through 'ere. Over there.' He pointed to some low, bush covered hills, about two miles to the north.

'I've been there, Billy. There's nothing there except scrub.'

'No, boss. Big hole in ground. Whitefella not see. Blackfella see.'

'What the hell's he talking about?' Mundine snarled. 'Holes in the ground that only blacks can see!'

'He may be talking about limestone caves,' Michael said. 'There have been a few found in these parts. Sometimes you have to fall into them before you know they're there. OK, Billy. Let's get the first load of barrels onto the wagon and you show us the way.'

4 June 1878 – The Otway Ranges

Michael was right; the place that Billy took them to was a large limestone cave, almost completely hidden from view by the thick scrub that grew profusely along the base of the hills bordering the ranges beyond. He led them to its mouth but refused to go inside.

'Mebbe spirits live 'ere, boss. Me carry barrels to cave but you take inside.'

'Why don't you just make him help us,' Mundine snorted? 'It's just bloody native superstition.'

'Because I respect Billy's beliefs, Mundine, even if I don't share them. His people have been here for a lot longer than us. They have a feeling for the land we don't understand.'

'Bloody nonsense! Mundine muttered to himself.'

It took four trips to get all the barrels off the beach and into the cave, but when it was done, they were jubilant, convinced that no-one would discover their cache before they returned to retrieve it. Their jubilation faded, however, as they returned to the homestead and spotted the blue police tunics outside.

'I thought you said the troopers would take hours to get here,' Mundine said.

'I did. But I didn't think we'd be away as long as this.'

'So, what do we tell them?'

'We'll tell them that we've been searching the coast for survivors.'

'What about the Abo? Can he be trusted to keep his trap shut?'

'Don't worry about Billy, he knows what to say. Isn't that right, Billy?'

'No worries, boss.'

'Okay, let's get up there and make our report.'

Geoffrey Glaston was standing next to a burly police sergeant as they rode up to the homestead. 'This is the good man who saved our lives, Sergeant,' Geoffrey smiled as he took Michael's hand. 'He and his worthy companion, Billy.'

'You mean the Abo?'

'This "Abo" is my head stockman, Sergeant. He's the one man around here that I'd trust with my life.'

'As you please, Mr. Burns.' The policeman turned to Mundine. 'And you are?'

'Ernest Mundine. I was a passenger on the *Nancy.* I've been helping Mr. Burns search for survivors.'

'Well, by the look of it you haven't found any. From what the reverend tells me, you were lucky to survive yourselves. The *Nancy* wasn't the first ship to come to grief along this coast, and she won't be the last. Anyway, you'd better come inside and get something to eat. Then I'll take your statements. I won't need one from the Abo. He can go back to his people. We'll start another search at first light tomorrow.'

They called off the search at nightfall on the following day. A dozen riders from Port Benson had joined the three police troopers and scoured the cliffs and beaches of that wild and lonely coast without luck. The only evidence of the tragedy that had befallen Captain Travis was an oar washed up on a beach several miles west of Lizard Head.

'Well, I suppose that's it,' the sergeant shrugged. 'They've obviously all drowned. I'll telegraph the news to Melbourne as soon as I get back.'

'What about the Glastons and Mr. Mundine?'

'We'll take them back to Port Benson. There's a paddle steamer due in from Melbourne in three days' time. I'll arrange passage for them. Now, if we can impose on your hospitality just a little more, I'd be obliged if we could stay here until first light and then we'll get on our way.'

* * *

The group departed at dawn, as planned. The Glastons were profuse in their expressions of gratitude to Michael and Billy, while Mundine merely shook Michael's hand and whispered, 'Now don't you get any ideas about moving those barrels before I get back.'

'Your gratitude overwhelms me,' Michael whispered back sarcastically.

Mundine shrugged and joined the Glastons aboard the police buggy. The trooper flicked his whip over the horses' backs, and they set off with the sergeant and the other members of the search party riding ahead. The last Michael saw of them was Amelia waving as the track disappeared into the stringybarks.

'Well, Billy, it's back to work for us until we hear from Mundine.'

'Me no like 'im, boss. Me no trust 'im.'

'Don't worry, Billy. He may be no good, but he's going to make me rich, you'll see. And I'll make sure you do all right too.'

Billy grinned. 'Thanks, boss.'

11 July 1878 – Melbourne

Mundine's letter arrived five weeks later. Michael picked it up with some other mail when he made his weekly trip into Port Benson. It had taken a week to get there and had been sitting in the post office for several days. He tore the envelope open and read a short note saying that Mundine planned to remain in Melbourne until the official inquiry into the loss of the *Nancy* was completed and would then travel overland with some bullock drays to meet him and retrieve the barrels of rum.

Michael stuffed Mundine's letter into his pocket and turned his attention to the other mail. There were the usual station accounts to be paid and a letter from the station owner complaining about the lower-than-expected returns from the last wool clip. Michael read them quickly and then turned his attention to the final piece of mail, an official looking envelope sealed with wax.

It was from a man who referred to himself as Cecil Cartwright Esq. Melbourne Agent for Lloyds of London, requesting his presence at a meeting of the board of inquiry into the sinking of the barquentine *Nancy*, to be held on 19th July at 212 Branston Street, Melbourne. The letter included a return ticket for the weekly paddle steamer service and promised that Lloyds of London would reimburse Michael for his time away.

'Bloody Hell,' Michael said to himself. 'That's only a week away.'

Fortunately, there was little to be done on the station at that time of year, and he realized that it would be to his advantage to get the whole matter of the ship's loss out of the way so that he and Mundine could retrieve the salvaged rum as soon as the excitement had died down. However, he felt nervous about having to face a board of inquiry. If they put him under oath, he knew he was going to have to commit perjury, and he was not sure he wanted to risk that. But the prospect of a handsome profit from the sale of that fine Jamaica rum overcame his anxiety. He put the letters into his saddle bag, secured his load of supplies onto his pack horse, mounted his own horse, and cantered out of town.

* * *

The weekly paddle steamer service that served the ports along Victoria's south coast docked in Port Melbourne early on the morning of the 18th of July As there was still a full day before the inquiry began, he thought it would be a good idea to visit Mundine so that they could ensure they had their stories straight. So, as soon as he was ashore, Michael took a horse-drawn cab to the address Mundine had listed on his letter. It was a small and somewhat seedy establishment near the river, catering primarily to seamen and impoverished farmers visiting the metropolis. The proprietor, a hard-faced woman of indeterminate age answered Michael's knock.

'We're all full up.'

'It's not a room I'm wanting,' Michael explained. 'I'm here to see one of your guests, Mr. Ernest Mundine.'

'Never 'eard of 'im.'

'But you must have. He wrote a letter to me a few weeks ago, giving this address.'

'Like I told yer, I never 'eard of 'im.'

'Are you certain? He's about fifty, average height but heavyset. He's in the importing business. He was one of three survivors from a ship that got wrecked near Port Benson about five weeks ago.'

'The *Nancy* you mean?'

'Yes.'

'Well, I don't know anything about a bloke named Mundine, but I did have a couple who got rescued from that ship – a reverend gentleman and 'is wife.'

'Reverend Glaston?'

'That's 'im. 'E and 'is missus stayed here a few days until somebody from the church came an' took 'em somewhere else.'

'Do you know where they went?'

She shook her head. 'You could try the Congregational Church in Russell Street I think it was them as arranged a place for 'em to stay until they sailed for Sydney.'

'Are they still in Melbourne?'

'Dunno. You'll 'ave to ask at the church.'

Michael thanked her and made his way to the Russell Street Congregational Church. He found the minister, a tall, ascetic looking man, working in his study adjacent to the chapel.

'My dear chap,' he said when Michael introduced himself, 'I am honoured to meet you. Geoffrey and Amelia told me all about you and the way you rescued them from that ship. It's not often one gets to meet the agent of God's deliverance.'

'I only did what anyone would do in those circumstances, sir. And much of the credit must go to my Aboriginal stockman.'

'Yes, indeed. The Glastons spoke very appreciatively of him.'

'Are they still here?' he asked.

'I'm afraid you're too late. They left for Sydney two weeks ago. Geoffrey Glaston has taken up the ministry of the Morrison Street Congregational Church. But I can give you their address if you wish.'

Michael's puzzlement showed on his face . 'Thank you, Reverend. I'd appreciate that. And perhaps you could also direct me to Branston Street. I've been asked to appear before a board of inquiry into the loss of the *Nancy*.'

The minister stopped writing. 'You must be mistaken, Mr. Burns. The board of inquiry met just before the Glastons left for Sydney. I accompanied them to the very address you spoke of. The whole thing was over in little more than an hour. The board studied the report of the Port Benson police and also listened to the testimony that the Glastons gave and that of the other survivor. It found that the ship had been wrecked due to a storm and faulty navigation on the part of the captain, and that he, his crew and the cargo had been lost.'

'You say the other survivor was there to give evidence, too.'

''Yes, a businessman named Mundine. A somewhat disreputable character, from what Geoffrey Glaston told me.'

'And what happened to him?'

'The last I heard was that he had received a substantial payment from the insurance company to cover his losses and had left Melbourne.'

'Do you know where he went?'

'No. Why do you ask?'

Michael made no reply. Everything had suddenly become clear to him. The letter requesting his presence at the board of inquiry had been a fake. Mundine must have paid someone to write it. He must have arranged it knowing that Michael would respond by travelling to Melbourne, and that would give Mundine a free hand to recover the hidden barrels while he was away.

'My dear fellow,' said the minister, rising from his seat and taking Michael by the arm. 'Are you alright?'

Michael fought to regain his composure. 'Thank you, yes; I'm all right. I just felt dizzy for a moment.'

'Would you like to sit down for a moment? I could get you a glass of water, or some tea if you'd prefer.'

'Thank you, Reverend. That's very kind of you, but I think I'll just be on my way. Thank you for your help.'

He turned quickly and made his way back into the street, hoping that the clergyman had not been able to recognize in his face the fury he felt in his heart. He strode along the blue-stoned pavement, his mind racing as he shouldered past other pedestrians, who glared at him angrily. It had been five days since he'd left home. If he'd stayed in Melbourne for the supposed meeting on 18th July it would then be another week at least before the paddle steamer returned to Port Benson. Mundine would have had plenty of time to retrieve the cached rum and make his escape before Michael returned.

The only thing to do, he thought, was to get back home as quickly as he could. He remembered that the paddle steamer that had brought him to Melbourne was due to depart for another round trip that afternoon. With luck he might get to the wharf before it left. He hailed a passing cab and spent the next hour fretting impatiently as the driver slowly negotiated the busy Melbourne streets until they eventually arrived at Port Melbourne, where the paddle steamer was taking on its last pieces of cargo before setting sail.

7

22 July 1878 – Otway Ranges

It was still early morning when Michael and Billy arrived at the cave. Michael jumped from his horse and ran to where he thought the entrance was located, cursing furiously as he pulled the thick scrub aside but failed to find it.

'Over 'ere,' boss.' Billy, with his native ability to read the country, had gone straight to the spot where a small opening, completely hidden by the vegetation, led into the cavernous interior. He held the scrub aside as Michael rushed inside. It took a while for his eyes to adjust to the darkness, but the barrels were still there. Michael breathed a sigh of relief. He struck a match and lit the small oil lamp in his hand and walked over to where they were piled. It was only then that he realized that the stack was much smaller than when he had last seen it. He held the lamp close to the stack and looked for the distinctive letter P, but none of them seemed to have it.

'The swine!' Michael roared. 'He's taken the premium rum and left me the *rot gut.*'

Immediately, it became clear to him what Mundine had done. He'd promised Michael half the barrels, and Michael had assumed he'd meant half of the premium rum as well as half of the cheap stuff. In reality, he'd been left forty barrels of cheap liquor worth a fraction of what they'd salvaged from the wreck.

He began to curse Mundine, giving vent to all the pent-up suspicion and anger of the past few days. In one breath he damned Mundine to the hottest part of Hell, and in the next vowed to track him down and send him there. As he paced back and forth, he took out his rage by aiming a kick at one of the barrels. The barrel rocked and Michael, now nursing a sore toe, noticed something fall from it. He held the lamp high and saw a brown envelope lying on the ground. He picked it up and recognized it as having come from the oil-skin package he'd rescued from the wreck and given to Mundine, except that now it had his name on it.

He opened it and took out the certificate indicating that Ernest Mundine was the owner of five hundred shares in the *Melbourne Omnibus Company.* With it was a letter, signed by Mundine and witnessed by some other person, assigning the shares to Michael Burns.

'Perhaps he's not quite the scoundrel I thought he was,' Michael said to himself. 'He hasn't robbed me completely of what we agreed on; just most of it.'

He went outside and found Billy walking around staring at the ground.

'They go this way, boss. Twelve bullocks and two wagons. Three whitefellas.'

Michael followed his pointing finger. The evidence that bullock drays had been there was clear now that Billy had pointed it out, but he doubted he would have seen it by himself.

'How long since they were here?'

'Week mebbe, boss. Looks like they go through bush to coach road.'

Michael nodded. That made sense. The overland route from Port Benson to Geelong and then north to Melbourne lay a few miles to the south. Mundine could be two hundred miles away by now. That meant that the rum might already be up in the gold fields, in any one of a score of settlements.

'How long do you reckon you could follow these tracks?' he asked.

Billy grinned. 'Long time, boss. Even whitefella do it. Them like mob of cattle go through bush.'

Michael looked again at the barely visible wheel marks and wondered if Billy was exaggerating. But even in the short time he'd worked in the bush, he'd witnessed the uncanny ability of the natives to read signs that no white man could see. If Billy said he could follow Mundine's tracks, Michael knew that he meant it.

'Okay. We'll return to the homestead and get what we need. Then we'll go after Mundine.'

Billy grinned. 'No worries, boss.'

* * *

It was the Southern Ocean that finally proved too much for Billy's skills as a tracker. Michael expected that Mundine would have turned north and headed for the goldfields. But he was wrong. The tracks led them to a sheltered inlet twenty miles east of the cave where the rum had been hidden.

'Whitefellas unload wagons 'ere, boss,' Billy said, pointing to the corner of a sandy beach that was sheltered from the ocean swell.

'Are you sure?'

'Yeah, boss,' he pointed to several barely visible marks on the ground where the grass ended, and the sand began. 'Barrels fall 'ere. They roll 'em down to beach.'

Michael tried to read the signs that were so obvious to Billy, but all he could do was nod and pretend that he could see them too. He looked at the small waves breaking onto the beach and noticed how much calmer they were than those further down the bay, where the surf was larger.

'They must have had a ship anchored out there under the lee of the headland.'

'Where you think they go, boss?'

Michael picked up a rock and threw it out to sea in frustration. 'I don't know, Billy. But there's nothing left for us here. It's time for us to go home.'

They rode back in silence, Michael's thoughts alternating between anger and frustration. For the second time in as many years his hopes had been dashed. Two years earlier, after years of working his way from deckhand to 2nd mate of a Cape Horner, he deserted the ship in Port Melbourne and, along with most of the crew, made his way to the gold diggings near Ballarat, where fortunes were being made every week. But those fortunes, real though they were, came only to a few. Most of the diggers ended up back on the streets of Melbourne, destitute. Michael had been lucky to get the job of managing a remote sheep station east of Port Benson. But there was little future for him there, living in a slab hut, eating wallaby stew and listening to the haunting sound of didgeridoos as Billy's people chanted around their campfires – until the *Nancy* ran aground and 80 barrels of Jamaica's finest rum rolled into his hands. 'Damn that bastard, Mundine,' he cursed. 'Damn him to Hell!'

Eventually the tedium of the long, lonely journey began to have a calming effect on his mind, and he found himself more able to think clearly about his options. By the time they reached the homestead late the following day, Michael had a plan beginning to take shape in his mind.

'What we do now, boss?' Billy asked.

'I'm still thinking' about it. But my days of sitting around in this god-forsaken hole, looking after a rich man's sheep, while he and his missus live comfortably in Melbourne, are over. I thought Mundine had given me the chance to make some real money with that rum. But maybe I still can do some good with what he left me. I remember meeting a bloke in the pub at Port Benson – a seaman, like me – telling me there's a market for rum – any sort of rum – in the far north of Queensland. But I'll need money to get it there. Anyway, what's all this about 'we'? Are you planning to come with me?'

Billy grinned: 'Yeah, boss. Somebody gotta show you way.'

8

24 July 1878 – Sydney

Sydney in the late 1870s had shaken off its earlier image of a convict settlement and was beginning to look like a prosperous city. The unruly sprawl of dusty lanes and insanitary hovels had become major thoroughfares graced with fine sandstone buildings and an impressive town hall. Its location on the shores of the world's finest natural harbour made it the hub of the South Pacific, and the presence of so many ships from all over the world gave it a raffish, sailor-town ambience that pleased some of its citizens and appalled others.

Geoffrey Glaston was somewhat ambivalent in this respect. As minister of the Morrison Street Congregational Church, he deplored the free and easy morality that seemed to characterize the city's working people. His congregation consisted largely of respectable, middle-class families, who had prospered by hard work, sobriety and the opportunities afforded by this new land.

But there was another side to Geoffrey's personality. In his youth he'd read and re-read the journals of Captain James Cook and other adventurers who had followed in his wake. Something inside convinced him that his destiny was also to be found in those exotic South Seas. However, it was the story of John Williams of the London Missionary Society that eventually focused his aspirations. Williams opened up the South Sea islands to the spread of Christianity. He was everything that Geoffrey wanted to be - a man whose physical courage was matched by his devotion to God, and whose adventurous spirit had been channeled to achieve heavenly, rather than worldly treasure.

Journeying halfway around the world to become the pastor of a prosperous congregation in one of the Empire's newest cities was not quite in the same league as John Williams' missionary journeys. But it was a modest adventure, and Geoffrey was thankful that he'd been given the opportunity to do it. He was even more thankful that he was married to a woman who was happy to support him in his work, believing that his calling was hers too.

The Morrison Street Congregational Church manse was a modest but comfortable cottage that overlooked one of Sydney Harbour's many bays. In the short time they'd been there, Amelia and Geoffrey had developed the habit of sitting together on the porch each afternoon as the sun went down, gazing out to the west, where the harbour narrowed to become the Parramatta River. Early in their marriage they learned the importance of talking together about the experiences of the day and sharing their hopes and dreams. The manse's porch was a wonderful spot for doing it.

As they sat together that winter afternoon, watching the last streaks of indigo and red fade in the western sky, Amelia turned to Geoffrey and took his hand in hers. 'It's so lovely here, my dear. How fortunate we are.'

Geoffrey smiled. 'And to think how close we came to not making it! It's hard to imagine it actually happened. Do you remember telling me that God hadn't brought us this far to abandon us now?'

'Yes, I do. And I also remember the Good Samaritan He sent to help us.'

Geoffrey nodded reflectively. 'I wonder what Mr. Burns is doing now?'

'Probably still managing that huge sheep farm, I suspect.'

'Sheep station, you mean; that's what they call them here.'

'Well, station or farm, it's all the same. But it did seem such a lonely and inhospitable place; so far from civilization and with only natives for company.'

'Don't forget that we also owe our lives to one of them.'

She sat quietly for a few moments, then said: 'You know Geoffrey, I really wish we could do something to show our gratitude - something that might make their lives easier.'

'I know, and I feel the same. But all we have is my stipend, and if it weren't for the generosity of people in the church, we'd be sitting on fruit boxes and sleeping in hammocks.'

'Yes, I suppose you're right.'

Geoffrey picked up the afternoon newspaper lying next to the sofa and began to read about developments in the city, while Amelia's thoughts returned to that lonely stretch of windswept coastline in Victoria.

'The furnishings of Mr. Burns' slab hut weren't much better than fruit boxes, either.'

'Yes, I remember.'

'And he seemed so lonely.'

'Yes.'

'Geoffrey, are you listening to me?'

'Of course, my dear.'

'Then put that newspaper down!'

He immediately did as he was told - experience had taught him that life was simpler that way - and tried to show that she now had his full attention. 'Now, my love. You were talking about Mr. Burns.'

'Yes. We didn't come out here to make money. We came because we felt called to a mission. And remember how you always used to say that you didn't want to become another 'tea-sipping' parson, listening to the complaints of elderly matrons.'

Geoffrey grinned. 'Well, it's possible I could still end up like that here at the Morrison St. church. Sydney has become quite respectable these days.'

'Well, I want us not to forget why we are here.'

'By becoming too settled and comfortable.'

'Exactly.'

'So, what does this have to do with Mr. Burns?'

'I don't know . . . yet.'

Geoffrey looked at her quizzically, but no further information was forthcoming. So, he picked up his newspaper and returned to the state of the colony, while Amelia continued to ponder.

* * *

Two days later, as Geoffrey returned from his hospital visitation and joined Amelia on the porch, she greeted him with a kiss and a handful of envelopes. 'This one's from England,' she said.

Geoffrey took the letter from her and looked at the postmark. 'It's from Maidstone in Kent. Do we know anyone from there?'

Amelia shook her head. 'Open it and find out.'

Geoffrey took a kitchen knife and slit the envelope. A single sheet of paper fell out with something pinned to it. He picked it up, his eyes wide with astonishment.

'What is it? Tell me what it is.'

Geoffrey read the letter carefully and then examined the bank cheque pinned to it. 'It's a letter from a congregation in Maidstone commending us to God's care in our new ministry and sending us a bank cheque for fifty guineas to use as we see fit.'

Amelia snatched the letter from his hand and read it for herself. She turned to him, her eyes shining. 'This is it, darling!'

'This is what?'

''This is how we can express our gratitude to Mr. Burns.'

'You mean we should give him some of the money?'

'No. Give him all of it.'

'Steady on, my love...'

'But we are so much more comfortable than he is, Geoffrey. God has provided us with everything we need. It's the least we can do for the man who saved our lives.'

Geoffrey was not convinced. 'I'll think about it,' he said.

* * *

Michael received Geoffrey's letter two weeks later when he made his weekly visit to Port Benson. The Post Office was his last call after he'd loaded the dray with supplies. Apart from a letter from the station owner, the only other letter was from an address in Sydney. Somewhat mystified he decided not to wait until he got back to the homestead but to read it there and then.

He was as surprised by the bank cheque that fell out of the letter as the Glastons had been by the original that had been sent to them. But when he saw that it was made to him, his surprise turned to amazement. With mounting excitement, he opened the accompanying letter to see who it was from.

'Well, I'll be damned,' he said out loud. 'It's from Reverend Glaston.' He immediately felt a twinge of guilt about using a mild profanity, but curiosity soon dispelled that, and he began to read the letter.

My Dear Mr. Burns,

Amelia and I thank our gracious Lord every day for you and your native companion who rescued us from what would certainly have been a watery grave. You will be glad to know that we are now safely and happily settled in our new home in Sydney, where we have been received most graciously by the congregation of the Morrison Street Congregational Church. The enclosed cheque is our expression of gratitude to you and is for you to use in whatever way you choose. Our hope and prayer is that it might enable you to find a more comfortable and rewarding way to earn your living, and also, perhaps, to make your native stockman's life a little easier. May God bless you both.

Yours gratefully
Geoffrey Glaston (Rev'd)

He rode back to the homestead with his mind racing. He felt quite humbled by the Glastons' generosity – even though it was probably true that they owed their lives to him. But he also sensed that this was the opportunity he'd been waiting for, and by the time he got to the homestead he had a plan already formed in his mind. He explained it to Billy as they un-harnessed the horses.

'Were getting out of here, Billy.'

'Where we go, boss?

'Cape York.'

'Where Cape York'

'Long way, Billy. Right at the top of Australia. Farther than you've ever been.'

'We take horses, boss?'

'No Billy. We're going on a ship. There's a schooner lying idle in Port Benson. I met her skipper in the pub while I was there. He's lost his crew – they've all buggered off to the goldfields, like I did. I'm gonna hire him to take those barrels of rum to where the locals are even more thirsty than the miners on the goldfields.'

'How 'e sail there if 'e got no crew?'

'You and I will be his crew, Billy.'

'Me know nothin' about ships, boss.'

'You soon will, Billy. But first I have to write a letter of thanks to Rev. Glaston. Then we'll take it to Port Benson to post it and talk to the skipper of the *Wahini.*'

'You gonna tell 'im your plan, boss?'

'Hell, no. I don't think the good reverend would approve of me using his generous gift to get into the sly-grog trade.'

'What you tell 'im?'

'I'll just tell him that I'm about to make an investment in the colony of Queensland's economic growth, and if it pays off, I'll make sure some of the benefits flow back to him as thanks for his kindness.'

PART TWO

5 March 1886 – Cape York Peninsula

The south-easterly trade wind, blowing at a good 20 knots, was dead astern of the large ketch making her approach to the tiny township of Refuge Bay. Situated north of Cooktown, it was the last European settlement before Cape York, Australia's most northerly point. It lay under the protection of a large headland that provided good protection from the worst winds, but allowed easy access for approaching vessels, due to the fact that it was one of the few spots along that long, lonely coastline that had a deep-water channel leading into it. Unfortunately, the tide ran very fast in that channel, requiring careful handling of the sails in order to anchor before running onto the mangrove swamps.

Captain Michael Burns, master of the schooner *Wahini*, riding at anchor close to the town beach, watched the ketch through his brass telescope as she made her final approach.

'Will you look at that!' he said. 'She's being sailed by a bunch of women.'

Bernie Matthews - Michael's business partner and co-owner of the *Wahine* - took the glass from him and looked for himself.

'Looks like they're gonna gybe and bring her back up to the wind. Why the hell don't they just let the mains'l run free and drop the anchor?'

Michael grabbed the telescope from him and scanned the vessel again. 'Because they've got no bloody anchor, look!'

Bernie looked again. Sure enough, the cathead – a projecting timber beam on the bow that held up the anchor – was empty.

He had hardly finished his words when an unexpected gust caught the gaff- rigged mainsail and swung it violently from one side of the deck to the other, causing the vessel to lurch precariously and heel over on its starboard side.

They watched with mounting anxiety as the vessel yawed crazily until it came under the shelter of the headland and the pressure of the wind dropped, enabling the women to regain control of the sail and haul it inboard. The ketch, still heeling to starboard, then began to pick up speed and cut through the white flecked waves into the calmer waters of the anchorage.

'Nicely done!' Bernie muttered appreciatively.

Michael could see a woman wrestling with the ship's wheel, skillfully bringing the ketch off the wind sufficiently to slow it down, then turning slightly back into it to prevent the vessel going onto the opposite tack. However, a sudden gust of wind, funneling down a small valley behind the headland, hit the unsuspecting vessel and pushed it over onto its beam. The woman at the helm was thrown bodily against the starboard rail, while the wheel itself spun out of control. For one anxious moment it seemed likely that the fast-running tide might sweep the ketch broadside into the mangroves. But the woman immediately sprang back to the wheel and brought the vessel under control, steering the ketch away from the shallows and into deeper water.

Michael sprang into action. 'Bernie, get the boys from below; and bring up the spare anchor.'

He jumped down into the *Wahine's* boat, which was floating alongside the schooner, soon to be joined by Bernie, Billy, and the three burly Kanakas who made up the rest of their crew, one of them carrying the spare anchor.

'Put your backs into it, lads,' Michael urged. But the oarsmen needed no encouragement. The Kanakas were young and hard muscled islanders who had learned to paddle canoes through ocean swells almost from the time they could walk. It didn't take them long to cut across the placid waters of the anchorage to the shallows where the ketch lay pointing into the wind but drifting with the tide. There they found six Polynesian women, eagerly waiting to help them aboard. One of them, whom Michael recognized as the woman he had seen at the ship's wheel, came up to him and took both his hands in hers.

'Thank God you're here to help us, sir. We've been trying to find our way here for more than a week.'

In other circumstances Michael would have enjoyed the experience of having her holding his hands and looking thankfully into his eyes, because she was as beautiful a young woman as he had ever seen. She was slim, of medium height, with long raven hair and eyes that flashed like black pearls. Like the other women, she clearly had Polynesian blood, but her slim figure and the shape of her eyes suggested she was probably Eurasian, too. However, the urgency of the moment cut short his reverie. He withdrew his hands from hers and pointed to the empty cathead.

' 'I see you have no anchor.'

'Yes,' she said. 'We lost it a week ago.'

'We'll have to use ours, then. We need to try to kedge you away from the shallows. We have a falling tide and every minute counts.'

'What do you need us to do?' she asked.

'Just leave that to my lads and pray that she doesn't get pushed further up onto this bank.'

'That's something we can do, sir. We're all missionaries.'

Michael looked at her with surprise, not knowing what to say. He grunted acknowledgement and then joined Bernie and the crew, who were already attaching their spare anchor to what remained of the ketch's anchor cable.

Using a block and tackle, they swung the heavy anchor into the centre of the *Wahine's* boat. Michael and Billy then rowed it back into deeper water.

'This should do it,' Michael said. 'Let's get it over the side. Careful now, it's heavy enough to capsize the boat if we lose the trim.'

The boat began to tip alarmingly to one side as they heaved the anchor over the gunwale and dropped it into the milky blue water, where it quickly disappeared, settling into the sandy bottom twenty feet below. Michael then waved to Bernie, who by this time had the other end of the cable lashed to the ship's capstan.

'OK, start winching.'

Bernie and the Kanakas inserted the bars into the capstan and began to push it around. Each partial revolution caused the gearing to clank as the cable pulled tight against the anchor, pulling the ketch further into the safety of the anchorage. Michael winced as he heard Bernie cursing loudly, wondering what the beautiful missionary lady was thinking of them. But, to his astonishment, he saw that she and the others were gathered around the taffrail, their eyes closed and their mouths moving silently. He realized they were praying, just as he had unwittingly suggested.

For one awful moment Michael thought they were going to fail. The falling tide had caused the ketch to settle into the sand. Then, almost imperceptibly, they felt something begin to move. Sweating and cursing, they continued to push against the bars until inch by inch the ketch began to slide slowly back into deeper water. Bernie and his men kept the pressure on the capstan while the women at the taffrail opened their eyes to see water beginning to move under the stern.

'You've got it, Bernie. She's sliding off.' Michael waved his hat in jubilation. Then, with a few more revolutions of the capstan, the ketch was clear of the sandbank and afloat. They continued cranking until the vessel was directly over the anchor and, with the cable now vertical, they hauled it aboard.

'We'll use our boat to tow her closer to the beach,' Michael said. 'We can raft her up to our vessel. She'll ride safely there, away from this bloody current.'

He suddenly realized what he'd said. 'Sorry, ma'am. We don't get too many missionary ladies in these parts.' The young Eurasian woman, who appeared to be the leader of the group of missionaries, took his hands again and looked at him with an intensity he found quite disconcerting. 'How can we ever thank you, sir? And we don't even know your name.'

'I'm Michael Burns, ma'am, master of the schooner *Wahine,* and this is my partner, Bernie Matthews.'

Bernie removed his hat, wiped his greasy hands on his trousers and took the lady's hand gently. 'Pleased to meet you, missus. Sorry about my bad language back there.'

She smiled. 'My name is Sele Saena. These other ladies and I were on our way to Cooktown where we're to work as teachers with the islanders who live there. We left Samoa more than three weeks ago, but a week ago we ran into a storm and sea water somehow got into our water casks. So, Captain Mason, the master of this vessel, put into an island close to Warrior Reef and went ashore with his three crewmen to fill the casks with fresh water. The next thing we knew was he came rowing back alone, screaming for us to cut the anchor cable.

'Then we saw canoes full of natives being launched from the beach, obviously intending to attack our ship. Their leader was a huge white man, although his skin was burnt brown by the sun. Captain Mason didn't even try to get his boat on board. He climbed aboard and when he saw that we had managed to cut the anchor cable he got us to help him raise enough sail to get under way. We were very lucky to escape before the canoes reached us. He told us that his crew had been butchered as they went in search of water while he had been with the boat. He barely escaped himself.'

'Did he say anything else about this white man?'

'Only that the natives appeared to be terrified of him and that he wore a string of shrunken heads around his neck.'

Michael grimaced slightly. 'I've heard talk of a wild white man up in that area. You were lucky to escape. Where is Captain Mason now?'

'He's down below in his cabin. He was struck in the shoulder by an arrow. He was able to help us raise the sail and get the ship under way, but soon after the wound became infected, and he started to drift in and out of consciousness. He was able to give us enough instructions to keep the vessel going and told us how to get to Refuge Bay; and we've been doing our best to manage the ship and follow his instructions. Fortunately, we're all Polynesian, as you can see, and we're familiar with the sea; but not in vessels as large as this one. But we really need to get him ashore for medical help.'

'You were unlucky to have had a fast-running tide and a 20-knot wind to contend with. I doubt I could have kept your ship out of the mangroves without an anchor. It was an impressive bit of seamanship!'

She smiled appreciatively and led Michael below to a small cabin at the ship's stern where a man lay tossing deliriously on a cot. Michael reached down and felt the man's brow: he was burning with fever.

'There's an Aborigine mission station ashore,' he said. 'The missionaries are used to treating the natives for spear wounds. They should be able to do something for him. We'll get him into the boat and take him there. But where's the arrow that caused the problem?'

Sele turned to a small cupboard and produced a broken arrow. I had to break it off and push it through his shoulder to get it out,' she said. 'Otherwise, he would have died.'

'You did that, yourself?'

'Yes. It had to be done.'

Michael looked at her again and nodded approvingly.

5 March 1886 – Refuge Bay

The mission station stood at the top of a small hill looking down on the pristine waters of Refuge Bay and its untidy conglomeration of shacks that littered the beachfront. Michael explained that they belonged to a motley group of characters who made their living fishing for beche-de-mer – the sea cucumber so richly prized in China.

'Most of them head south when the cyclone season begins around December,' Michael explained. 'But their women stay here.'

'Why don't they take their wives with them?' Sele asked.

'They aren't wives in the usual Christian sense, ma'am,' Michael replied. 'They are native women; some of them from the local Aborigine tribes and others from the islands to the north.'

'Do you mean they're concubines?' Sele looked shocked.

'That would be putting it nicely,' Michael replied, anxious to change the subject.

They carried the semi-conscious Captain Mason on a canvas stretcher as they climbed the hill to the mission house. A grey-haired man was standing on the veranda waiting for them.

'It's Captain Burns, isn't it?' he asked, offering his hand to Michael. 'I hear that you've been delivering supplies to our general store.'

'That's right, Dr. Wakeley. And this lady is Miss Saena; a missionary like yourself.'

Dr. Wakeley's eyes opened with surprise and delight. 'Miss Saena, you are most welcome. We've heard so much about you. But I didn't expect to see you here. I thought you were going to Cooktown.'

Sele took his outstretched hand with both of hers. 'And I'm so glad to see you Dr. Wakeley. We have someone here who needs your help.'

Wakeley hurried down the veranda steps and looked at the white-faced man on the stretcher. He felt his brow; then, taking out his pocket watch, he timed the sick man's pulse rate. His brow furrowed with concern.

'We need to get this poor chap inside where I can attend to him properly. What happened to him?'

'He was shot through the shoulder with a native's arrow, several days ago,' Michael answered. 'Miss Saena managed to get the arrow out.'

Wakeley pulled the sheet away from Mason's shoulder and gently removed the dressing covering the wound. 'How long ago did this happen?' he asked.

'About a week ago,' Sele told him.

'How did you get the arrowhead out?'

'I had to push it through the other side of his shoulder and then break it off so that I could withdraw the shaft.'

He nodded approvingly.

'Not many women would have had the stomach to do that,' Michael added. 'He would've been in terrible pain. How did you manage to hold him still enough to do it?'

Sele looked at him sharply. 'My dear Captain Burns, women have the *stomach* to bear children, you know. I doubt many men would be able to do that! Anyway, I was able to calm him.'

Wakeley looked at her admiringly. 'Ah yes. Geoffrey Glaston told me about your amazing ability to do that.'

Michael, still smarting slightly from Sele's retort to what he thought was a compliment, looked up in surprise. 'Did you say Geoffrey Glaston?'

'Yes. He is the mission superintendent at Cooktown. He arranged for us to open this medical mission station. But we can talk more about that later. First, we must see to this poor chap's injuries.'

Later that evening Michael and Bernie accepted Dr. Wakeley's invitation to join them for dinner at the mission house. Mrs. Wakeley met them at the door and led them into the parlour where Sele and the other Samoans were waiting. Sele smiled warmly at them both, though her eyes seemed to rest a little longer on Michael's face.

'How is Captain Mason?' Michael asked.

'I'm glad to say that half an hour ago he was sitting up and taking some broth Mrs. Wakeley made for him. I expect him to make a complete recovery. He's a strong man and should be up and about in a few days.'

'Well, that is good news, Doctor. He has you to thank for that.'

'I think it would be more appropriate to say that he has Miss Saena to thank. If that arrowhead hadn't been removed, he would surely have died of blood poisoning.'

Michael looked at Sele, seated opposite between two other Samoans. 'I still find it hard to believe that you ladies were able to hold him down while you pushed that arrow through his flesh. He's a big man; he must have struggled like hell...' He reddened slightly, thinking that his terminology might not have been appropriate to use with missionaries, but they seemed not to mind.

It was one of the other women who gave the answer. 'Sele do what she always do. She pray, then she say to captain, "Be still, now." And he lie quiet while she push arrow through.'

Michael looked at Sele, who seemed to be paying no attention. Then he turned enquiringly to Dr. Wakeley. 'Well Doctor, you're a medical man, what do you think?'

Wakely laid down his knife and fork and stared absently for a moment. 'As a man of science, I am trained to look for logical answers to life's seeming mysteries. As a man of faith, I also believe in a spiritual reality that transcends mere physics. This has often caused me some consternation. However, I've come to see that neither I nor my medicines heal people. The healing is within them. Wounds heal and the cells of the body are renewed. My ministrations merely help nature do its own job. So, in that sense I can say that the healing comes from God, and medical science is merely the tool.

'But I also believe that there are powers of healing within the mind - powers which also express the healing power of God. I believe there are some people - not many, but some - who are able to channel another form of healing – one that is every bit as efficacious as my scientific ministrations. From what Geoffrey Glaston has told me about Miss Saena, she is such a person.'

'She always like that,' one of the other Samoans added. 'Even when she little girl.'

The others nodded their assent while Sele said nothing, concentrating on her meal.

'I've seen the natives do things that don't make sense to us whitefellas.' Bernie added. 'I've seen grown men - strong men too - just sicken up and die for no reason. And then later we learned that they'd had the bone pointed at them by some witch doctor type of bloke, miles away.'

'What do you mean by "pointing the bone"?' Sele asked.

'The Aborigines believe that certain men, called kurdaitcha men, have the power to kill others by magic. They have a special bone called a kundela that the kurdaitcha man points at the victim after he's tracked him down. The victim always dies in agony.'

'Perhaps that's because it's all in the victim's mind,' Mrs. Wakeley added. 'They knew the bone had been pointed, and they believed it meant they would die, and so they convinced themselves that's what would happen, and it did.'

'That's what I used to think, missus; 'til I came across coves what up and died not even knowing that the bone had been pointed at them. The kurdaitcha men had done it from a distance.'

Dr. Wakely nodded his head thoughtfully. 'As I said, I'm a man of science and also a man of faith. I think there's a spiritual dimension to our existence that we Europeans are largely unaware of. I'm convinced of the reality of spiritual evil, just as I believe in the reality of spiritual good. After all, the New Testament does say that *"We wrestle against spiritual wickedness in high places."*'

'But when the followers of Jesus use spiritual powers, it's for good purposes, not for evil,' Sele said quietly. 'That's what Geoffrey Glaston taught me.'

Michael's ears pricked up at the mention of Geoffrey Glaston's name. 'You keep talking about Geoffrey Glaston. I once knew a man by that name. He was a reverend. He and his wife, Amelia, were shipwrecked near to where I once lived, just outside Port Benson in the colony of Victoria.'

'Well, there's a coincidence,' Wakeley answered. 'There can only be one Reverend Geoffrey Glaston with a wife named Amelia who got shipwrecked off Port Benson; and that has to be our mission superintendent at Cooktown.'

'I thought he was a minister in Sydney,' Michael said.

'He was, until he felt a call to go to Samoa as a missionary,' Wakeley answered.

Sele looked up from eating and said quietly. 'He was the Principal of my Bible School in Apia, where I grew up. He taught me, and all of us, to be missionary teachers.'

'And now he's back in Australia?'

'Yes. He returned a year ago,' Wakely answered.

'Amelia was suffering from recurring bouts of malaria,' Sele added. 'She nearly died and so the mission authorities thought it better for them to come back. They wanted Geoffrey to become the General Secretary of the missionary society. But he asked to be sent to North Queensland where he could minister to the local natives and the islanders living here.'

'Pity you weren't able to work your healing powers on Mrs. Glaston, too,' Bernie added mischievously.

Wakely and his wife both glanced at him reprovingly, but Sele responded with a smile. 'God works in mysterious ways, Mr. Matthews; don't you agree Captain Burns?'

Michael looked at her wistfully. 'He does indeed, ma'am. He does indeed.'

5/6 March 1886 – Cape York Peninsula

The *Wahine* was due to sail for Melbourne on the next morning tide. Michael offered to take Sele and her companions to Cooktown, though Sele was concerned that this might delay his voyage south.

'It won't be a problem, ma'am,' he said. 'With a decent breeze we'll reach Cooktown in a couple of days. We'll deliver you to the Reverend Glaston and be on our way again before dark. I'm hoping for an easy run down to Melbourne so that I can return with supplies for these northern settlements.'

'What sort of things will you be bringing back?'

'Oh, flour and other necessities of life that aren't available up here,' he answered, vaguely. 'Now, if you and the other ladies can arrange to be down at the waterfront by first light tomorrow, I'll have a boat waiting to bring you and your luggage aboard and we'll be on our way.'

Sele took his hand in hers and smiled at him in a way that made his heart race. 'Dear Captain Burns, how can we ever thank you for your kindness to us?'

'That won't be necessary, ma'am. It's my pleasure to be of service.'

'Then we shall be there at the beach at first light, just as you said.'

Michael touched the peak of his cap and turned to leave, signaling to Bernie that it was time to go. It was then, as they walked back down the hill, that Bernie revealed his own surprise news- something he'd been wanting to reveal for a while but had been reluctant to do for fear of making life harder for Michael. They'd been in partnership now for nearly ten years, providing a lifeline to remote northern communities, shipping supplies through uncharted waters filled with reefs and subject to cyclonic winds. They had made a good living – especially through the sale of illicit liquor – and the partnership seemed set to prosper even more with the recent development of the pearling industry.

'I've got something I need to talk to you about, Michael,' he said. I've been givin' it a lot of thought and I think my days at sea are over. I've done pretty well these past few years, especially since you now own the half share in the *Wahine* that used to belong to the bank.'

'It still does,' Michael grimaced. 'It's just that I now owe them the money instead of you. So, what do you plan to do?'

'I'm going to look around for a nice little business in Cooktown. I've always fancied a ship's chandlery or a store to outfit gold prospectors – something like that.'

'And when do you plan to do this?'

'Well, you probably won't want to hear this, but I want to do it now.'

'Now? Do you mean when we get to Cooktown?'

'Yes. I know that means you'll be shorthanded, but you and the boys will manage.'

'Oh, I'm not worried about being one man short. You've been more like an owner/passenger anyway since you took me on as your partner and made me skipper. I'm more concerned about you needing more time to think about this.'

'I've been thinking about it for weeks. And now's a good time to do it.'

'Why?'

'Because I reckon there's gonna be another gold rush here.'

Michael looked at him quizzically. 'What do you know that I don't know? Has someone been talking to you?'

'I've been talking to an old prospector I've known ever since I first came up here. He's seen things up there in those ranges.'

'What sort of things?'

'Rocks. The sort you always see when there's gold around. But you keep that to yourself.'

'So, you plan to go prospecting again?'

'No, mate; that's a mug's game. I intend to help spread the rumour about gold up there and then provide the prospectors with the things they need to go looking for it. But I will make one trip to stake my claim before the rush starts.'

Michael realized Bernie wasn't about to divulge further information, so he shrugged his shoulders and said: 'Well, if you're sure that's what you want to do, I hope you make a go of it. But what about your half share in the *Wahine*? Do you intend to keep it?'

'Of course! With your head for business, it's bound to keep makin' money. And the blokes up here still have powerful thirsts.'

Michael looked around anxiously and then remembered that the missionaries were no longer around to hear that last comment. 'Well, I'll be sorry for not having you on board, Bernie.'

'Don't make me laugh, Michael. There can only be one master aboard a ship – even one the size of the *Wahine.* Having the former skipper around, like you've had these past months, has to be a real pain.'

Michael grinned. 'OK, Bernie. I'll put you ashore at Cooktown with the ladies and then keep on making profits for both of us.'

'That's what I hoped you'd say!' They shook hands and climbed into the boat waiting to take them back to the schooner. As soon as they were aboard Bernie went below deck, leaving Michael to prepare the vessel for an early departure, and to contemplate his new freedom.

* * *

The Wakeleys came down to the beach next morning to say goodbye. Further up the beach a villainous looking group of men, most of them intoxicated, staggered out of the general store – which also served as a pub, adding their farewells and thanking Michael for the much-needed barrels of flour.

'How curious it is to have flour stored in barrels rather than bags,' Sele remarked. 'Do you always carry it that way?'

'It's so we can float them ashore,' Michael answered quickly, anxious to change the subject. 'Many of these little settlements don't have wharves for ships to tie up to.'

'Flour is an important commodity up here, my dear,' Mrs. Wakeley added. 'And so is rum, as you can see from those ruffians over there.'

'Let's not go into that, my dear,' Wakeley said. She, however, would not be deterred.

'The colonial government has tried all sorts of things to prevent the sale of spirits in these parts. But there are some people who seem to know ways of overcoming the difficulties.' She looked at Michael, who pretended not to hear. 'You only have to look at those men over there to see the effects of it. And what it does to the natives, especially the native women, does not bear repeating.'

Wakeley gave her a reproving look and then turned to Michael who was helping the missionaries into the boat. 'We're in your debt, sir. It's kind of you to take the ladies to their destination, free of charge.'

'Not at all, Dr. Wakeley. It's the least that I can do, knowing what valuable work you missionaries do in these parts.'

'Please give my very best wishes to Geoffrey Glaston when you get to Cooktown.'

'I shall indeed. I'm looking forward to meeting him again. Goodbye doctor; ma'am.'

One hour later they were on their way, sailing close-hauled with a steady fifteen knot breeze coming almost across the starboard bow, causing the *Wahine* to heel well over on her port beam. Sele watched delightedly as the white flecked foam surged past the gunwales.

'Would you like to take the wheel, Miss Saena?'

Sele looked over her shoulder to where Michael stood at the ship's wheel. 'Do you really trust me to have control of your ship after having seen what I did to Captain Mason's ketch?' she laughed.

'Conning a vessel like that into a narrow anchorage in a strong wind would test the skills of any seaman,' Michael replied. 'I'm amazed that the six of you were able to sail that ketch for all that time on your own and actually find your way to Refuge Bay.'

'Well, we are Polynesians, you know. The sea is in our blood. I grew up sailing outrigger canoes from our home in Apia. My brothers and I would often go out through the reef to the open sea to visit villages along the coast. My father also had a small cutter. He got it from a German trader, who taught him how keel boats work. So I was not without some experience; and we did get plenty of advice from Captain Mason until he became too delirious to talk rationally.'

'In that case you should have no problems whatsoever in taking the *Wahine* out into the Coral Sea.'

'You will stay by me, Captain Burns; just in case.'

'It will be my pleasure, Miss Saena.' Michael had never spoken a truer word.

Under the steady pressure of that fifteen-knot breeze the *Wahine,* with all sail set, surged along the channel. Sele quickly became accustomed to the feel of the wheel as it responded to the pressure of the water against the rudder. Under Michael's instruction she learned to watch the leading edge of the jib, making sure that it held the wind, and then bearing away slightly to port whenever it began to shimmer.

Michael stood behind her, with one hand gripping the boom that was hauled in almost to the ship's centerline. He watched appreciatively as her hands deftly responded to every slight change of wind direction, while also gazing at the shape of her neck and the profile of her face. To say he was quite smitten with her would be an understatement. But something told him he was out of his depth. The girls he'd grown up with in the Black Country slums were mostly ragged street urchins, with matted hair and snotty noses. By the time he'd started to show interest in girls he was living in the all-male world of a ship's focs'l, where romance was mostly hidden under layers of misogynistic lust.

Yet he'd long dreamed of meeting someone to whom he could really give his heart – as well as his body. But what decent girl would be interested in a man who spent most of his life away from home – and was a rum runner to boot. Certainly not someone like Sele Saena. Not only was she exotically beautiful, but she had a grace and dignity that would enable her to move in the highest circles without embarrassment – even though she was of mixed race. Perhaps one day he also might be able to move in those circles, but for now all he could do was dream.

'We'll soon be weathering the headland,' he told her. 'The wind may seem to drop as we come under its lee, so I suggest you steer a little more to port so that we don't risk losing way.'

'Aye, aye, skipper,' she replied with the slightest hint of a chuckle in her voice.

Suddenly, out of the blue, a strong gust of wind caught the *Wahine* and caused her to heel alarmingly on to her port beam. Sele gave a little scream of alarm while hanging firmly on to the ship's wheel. Michael immediately let go of the boom and reached over her shoulder to take the wheel with his left hand, while simultaneously reaching round her waist to grip it with his right. He held the ship steady on its course until the gust of wind passed and the *Wahine* resumed her previous trim.

'My apologies, Miss Saena,' Michael mumbled. He withdrew his hand from the ship's wheel and returned to his previous position. He also noticed that a distinct blush was showing through Sele's golden skin.

'That gust of wind was what we call a bullet. The wind sometimes gets funneled down the valley between the headland and the hill next to it. I should have warned you that it might happen.'

'Please don't apologize, Captain. Your quick thinking clearly kept me from making the same mistake that brought us to grief on Captain Mason's ketch. Do you want me to continue steering or would you prefer to do it yourself?'

'I think you're doing a wonderful job, Miss Saena. I'd be happy for you to continue as long as you wish.'

She looked over her shoulder and smiled at him. 'Then I shall continue, but only as long as you're there to help me.'

Thirty minutes later they were beyond the headland and out into the Coral Sea. Under Michael's guidance, Sele brought the schooner onto the opposite tack, this time with the wind blowing across the port bow and the sails close-hauled to the starboard side.

'You did that very well, Miss Saena,' Michael said. 'The ship went about with hardly any loss of speed through the water. We'll make a sailor out of you yet.'

Sele flashed another smile and laughed. 'Well, I did tell you that I'm part Polynesian and all Polynesians are sailors. Anyway, you were there at my side telling me everything I had to do.'

The thought crossed Michael's mind that he'd like to be at her side telling her what to do permanently, as he watched her hair flying in the wind – although he sensed that the reality might be the other way round.

'How long should it take us to get to Cooktown?'

'If this wind holds steady, we should get there the day after tomorrow,' Michael replied. 'We'll hold this course for about four hours. That should bring us close to the outer reef. Then we'll go about onto the other tack and should have a straight run south to Cooktown.'

'Oh, that'll be good. I'm so looking forward to seeing the Glastons again. They're such a dear couple and taught me so much.'

'You said earlier that you had studied in his Bible School?'

'Yes. I felt God's call to be a missionary teacher.'

'I thought all the missionaries were Europeans – begging your pardon, Miss Saena; I don't mean to imply that islanders can't teach.'

Sele smiled. 'You keep apologizing, Captain. There's no need, I assure you.'

Michael smiled sheepishly.

'Most people don't realize that more Samoan missionaries have gone to the islands of the Pacific than from anywhere else. And most of the stories you hear about missionaries in cannibals' stew pots were actually about Samoans.'

'I didn't know that.'

'When John Williams first arrived in Samoa, my people responded to his message with great enthusiasm. My grandfather's older brother, who was the supreme chief of all Samoa, was one of the first to be baptized. It was John Williams himself who established the Bible School I went to.'

'And your grandfather's brother was the supreme chief!'

'Yes. He was my father's uncle. My mother was Eurasian, half English and half Chinese. Her mother - my grandmother - was the daughter of an English trader. When he died, she married the son of his Chinese business partner. The two of them inherited the business and became quite wealthy, trading with the Samoan chiefs for copra. That's how my mother came to meet my father.'

'Ah, so that explains why you speak English like an English lady!'

Sele smiled. 'The missionaries also taught me well.'

'And you're related to the Samoan royal family,' Michael added. 'That makes you a princess.'

Sele laughed. 'Perhaps not quite like your British princesses.'

'Oh, I think you're much more of a princess than any of them.' Michael suddenly realized that he was blushing and turned to look up at the mast-head so that she wouldn't notice. But she had and was surprised at the quiet glow of pleasure it created.

8 March 1886 - Cooktown

The sun was still low in the eastern sky as Sele came up on deck in time to see the *Wahine* enter the mouth of the Endeavour River. Michael was standing at the ship's wheel, carefully navigating the schooner across the river bar. She looked out over the rail to see an unruly conglomeration of wooden buildings, stretching from the river's edge up and over the low hills beyond it.

'Good morning, Miss Saena. I hope you slept well.'

'Good morning, Captain. I did, thank you.'

'How do you like your first view of Cooktown?'

'It's larger than I expected.'

'Yes, it's always a surprise to see how quickly gold rush towns grow. It was the same on the Victorian goldfields when I first came to Australia.'

'Did you come to Australia hoping to find gold?'

'No ma'am. I was second mate on a windjammer that used to sail from Liverpool to Melbourne via the Cape of Good Hope, then back around Cape Horn, loaded with wool. On my fourth visit I jumped ship, along with most of the crew, and headed off to the goldfields, convinced I'd make a fortune.'

'And did you?'

Michael smiled ruefully. 'No, ma'am. But some did, and some keep on doing it, including men who left Victoria to come up here.'

I know that Cooktown is booming and is less than twenty years old but I've never really learned its history. When did it all start?'

'It was back in 1873. A prospector named Mulligan discovered gold on the Palmer River. Once the word got out it started a new gold rush to these parts. The Queensland Government sent a man named Dalrymple up to find a suitable place for a port. He chose this very river and named the new settlement Cooktown - after Captain Cook.'

'And the Endeavour River must have been named for Captain Cook's ship.'

'Yes.' Michael pointed back over his left shoulder. 'It was further down the coast that the Endeavour nearly came to grief when she ran across a reef one night. Cook managed to get her into this river and careened her on that beach over there,' he pointed to a stretch of white sand just off their port bow.

'So, nothing really happened then for a hundred years.'

'No, ma'am. Apart from the natives and a few villains who fished these waters for beche-de-mer, there was no-one here until the gold seekers arrived; and they came in their thousands, from all over the world, including from China.'

'From China too?'

'Oh yes, ma'am. Wherever there's a gold rush you'll always find Chinamen. We had them down in Victoria too; thousands of them. There were some pretty nasty incidents too. The white diggers resented them and there was talk of lynchings. But most of the ones who died up here got killed by Aborigines.'

'Why?'

'Well, to avoid trouble with the white diggers in Cooktown, the boats that brought them here used to drop them off in little coves and creeks along the coast and let them take their chances, finding their way to the goldfields through the bush. The local tribes by this time had suffered enough at the hands of the whitefellas and didn't differentiate between them and the Chinamen, who were easy targets as they tried to find their way through all that rainforest out there.'

'How horrible! And all this has grown from nothing in fifteen years?'

'Amazing, isn't it? But that's what gold fever does. In the first year the population grew to around thirty thousand. Anyway, I've bored you enough with the history lesson. I can see the town wharf coming up, so if you'll pardon me, ma'am, I'll bring the ship alongside.'

'Oh, you've not bored me at all, Captain Burns. It's a fascinating story. I shall look forward to hearing more about it later, perhaps. Now, you carry on with your duties.'

He smiled and touched the brim of his cap, quietly delighted by her rapt attention. Sele stood well away from the crew as they took in the mainsail and prepared to come alongside the wharf, but Michael noticed her eyes were still on him, and it made his heart race. With the wind now little more than a light breeze blowing across the *Wahine's* port beam and the tide beginning to ebb, it was relatively easy to edge the schooner gently up to the wharf, where the Kanakas jumped ashore to secure the bow and stern lines.

'That was beautifully done, Captain Burns,' Sele said admiringly. 'I hardly felt a bump as we touched the wharf.'

'Thank you, ma'am. It wasn't difficult in a light breeze. But you have to know your ship and how she responds. Fortunately, *Wahine* is a very responsive lady.'

'I suppose you wish all the ladies you had dealings with were the same,' Sele asked mischievously.

Michael looked surprised. It was not the sort of comment he expected from a missionary. He wasn't sure how he ought to answer her, so he just smiled. But it did make him wonder if she, perhaps, was offering him some encouragement. It both thrilled him and scared him.

A middle-aged couple detached themselves from the onlookers who had been watching the schooner's arrival and made their way to the gangway being secured to the ship's side.

'It looks like we have a reception committee,' Michael said.

Sele looked up and her face beamed. 'It's the Glastons. How on earth did they know we were about to arrive now?'

Apart from a receding hairline and a deep suntan, Geoffrey Glaston had not changed much since Michael had rescued him from the wreck of the *Nancy,* ten years earlier. He was still slim and energetic looking, and his grey-blue eyes had the same intensity Michael remembered from their earlier meeting. Amelia, though, looked tired and unwell; even though her face was wreathed in smiles. Sele's feet had barely touched the wharf timbers before she hugged her to herself with an enthusiasm that surprised Michael, who thought of missionaries as always being very reserved.

Geoffrey waited patiently for his wife to finish her greeting and then took Sele's hands in his and kissed them gently. 'My dear Sele,' he said. 'Thank God you and your companions are here safe at last.'

He turned to the others who had followed her ashore and joined Amelia in greeting each of them warmly. 'We heard last night about how your ship had been attacked up in the islands and how you had managed to escape and get to Refuge Bay.'

'How on earth did you find out so quickly?' Sele asked.

'One of the local beche-de-mer skippers was at Refuge Bay when you arrived. He got the story from one of the Kanakas aboard this ship. The story is all over Cooktown. But let's not talk about that now. You and your companions must come straight to the mission house where you can have a bath and refresh yourselves. Then you can tell us about your adventures.'

'Thank you, Geoffrey. That will be lovely. However, before we do, I want you to meet Captain Burns, who helped us save our ship after we ran it aground at Refuge Bay. He was kind enough to give us free passage to Cooktown.'

'Bless my soul!' Geoffrey exclaimed as he recognized Michael. 'Amelia, look who it is!'

Amelia put her hand to her mouth to stifle her gasp of surprise. 'My goodness; Mr. Burns! Is it really you? I can't believe it.' She ran to him and embraced him as warmly as she had Sele, until Geoffrey restrained her.

'Now, my dear, we mustn't embarrass Mr. Burns; or should I say Captain Burns.' He pumped Michael's hand. 'My dear chap, I can't tell you how glad I am to see you! Once again, we're in your debt. But what are you doing as captain of a schooner? I thought your job was running a sheep station.'

'It's a long story, Reverend Glaston,' Michael grinned. 'But I spent a few years at sea before I took up that job managing the property in Victoria. Thanks to your generosity in sending me that money all those years ago, I was able to work my way up to the point where I could purchase a half share in the *Wahine* and become master of my own ship.'

'Well, we are both so delighted to hear that,' Amelia said. 'If it hadn't been for you neither of us would be here today.'

'And, if it were not for Michael, I would still be stranded in Refuge Bay,' Sele added, looking at him warmly, while he smiled shyly.

So, it's Michael is it, not Captain Burns, Amelia thought to herself.

'And what about that other chap who was with us; what was his name?'

'Mundine.'

'Yes, that's it. Mr. Mundine. Have you any idea what happened to him?'

'No, sir. I haven't heard of him in several years, though I would like to meet up with him again.'

'Well, I don't think I want to meet him again,' Amelia said. 'He didn't seem like a very nice person.'

'No, ma'am. I can assure you that he's not a very nice person.'

Their conversation was interrupted by Billy and the rest of Michael's crew carrying the missionaries' luggage ashore.

'Where you want us put this, boss?'

Geoffrey's eyes widened with delight. 'Amelia, look who else is here!'

They took Billy's hands in theirs and patted his back delightedly, much to his embarrassment.

Michael looked enquiringly at Geoffrey. 'What would you like the boys to do with the ladies' luggage?'

Geoffrey pointed to a pony trap standing at the back of the wharf. 'The mission house isn't far,' he said. 'We can walk there while our driver takes the bags in his cart. You will stay for lunch, Captain Burns? Your fellows are most welcome to join us too.'

'Thank you kindly, Reverend; but we ought to be on our way.'

'Oh, Captain Burns, surely a couple of hours won't make any difference to your voyage back south,' Amelia interjected. 'And I'm sure Sele would love to have you stay with us just a little longer,' she added mischievously.

Sele's cheeks reddened slightly. 'Yes, Captain Burns. You must join us. We have so much to thank you for.'

Michael shrugged his shoulders. 'Well, how can I refuse such an invitation? But I think my lads would feel out of place, so I'll leave them to take it easy here for a couple of hours. The tide turns again just after noon. If I can be back on board by 2 o'clock we'll be in a good position to cross the river bar just before the next high tide.'

'Then it's settled,' Geoffrey beamed. 'Come, my dear. Let's show our guests the way to our house.'

The mission house stood at the top of a road that wound its way up a small hill above the town and looked out along the river towards the sea. It was high set on hardwood piles that allowed the cooling sea breezes to float through and surrounded by a veranda. A large poinciana tree, its orange-red blossoms in full bloom, helped shade the corrugated iron roof from the heat of the morning sun. The breeze also carried the sound of distant surf crashing on the coral sand and the intoxicating aroma of jasmine and gardenia. Amelia led them onto the veranda where they all turned to look at the view.

'What a lovely spot!' Sele exclaimed.

'And quiet too,' Geoffrey added. He pointed to the town below. 'It gets pretty noisy down there, especially once the sun has gone down and the pubs fill up.'

'There can't be many of them in a town this size, can there?' Sele asked.

'My dear, unbelievable though it may sound, there are more than sixty. And when the gold miners come into town to join the pearlers and bech-de-mer fishers, this pretty little township turns into a vision of Hades.'

'But how do they manage to get hold of so much liquor?'

'There are unscrupulous captains who keep the local publicans supplied with beer and rum – especially rum,' Geoffrey explained. 'In some places they actually bring it ashore in flour barrels to avoid the attention of the authorities.'

Sele stole a quick glance at Michael and noticed he had quietly walked away.

It was well into the afternoon before the *Wahine* set off downstream against the rising tide. Michael was anxious to cross the river bar about one hour before high tide. That way he could be sure of having plenty of water under the keel as his schooner crossed the constantly changing sandbanks. He had intended to be on his way by 2 o'clock but had found it difficult to tear himself away from the enchanting young woman he'd only known for a couple of days, but whom he couldn't stop thinking about.

Sele was also sad to see him go. She stayed on the wharf, watching his ship beat against wind and tide until it rounded a bend in the river and momentarily disappeared from sight. Michael, gazing through his telescope, could still see her standing there, waving with her arm stretched high above her head, her raven black hair blowing in the wind, contrasting sharply with the demure, white skirt that fluttered around her ankles. He wondered if she was as sorry to see him go as he was to leave her; but he thought that was too much to hope for. Even so, he knew that nothing was going to keep him from coming back.

While Geoffrey wandered back into the house Sele and Amelia walked to the top of the hill Captain Cook had once climbed, hoping to see the way through the sandbanks beyond the mouth of the river. By the time they reached the top the *Wahine* was just a small white shape on the wide expanse of the ocean beyond. They paused for a while to watch.

'He's a handsome rogue, that Captain Burns,' Amelia said.

Sele nodded, 'Yes, he is.'

'But he's still a rogue, my dear. You must remember that. Those ships sailing to Cape York don't just carry flour and tea, you know.'

Sele nodded. 'But he has kind eyes.'

Amelia sighed and shook her head.

29 March 1886 - Cooktown

Three weeks after the departure of the *Wahine,* a barquentine with a black hull dropped anchor in the Endeavour River. Geoffrey Glaston had been watching its progress up the river through his telescope, which he kept mounted on a tripod near his study window. He always took great interest in the comings and goings of vessels in the port – most of them schooners and small cutters. Some were regular visitors, and he could recognize them without having to search for their names. But even though this one was new to him, there was something vaguely familiar about it.

The ship swung slowly at anchor and eventually Geoffrey was able to read the name, *Hoylake,* emblazoned across its stern. Where have I heard that name before, he asked himself? He thought about it without success as he paced back and forth across his study floor. Then he decided to ask Amelia who was in the kitchen cleaning up after breakfast.

'Darling, does the name *Hoylake* mean anything to you?'

'Yes, it's a seaside town in Lancashire.'

'I know, but have you ever heard of a ship with that name?'

Amelia thought for a moment. 'Wasn't that the name of the ship we saw in Kingston when we were on the *Nancy*; the one that Captain Travis was trying to race to Melbourne when we ran aground?'

'Yes, of course! I remember now. She was loading a cargo of rum for Australia too.'

'And when you found out that rum was to be the *Nancy's* cargo you nearly cancelled our passage,' Amelia chuckled.

Geoffrey smiled. 'If I could have afforded it, I would have. That ship was accursed, I do believe.'

'Well, if it was, it was because of the type of man who was running it. But why do you ask?'

'Because the *Hoylake* has just dropped anchor. Come and see for yourself.'

Apart from a noticeable loss of hair, Ernest Mundine had not changed all that much in the last eight years. He was still overweight, foul mouthed and cunning. He was also considerably wealthier. He stretched his legs and leaned against the jolly boat's transom as a couple of Malay seamen rowed him ashore.

Looking back over his shoulder he watched a huge bear of a man roaring orders to the barquentine's crew and smiled to himself. He had first met Captain Homer - master of the *Hoylake* and commonly known as *Bulldog* - at the official inquiry into the loss of the *Nancy* in Melbourne. Mundine considered it to be one of the more fortuitous events of his life. Homer, like Captain Travis, was a hard drinking, hard swearing sea captain of the old school, who was not averse to flaunting the law if it meant a good profit, and would drive his crew – cutthroats like himself – mercilessly by sheer force of his size and personality.

Mundine was not the sort of man to feel easily intimidated – especially by a business partner. But *Bulldog* Homer frightened him. The sheer size of the man, his brutal reputation and his evil smile - made all the more sinister by two gold front teeth – ensured that Mundine took care never to antagonize him.

Homer, for his part, had been more than willing to allow Mundine to charter his vessel for a couple of trips to Cape York with her hold filled with barrels of rum. But it was not the profits from rum-running that had made them prosper. They'd discovered that the really big profits were to be made in providing the burgeoning sugar industry with black labourers to work the cane fields that had mushroomed along the fertile coastal river flats further south.

Those labourers were mainly Melanesians, but sometimes they included natives from the islands of the Torres Strait. Wherever they came from they were all known as Kanakas - islanders who, in theory, had volunteered to work in Queensland as indentured labourers for three years at a rate of up to ten pounds a year. When their time was up, they were supposed to be taken back to their islands, where, loaded with trade goods purchased with their wages, they would be considered wealthy men.

Sadly, as the demand for cheap labour grew, the trade attracted the worst type of sea captains, rogues like Homer who would lure unsuspecting natives aboard their ships, then force them below decks, seal the hatches and sail on to some other unsuspecting island, where they would repeat the process until their holds were full of kidnapped Kanakas, destined for the Queensland cane fields.

While many indentured labourers were properly recruited, the *Blackbirders,* as these unscrupulous ships' captains came to be known, made their fortunes by delivering their human cargoes to equally unscrupulous planters prepared to pay cash on delivery for islanders whom they treated little better than slaves.

Mundine had hit on what he considered to be a particularly ingenious method of luring natives on board Captain Homer's ship. Since the middle of the nineteenth century the islands of the southwest Pacific had proved to be fertile soil for the Christian message. Wherever the missionaries went, inter-tribal warfare, cannibalism and head hunting all but disappeared – along with other aspects of indigenous culture - to be replaced by a piety that would have delighted Queen Victoria herself.

Mundine soon learned to avoid those islands where the missionaries lived and to seek out places that had received only a partial exposure to Christianity and were curious to learn more. He would go ashore, pretending to be a missionary, and then invite the men of the village aboard his ship to join in their worship service. The men would be ushered into the hold, where they were told the service was to be held. Then, before they had time to react, the hatches would be sealed, imprisoning them below deck. Any women or children who happened to come aboard would simply be thrown overboard and left to swim ashore – or drown.

But, unlike many others in that nefarious trade, Ernest Mundine realized the bonanza wouldn't last forever. On his occasional visits to Brisbane, the capital of the colony of Queensland, he'd sensed a change in public opinion. People were becoming increasingly aware of the dark side of the trade in native labour, and there was talk of the colonial government banning it. There was also growing opposition from people who saw it as a threat to the employment of white workers.

But then he came up with an idea. An increasing number of planters, anxious to do the right thing, were looking for ships to return their indentured labourers to their homes. There wasn't much profit in it and competition for these human cargoes wasn't great. However, Mundine realized that the Queensland government, already talking about becoming part of a new and independent *White* Australian Federation, would be more concerned about keeping cheap native labour out than what might happen to those who were sent home. And that was why he had come to Cooktown, in order to meet an agent of the German New Guinea Company, recently arrived from Rabaul on the inter-island steamer.

As the ship's boat neared the town wharf he looked back to where the *Hoylake* rode at anchor and smiled as he saw groups of Melanesian men lounging against the ship's rail, looking at what they thought would be their last sight of Queensland before returning to their villages in the Solomon Islands. Some of them even waved to him, but he didn't wave back. 'Black gold,' he said to himself. 'Black gold, that's what they still are.'

* * *

Germany was the most recent competitor in the European game of colonizing the world. It had been less than twenty years since she herself had become a federated nation, but she had already joined the scramble for overseas possessions, some of which were now in the South Seas. The largest of them was in New Guinea, the northern half of the huge, unexplored land mass to the north of Australia. Further to the east they occupied New Britain, New Ireland and the islands of the Bismarck Archipelago. The New Guinea Company had been formed to exploit the natural resources of these new colonies, including the development of copra plantations.

Klaus Stein had been with the company since it first opened its base in Rabaul. A tall, slim man with a sun tanned and pockmarked face, he looked every inch the successful South Seas official in his cream suit and pith helmet. Mundine found him waiting in the saloon bar of the *Capricorn* Hotel.

They shook hands and ordered beer, which they took to a quiet booth in a corner, away from listening ears.

'You have the cargo you promised in your letter, Herr Mundine?'

'I do; ninety-five serviceable natives, all of them with three years' experience working the cane fields around Mackay. We picked them up five days ago.'

'And they are all docile; no potential mutineers among them?'

'They're all very contented at present, Herr Stein. They think they're on their way back to their villages in the Solomon Islands. When we get to where you want us to deliver them, we'll tell them it's just a short hop from there to their islands. They'll be glad to go ashore to stretch their legs after being cooped up in the ship's hold. Once they're ashore it's over to you and your men.'

Stein nodded. 'Good. But there must be no word to anyone that my company is involved. This is a private arrangement between the two of us and my friends who run the plantations. I don't want questions being asked by my superiors because the British Government has complained to Berlin. Do you understand?'

'Perfectly. It's also in my interest that this little deal be kept quiet. I imagine that you might want more cargoes in the future.'

Stein smiled. 'Indeed, Herr Mundine. I have many friends in the islands that need cheap labour. The local tribes are too wild and primitive to be any value. Your Kanakas are just what we need.'

'Then we agree on the price; seven English pounds per head?'

'Agreed.'

'So where is it that you want them delivered?'

Stein took a large sheet of heavy paper from his inside pocket and unfolded it on the table before them. It was a map of the southwest

Pacific. Stein pointed to a large island at the northern end of the Solomon Islands group.

'Here,' he said, pointing to a spot on the eastern side of the island.

Mundine looked carefully at the map. 'Bougainville,' he said.

Stein nodded. 'And the place you are to go to is called Makunai. It's a native village on a bay that provides good protection from heavy winds. There are several new plantations in that area, all in need of labourers. You are to take the Kanakas there and make contact with a young man named Gunter Stein.'

Mundine raised his eyebrows at the mention of the name.

'He's my nephew. He owns one of the plantations.'

'How will he know when to meet us?'

'Don't worry about that. The natives have a way of passing information very quickly. He'll be told as soon as your ship is within sight of Bougainville.'

'And the money?'

'You will receive your money as soon as the Kanakas are ashore.'

They finished their beer, shook hands and Mundine returned to the wharf where the two Malays were waiting to row him back to the ship. As they cast off Mundine lounged across the stern and did some mental arithmetic. They had already been paid two pounds per head to take the Kanakas home. The Germans would pay them another seven pounds when they reached Bougainville. That made nine pounds for each native. Multiplied by ninety-five, the total came to eight hundred and fifty-five pounds. Not a bad profit, particularly when the overheads were so low. After all, taro and ship's biscuit didn't cost much.

Had he not been so pre-occupied with his calculations he might have recognized the couple who were staring at him from the town wharf. Geoffrey and Amelia Glaston had strolled down the hill to take a closer look at the ship that had been racing the one that had nearly taken their lives. They spotted Mundine as soon as he came out of the hotel.

'It is him; I'm sure it's him,' Amelia said.

'It can't be, my dear. It would be too much of a coincidence,' Geoffrey replied.

But as they reached the wharf and got a closer look at the figure sprawled across the back of the boat, they turned to each other and both said, 'It is Mundine.'

'What on earth is he up to here?' Amelia asked.

Geoffrey shook his head. 'No good, my dear. Of that you can be sure.'

14 May 1886 – The Solomon Sea

Using the same passage that Captain Cook had discovered more than a century earlier and now bearing his name, Captain Homer navigated the *Hoylake* through the dangerous waters of the Great Barrier Reef and out into the Coral Sea, setting a course for the Solomon Islands and then due north along the eastern side of Bougainville.

The joy of his human cargo was palpable as they saw the mountains of their native islands in the distance, believing they were soon to be put ashore at the villages from which they'd been recruited – or kidnapped – years before.

However, the further north the ship sailed the more puzzled some of them began to feel. The rugged coastline they now saw to the west was similar to what they remembered, but none of them were able to see landmarks they actually recognized. They began to talk among themselves, questioning each other as to where they might be. By the time the *Hoylake* dropped anchor off Makunai they were convinced something was afoot and were ready to erupt.

'The natives seem restless,' Mundine muttered.

'So would you be if you were about to get sold to a German,' Homer replied.

'Any sight of 'em yet?'

Homer scanned the settlement through his telescope. 'It looks like there's a bit of activity down on the beach.'

Mundine took the glass from him and saw figures beginning to emerge from the trees. A few of them were Europeans, but most were Melanesians. Some were carrying rifles. He saw several natives drag a small boat across the narrow belt of sand and into the waves lapping the shore. Two of the Europeans followed them to the water's edge where a couple of natives carried them to the boat. As soon as they were seated, the natives jumped aboard, four of them taking the oars while the others, all armed, squeezed in as best they could.

A Malay seaman secured a rope ladder over the *Hoylake's* side and the two Europeans climbed aboard. The first was a young man in his early twenties and the other an older man of indeterminate age. Captain Homer stood ready to meet them with Mundine standing behind him.

'Welcome aboard my ship, gentlemen. I am Captain Homer, and this is Mr. Mundine. Do you speak English?'

'I speak English,' said the younger man. 'I am Gunter Stein, and this is Herr Muller. Herr Muller speaks no English. I believe you have met my Uncle Klaus, an official of the New Guinea Company.'

The young man's English was good, but he spoke with a heavy German accent.

'I had the pleasure of meeting your uncle in Cooktown two weeks ago.' Mundine stepped forward to shake their visitors' hands. 'He told me that you have established copra plantations on this side of the island.'

'That is correct,' Stein replied. Uncle Klaus's company has already established many plantations in New Guinea. We hope to do the same here.'

'And you need natives to work them,' Homer added.

'Ya.'

Mundine smiled. 'Well, as I promised your uncle, we have over ninety for you; all of them accustomed to working on plantations.'

Stein turned towards the hatch covers which were now securely fastened. But they weren't able to block out the sound of angry men below, demanding to be let out.

'They do not seem glad to be here. How do you intend to get them ashore without a riot?'

Homer stepped forward. 'Just leave that to me, sir. But tell me; why don't you just get your workers from the savages who live here?'

'We are still few in number, Captain; and the local chiefs are happy to allow us to establish our plantations as long as we give them trade goods and treat their people well. They even provide us with warriors, whom we have trained as our police.' He pointed to the armed natives in the boat below. 'But I don't think they would be so happy if we started taking their men to work the plantations – not yet anyway. Perhaps that will change when there are more of us here.'

'But they don't mind if you use natives from other islands, eh!'

Stein nodded and then turned to his companion, who spoke anxiously to him in German, pointing to the hatch covers.

'They're worried about whether we can get these Kanakas ashore quietly,' Mundine whispered. 'Are you really sure you know how to do it?'

Homer's face twisted into an evil grin. 'You'll see, matey. Now, invite our guests to my cabin for some of that rum you've been selling. Meanwhile, my lads can start getting things ready while those Kanakas exhaust themselves in the heat down below. They'll quieten down soon. By the time the sun is at its highest they'll have trouble even breathing down there.'

He walked over to the ship's galley and beckoned to the Chinese cook who trotted obediently to his side.

'Get your fire going as hot as you can and fill every container you've got with water. Let me know as soon as it's all boiling.'

The cook nodded and scurried off to fill containers with water and then stoke his fire, while Homer whispered something to Harris – the ship's mate. Then he returned to his cabin where the two Germans were waiting with Mundine.

'Well gentlemen. I believe we have time for some refreshments before we transact our business. Mr. Mundine, would you kindly pour these gentlemen a drink.'

Thirty minutes later the cook tapped softly at Homer's cabin door and announced nervously that he had several gallons of water boiling on the galley stove. Homer leapt to his feet.

'Follow me, gentlemen. Now I will show you how to handle an unruly mob without actually killing anyone.'

They followed him to the main deck, where he barked an order to Harris, who then shouted orders to six members of the crew. They ran to the master's cabin and returned carrying an assortment of firearms. One of them handed a brace of revolvers to the mate who stuck one in his belt and handed the other to Homer. Homer checked that each of the six chambers was loaded, then stuck the pistol into his belt too.

'Right, take up your positions,' he ordered.

The armed seamen fanned out in a semi-circle behind Homer and the mate, facing the hatch cover.

'Bring the buckets,' Homer ordered.

The cook and his assistants hurried forward, carrying buckets of boiling water, still bubbling after having stood for several minutes on the galley fire.

'Now, open the hatch cover.'

Three seamen removed the locking pins and dragged the heavy cover back. Immediately an invisible cloud of hot air, mixed with the stench of excrement and unwashed bodies rose from the bowels of the ship. The whites of dozens of eyes could be seen through the blackness of the interior, and a howl of relief mingled with rage arose from below. A dozen of the boldest Kanakas came scrambling up the ladder, intent on taking vengeance on the men who had caused them so much suffering.

Mundine went white with fear. The *Hoylake's* crew numbered less than twenty, and even though some of them were armed, if the ninety-five Kanakas were determined enough, they could easily overpower them. He looked at Homer and saw a malicious smile on his face as he and the mate picked up two of the buckets. They waited until the first Kanaka scrambled over the rim of the hatch and then they hurled the scalding water at their heads and bare chests.

The men screamed in agony as the boiling water scalded their skin, and they fell back onto the men climbing the ladder behind them. Homer and the mate then picked up the other buckets and emptied them onto the struggling mass of bodies below, causing more screams as the scalding water poured over their half-naked bodies.

Homer then drew his pistol and beckoned for his armed seamen to follow him. He climbed down a few steps of the ladder to a point where he was silhouetted against the light and fired a couple of shots into the bulkhead just beyond the Kanakas' heads.

'Stand back,' he bellowed. The noise of shouting immediately died down, apart from the agonized groans of the scalded men and the Kanakas huddled back into the deeper reaches of the hold.

'You fella Kanaka. You plenty fright now along me white fella,' Homer shouted at them in pidgin. 'Now, you fella Kanaka, you go up ladder plenty slow or we kill'm plenty.'

Mundine looked down at the terrified eyes, still white against the darkness of the hold, and realized that Homer had them under control. He stood back as the first few began to scramble through the hatch onto the deck and watched as other members of Homer's crew, protected by the armed seamen, fastened chains to their necks.

The last to come on deck were the scalded ringleaders, who groaned as the heat of the noonday sun increased the agony of their tortured flesh. One of them, a powerfully built Melanesian from Guadalcanal, though in great pain, was still defiant, and as he passed Homer he spat in his face. Homer responded with a roar of anger and clubbed the man to the deck with the butt of his pistol.

The two Germans, who had stood back watching all this happen, began to talk rapidly to each other in their own language. Mundine was worried. The older German did not seem happy at what was happening.

'What are they talking about?' Homer snarled.

Mundine walked over to Stein and said, 'I'm sorry about this unfortunate incident, Herr Stein. But Captain Homer had to restore order. As you can see it's all over now and there need be no more unpleasantness.'

'We're not concerned about your methods, Herr Mundine,' Stein replied. 'But we are concerned about these men you have delivered. They do not appear to be the tame labourers we were told we were to get. They seem ready to riot at the first opportunity.'

Homer joined the conversation. 'Please reassure yourself and your companion that that will not be the case. I've spent the last twenty years amongst these savages, and I know how to control them.'

'But how do you control a man who has half the skin scalded off his chest, yet still spits in your face, Captain?'

Another evil grin creased Homer's face. 'Just watch me, Herr Stein. It's all a matter of putting the fear of God – or the Devil - into these savages' minds.'

He beckoned to the mate. 'Get the cook to bring all the offal and blood from the bullock he slaughtered this morning. Then get the lads to set up a block and tackle from the lower yard. The mate grinned and gave the orders. Minutes later the cook appeared with a bucket full of bullock's innards.

'Throw it overboard,' Homer ordered.

The cook looked surprised. He was planning to use the offal in dishes that the Asian seamen appreciated, but he did as he was told and tipped it all over the side. As he did so, a couple of other seamen rigged a block and tackle to the outer end of the lower yardarm, with a rope from the deck running through it.

'Bring that one over here,' Homer ordered, pointing to the man he had clubbed.

The Kanaka had just regained consciousness as a couple of seamen grabbed him and dragged him over to where Homer stood. He grimaced in pain as their rough hands tore into his scalded flesh.

'Tie one end of that rope to his feet and haul him up to the yardarm.'

Moments later, the Kanaka was hanging from the block and tackle by his feet, his head level with the ship's rail.

'Swing him out,' Homer said.

'The sailors hauled on the braces and swung the yard arm, with the Kanaka hanging from it, out across the water.

'Now let him down.'

They released the rope, and the Kanaka fell headlong into the sea alongside the ship. They left him there for twenty seconds until Homer told them to pull him up again. The Kanaka rose from the water coughing and choking. Suddenly his eyes opened wide with fear. Cutting through the water, no more than twenty yards away, was the unmistakable shape of a black triangular fin.

The older German saw it too and grabbed his companion's arm as he pointed to it. Soon, everyone aboard the ship, including the chained Kanakas, had rushed to the side to watch the shark gorge itself on the floating remains of the slaughtered bullock. Some of them pointed further out to where several other fins were now visible, coming in fast to join the feast.

'Reef sharks, I think,' said Homer casually. 'But that big one over there is a bull shark. Nasty things, those bull sharks! I don't think he'll want to share his breakfast with the reef sharks, though; especially now that it's nearly all gone. Let's tempt him with something a bit juicier.' He turned to the men holding the rope. 'Let 'im down again.'

The two Germans turned to each other with a look of horror in their eyes. Even Mundine turned his eyes away. The sailors let go of the rope and the hapless Kanaka, now well aware of what was about to happen, fell screaming into the waves below. A great cry that then turned into a high-pitched wail erupted from the chained Kanakas as they watched the huge bull shark surge towards the twisting body, dangling half in and half out of the water.

'Pull him up,' Homer roared.

The horrified onlookers aboard the vessel watched in silence as the Kanaka was hauled out of the water just beyond reach of the shark's jagged teeth.

'Drop him again.'

Once again the terrified Kanaka, splashed into the sea, and once again the shark turned and cut through the waves towards him.

'Up again,' Homer ordered, and once again the helpless form eluded those serried teeth.

On Homer's orders, the Malays holding the rope repeated the ordeal twice again until the once defiant Kanaka appeared to be dead – drowned or killed by heart failure. They hauled him in, poured a bucket of water over his head and watched him regain consciousness; his face contorted with terror. Homer turned to the white-faced Germans with a look of satisfaction on his face.

'Well gentlemen. I don't think you'll have any more trouble with your new workers. Now, while my men take the Kanakas ashore, we can go to my cabin and partake of some more of Mr. Mundine's fine rum, and you can hand over the agreed payment.'

21 May 1886 - Cooktown

'I had the strangest dream last night,' Sele said. 'I was back on that small island near Warrior Reef, where our ship was attacked and where Captain Mason's crew was killed.'

'Really, my dear,' said Amelia, spreading marmalade on her slice of toast. 'Was it a nightmare?'

'Oh no! It was actually a powerful dream. The natives were begging me to stay with them and help them.'

Geoffrey looked up from his breakfast. 'They wanted you to help them?'

'Yes. They were actually pleading with me.'

Amelia looked at Geoffrey quizzically. 'My goodness; what a strange dream! Can it have a meaning, Geoffrey?'

'Well, I'm no Joseph with the ability to interpret dreams,' he said. 'But it does remind me of the story of St. Paul's dream about the man of Macedonia.'

'Come over and help us,' Sele quoted.

'Yes, that's the one. I think every missionary who ever lived has identified with that story.'

'But not very many can actually report having had a dream that confirms it quite so clearly,' Amelia added.

'Do you think this was a message to me, Geoffrey?' Sele asked. 'Or was it just the result of an over-active imagination?'

He smiled across the table. 'I don't think you're the sort of person who suffers from an over-active imagination, as you put it. But I do know that you have a remarkable capacity for insight into spiritual matters.'

'Do you remember that woman in Apia, the wife of the French trader?' Amelia asked.

'Helena.'

'Yes, that was her name. Do you remember how Dr. Thornton at the mission hospital told us there was no hope for her?'

Sele nodded.

'But you were convinced that God wanted to heal her,' Amelia said. 'And you insisted we all join you in prayer. You read that passage from the Epistle of James about the prayer of faith healing the sick. And that's what you did.'

'And a day later she was out of bed, and within a week she was looking after her husband and family as if nothing had ever happened,' Geoffrey added.

'It was a feeling I had inside me,' Sele explained. 'I just knew it.'

'And it's happened before, hasn't it?' Geoffrey said. 'I remember your father telling me the same thing.'

'Yes. But it's only happened to me a few times.'

'Well, I believe you've been given a gift that most of us don't have. And maybe this dream is something you should take seriously.'

'But Geoffrey,' Amelia protested. 'Those natives killed Captain Mason's crew. They probably would have killed Sele and her companions if they'd had the chance. We've all heard stories about how savage the people up there are.'

'I know, my dear. But remember what the gospel has accomplished in Samoa – and in other islands. Those people are no wilder than the Fijians and look what's happened to them since they became Christians. They put most Europeans to shame.'

'I think there must have been some reason why those warriors attacked Captain Mason,' Sele said. 'Perhaps they've had bad experiences with the crews of European ships.'

Geoffrey nodded. 'I've heard stories about pearlers abducting islanders and forcing them to become divers. The women, it seems, are particularly valued as pearl divers because they can hold their breath longer than the men. And – forgive me for saying this – they also serve the pearlers' baser appetites.'

Amelia looked away in disgust. 'Geoffrey, I really don't want to discuss such things at the breakfast table, and I'm sure Sele doesn't.'

'Of course not, my dear!' He ventured a glance at Sele, sitting across from him at the table, and noticed a slightly amused look on her face. He suspected it was more to do with Amelia's reaction than the subject matter.

They continued to eat their breakfast in thoughtful silence until Sele asked: 'Then what do you think I should do?'

Geoffrey pondered the question for a few moments and then looked up at her. 'I think you should pray for confirmation that what you sense from this dream really is a call for you to go and minister to those people.'

Amelia looked anxious but nodded her agreement. Sele merely smiled and said, 'That's what I think too.'

* * *

The morning air seemed more humid than usual. Geoffrey noticed it the moment he stepped out onto his veranda. It was the first indicator of the approaching wet season. He looked out to the mouth of the Endeavour River and saw a two-masted schooner nearing the river bar. He walked over to his telescope and trained it on the approaching vessel, now pitching and rolling as she crossed the river bar.

'Just as I suspected! It's the *Wahine.* I know who'll be glad to hear that.'

He went back inside where Amelia and Sele were setting the table for breakfast.

'Guess who's just entered the river,' he said.

'I've no idea,' Amelia answered.

'Captain Burns.'

He smiled inwardly as he noticed how quickly Sele stopped arranging cutlery and looked towards the veranda. Ever since the *Wahini's* departure he'd noted how Sele would frequently retire to a corner of the veranda and gaze out to the open sea. At first, he suspected she'd been thinking of her home in Samoa, but Amelia had convinced him it was Michael Burns who really occupied her thoughts.

'Captain Burns?' Amelia exclaimed. 'Are you sure, Geoffrey?'

'Well, it's his ship, anyway. Come and take a look.'

The three of them trooped out to the veranda and Geoffrey pointed the *Wahine* out to them.

'There she is. I dare say that one of those figures you can see might be Captain Burns himself. Here, does anyone want to take a look through my telescope?'

Amelia glared at him as he playfully polished the eyepiece. 'There you are, my dear,' she said to Sele. 'Your eyes are younger than ours. You take a look.'

Sele smiled nervously and bent over the telescope. She read the name, *Wahine,* emblazoned across the stern, and then moved it slightly so that she could see across the deck where crewmen were furling the sails. Her heart seemed to skip a beat as a tall, well-built man wearing a peaked cap turned to give instructions to a seaman standing near the stern.

'Yes, it is Michael… Captain Burns, I mean.'

Amelia gave Geoffrey a knowing look. 'Then we should put our bonnets on and go down to meet him. I'm sure he'll be coming ashore soon. We'll invite him to lunch. What do you think, Geoffrey?'

'That is a very good idea, my love. But I don't have a bonnet.'

She muttered something under her breath, then took Sele by the arm and ushered her back into the house, while Geoffrey followed, chuckling quietly.

Michael was already ashore as they reached the town wharf. 'Reverend Glaston, it's good to see you again.' He shook Geoffrey's hand enthusiastically then turned to Amelia and Sele. 'Good morning, ladies. You're both looking as lovely as ever.'

Sele reddened slightly, but Amelia laughed and said: 'You can always trust sailor to say the right thing to a lady.'

Sele held out her hand. 'Good morning, Captain Burns. We didn't expect you back in Cooktown so soon.'

'I have a contract with Burns Philp and Co to deliver trade goods to their posts in Cooktown and then around to Karumba. I also intend to stop at Refuge Bay to see my former partner. He's about to go prospecting. There are reports of people finding rocks up there that look like they might be gold bearing.'

'Just like happened here,' Geoffrey added. 'Anyway, you must come up to the house and dine with us. How long will you be here?'

'It won't take long to unload what we have for the local store. I hope to leave on the evening tide.'

'Oh, surely you can stay 'til morning,' Amelia protested. 'I'm sure you and Sele have so much to talk about.'

Sele reddened again, but Michael's eyes lit up. 'How could I refuse such a charming invitation? What time would you like me to come?'

'As soon as you're free, old chap,' Geoffrey said. 'The sooner the better.'

They dined that evening on the wide veranda of the mission house, watching the full moon rising above the Coral Sea and bathing them in its silvery light.

'What a beautiful evening it is!' Amelia said.

'Sitting here like this reminds me of our years in Samoa,' Geoffrey added. 'Do you remember, my dear, sitting with Chief Malietoa, feasting on freshly killed pork and all sorts of treasures from the sea?'

'I remember it very well. I also remember Sele's father being there with us.'

Michael leaned across the table to where Sele sat. 'Tell me about your father, Miss Saena.'

Sele smiled. 'My father was the royal orator, able to recite the genealogy of the Samoan chiefs back for more than a thousand years. My mother was the daughter of a Chinese merchant and his English wife. I hardly remember my grandparents. They both died while I was very young.'

'We met Sele the first time we visited Chief Malietoa,' Geoffrey added. 'She was only fifteen at the time, and almost as lovely as she is now.'

Michael looked across the table at Sele and nodded. 'Then she must have truly been lovely.'

Sele dropped her eyes, blushing furiously. Michael looked away, conscious that he had revealed more of his feelings than he'd intended. Amelia looked knowingly at Geoffrey, but he pretended that nothing had happened at all. They continued to eat their meal, the silence broken only by the gentle rustle of the wind in the palms. Michael ventured another glance across the table and was both surprised and delighted to see that Sele was looking at him. They both immediately turned their eyes away.

After the meal, as the two women cleared the table and retired to the kitchen, Michael and Geoffrey stayed on the veranda and talked about the rumours of another gold rush.

'Do you think there's any substance to it?' Geoffrey asked.

'Bernie thinks so. That's why he's decided to give up the sea and try his luck selling supplies to the prospectors.'

'But you don't feel any great urge to go looking for gold?'

'No. I learned my lesson on the goldfields in Victoria. Gold prospecting is a game of chance; there are always many more losers than winners. I want to be a winner.'

'You're not a gambler then?'

'I'd prefer to describe myself as a man who takes calculated risks, rather than as a gambler.'

'And your investment in the *Wahine* is such a calculated risk?'

Michael grinned. 'It's going to make me rich; and when it does, I'm going to repay your generosity to me with interest.'

Geoffrey patted Michael's knee. 'There's no need, old chap. That gift was the least we could do after you risked your life to save us.'

'Well, you're goin' to get it anyway. I'm not there yet, but I will be, you'll see.'

Geoffrey nodded. 'I think you will. But let's hope your partner doesn't get his fingers burnt.'

'Bernie is convinced that the high country inland from Refuge Bay is going to be the sight of another gold rush, and he's determined to be in the right place to benefit from it.'

'And do you think he's right?' Geoffrey asked.

'Well, when you think about how much gold has been taken out of here over the past fifteen years, it makes sense to assume that there are other places up here that might do the same.'

'And if there is another gold rush, what sort of things will you be providing? Not barrels of rum posing as flour, I hope.'

Michael's face reddened. Geoffrey Glaston was no longer the naïve young clergyman he'd first met. 'I don't expect that you, as a man of the cloth, would approve of it, Mr. Glaston. But those poor devils out in the diggings have precious little to bring a bit of cheer into their lives.'

'And rum does?'

Michael shrugged his shoulders. 'I suppose it does.'

'It also makes wild animals of them, Michael. You've seen what it does. And I'm sure you've heard about the way some of them treat the native women when they're intoxicated.'

'I've never held with that sort of thing.'

'But you've supplied the devil's brew that causes it.'

Michael looked uncomfortable. 'Does Miss Saena know?'

'I don't believe so.'

'How did you find out?'

'Dr. Wakeley told me. I think the local tavern keepers told him. Are you concerned about Sele knowing?'

'Of course.'

'And why is that?'

'Isn't it obvious?'

'Amelia thinks you're in love with her.'

'She's a smart lady, your wife!'

'So, are you?'

'I do care for her.'

Geoffrey put his hand on Michael's shoulder. 'She's a missionary, old chap. Her life is devoted to spreading the gospel. You can't really imagine she'd want to be associated with someone who makes a living from rum running.'

'What if I swore that I would never do it again?'

'You mean that you would stick to carrying the sort of goods that will benefit these remote communities?'

'Yes.'

'I'd like to believe that.'

'Maybe I never had the incentive before.'

'And what about Mr. Matthews, what will he do?'

'If gold is discovered up there as Bernie expects, we'll build wharf facilities at Refuge Bay. It has one of the few deep-water channels north of Cooktown. It's the obvious spot for bringing supplies and people in, and for taking them and their gold out.'

Geoffrey nodded approvingly. 'You seem to have it all worked out.'

'And if the population does grow, I'll build a church for Dr. Wakely.'

Geoffrey smiled. 'That's a very generous offer, Michael. But I'll not hold you to it. Let's see how successful Mr. Matthews is first.'

They sat quietly for a while, looking out at the moon which was now high enough to be reflected on the ocean beyond the river bar.

'Is Sele likely to stay in Cooktown?' Michael asked.

'Well, that's what we were expecting,' Geoffrey said. 'But she seems convinced that she's meant to go back to those islands in the Torres Strait.'

'Do you mean the place where Captain Mason was attacked?'

'Yes.'

Michael leaned forward. 'Then you must stop her. She'd be putting her life in danger!'

'I don't think I can,' Geoffrey said. 'Sele is a very determined young woman.'

'But she trusts you and respects your judgement.'

'Yes, Michael. But I suspect she's right and that she is meant to go there.' He placed his hand on Michael's shoulder. 'I think I understand what you are feeling, old chap. But this is something bigger than your feelings.'

7 June 1886 – The Torres Strait

The *Hoylake* was on her second return trip to Queensland after having delivered another cargo of returning Kanakas to the German planters on Bougainville. Mundine, however, was beginning to feel nervous.

'We should keep deliveries to the Germans down to one trip in three,' he argued. 'If word gets around that other ships in the area haven't sighted us where we're supposed to be, the authorities in Queensland will start to get suspicious.'

'I think you're right, Mundine,' Homer said. 'That's why I've been thinkin' about tryin' our luck elsewhere.'

'Where?'

'The Torres Strait. There's dozens of islands there, and there's a good market for native women as pearl divers.'

'You want to get into the pearling industry?'

'No, you fool. I just want to provide what it needs to get the pearls off the seabed.'

'I thought they used Japs for that.'

'They do. But they can't get enough of 'em, and the Japs want to be paid. But those native women are better than the Jap divers. They can hold their breath for three minutes. And the pearling skippers don't need to pay 'em wages. They can also use 'em to keep their crews happy at night.'

'Anyway, I've arranged a meeting with a few old mates I've had dealings with before. But first we need to get ourselves some women.'

Five days later the *Hoylake* dropped anchor in the lagoon of an island close to the south coast of New Guinea. Homer scanned the shoreline with his telescope but saw no sign of life.

'There's not a soul in sight, but don't be fooled. There's probably a hundred of 'em watching us right now, waiting to see what we're gonna do.'

'And what are we gonna do?' Mundine asked.

Homer gave an evil grin. 'The first thing is to arm the crew. You'd better get your revolver, too.'

He signaled to the mate, who went aft to Homer's cabin, unlocked the cabinet where the firearms were kept and began to issue weapons to the Malays already posted around the deck.

'I doubt they'll come at night,' Homer said. 'They're terrified of the spirits after dark. But they might try to board us at first light when they think we're all asleep.'

'Then what'll we do?' Mundine asked.

'Slaughter 'em, of course!' Homer replied. 'Follow me. I've got something to show you.'

Mundine dutifully followed him back to his cabin where Homer opened the gun storage cabinet. He pulled a stout wooden box and prized the lid off.

'There,' he said, pointing to the contents. 'That'll put the fear of the Devil into 'em.'

The box was filled with sticks of dynamite. Mundine picked one up carefully and examined it.

'Where did you get these?'

'I won 'em in a card game from a mining engineer who chartered my ship last year. He'd run out of cash by the time we reached Cooktown, so he paid his debts with this. Anyway, he's probably made a fortune in gold from the other boxes I let him keep.'

'And what are you planning to do with them?' Mundine asked.

Homer gave another evil grin. 'You'll see tomorrow.'

They came at first light, just as Homer had predicted. There were almost twenty war canoes loaded with warriors, their faces and chests daubed with white clay. The canoes skimmed swiftly across the lagoon as the warriors dug their paddles noiselessly into its still water. It was one of the Malays, peering over the starboard rail, who was the first to spot them, silhouetted against the eastern sky. He passed a whispered alarm back to Harris, who woke his sleeping captain, sprawled fully clothed across his bunk, a loaded revolver at his side.

'They're comin', skipper; dozens of 'em.'

Homer was on his feet in a flash. 'Take the other end of this,' he snarled as he reached for one of the rope handles on the box of dynamite.

Mundine staggered wearily out of his cabin as they ran past. 'Get your gun, Mundine. They'll be on us in minutes.'

By the time they reached the open deck the bosun had the armed Malays positioned around the ship ready to repel attack from any quarter.

'Wait for my order,' Homer bellowed. 'I'll flog the skin off any man who fires too soon.'

The war canoes began to make their final dash up to the anchored ship. Dozens of paddles flashed in the early morning light as the warriors put all their strength into covering the remaining distance as quickly as they could.

Harris saw a couple of canoes peel off from the others. 'Looks like they intend to come up under our stern and attack the port side,' he shouted.

Homer called out to the bosun, pointing to the two canoes. 'Take four men and cover the port side.' Then he waved his pistol in the air, signaling for his men to stand up from wherever they had hidden themselves. 'Now, lads; make every bullet count.'

The sailors opened fire, pouring a fusillade into the approaching canoes. Homer watched as a few of the shots found targets and warriors fell screaming. But most of the shots went wild.

Cursing and swearing he tore a rifle from the hands of a flustered seaman, who was trying unsuccessfully to work another round into the breach. He took careful aim and fired. A warrior standing in the prow of the leading canoe screamed and fell into the water. He pushed another round into the chamber, took aim again and another warrior collapsed.

'Pretty good shooting, eh Mundine!' Homer grinned as he casually lit a cigar. 'Now watch this.'

One canoe that had thus far escaped the ragged fusillade swept up to the *Hoylake's* starboard quarter. The yelling warriors dropped their paddles and began to brandish fearsome war clubs as they prepared to swarm aboard the ship. Watching them carefully, Homer, a stick of dynamite in his hand, casually took the cigar from his mouth and used it to light the dynamite's fuse. He then lobbed the stick into the midst of the packed warriors. They had no idea what it was, and none of them lived long enough to find out. The dynamite exploded with an ear-splitting roar and tore both the canoe and the men in it to pieces. Mundine, standing against the ship's rail, was knocked flat by the blast.

Homer pulled him to his feet and laughed. 'Keep your head down, you fool.'

He lit another stick and stood up. The first blast had had the desired effect on the other canoes. Men stopped paddling and stared at the shattered bodies floating in the lagoon with a mixture of awe and terror. Then one canoe began to surge forward again, its crew urged on by a tall native in a brilliantly feathered headdress, who lashed the paddlers into action with the staff of his spear as he waved a huge war club with his other hand.

'Looks like that's their chief,' Homer said casually, as he brought his arm back to throw.

Mundine watched anxiously as the fuse burned down almost to its base, then crouched on the deck, covering his head with his hands as Homer lobbed the stick into the approaching canoe. It exploded in the air, right above a warrior standing in the prow holding a crude form of grappling hook. He died instantly, as did the three natives behind him. The blast tore through the other tightly packed warriors, searing their bare skin and tearing off limbs. Their chieftain fell forward into the screaming mass of bodies and then stared with a mixture of amazement and horror at the bloody stump that had been his left arm. He pulled himself to his feet and with his remaining strength used his one good arm to hurl his spear at his tormentors. It caught a Malay seaman full in the chest. He fell to the deck shrieking with agony as Homer calmly pulled his pistol from his belt, took aim and shot the chieftain through the head.

By now, panic had swept through the whole flotilla. Men dropped their weapons, seized their paddles and began to dig furiously into the water, desperate to get as far away as quickly as they could. Homer's men continued to shoot at them as they fled. A few shots found their mark and more terrified natives fell screaming into the sea.

'Cease firing,' Homer roared. 'No point wasting any more bullets. You useless mongrels could hardly hit a brick wall at twenty paces.' He turned to Mundine and grinned wickedly. 'The rest of it will be a piece of cake.'

He called out to Harris: 'Get the boats over the side. I want the bosun and a dozen good men with me - all of them armed. Put the leg irons in the boats too. I'll command the shore party, and you will stay with the ship. I doubt there'll be any more trouble from that lot,' he gestured towards the fleeing canoes. 'But keep an armed watch until we get back.'

The mate acknowledged the orders and began to organize the crew to launch *Hoylake's* two longboats. The bosun, a huge man with a broken nose and narrow vicious eyes, took command of one, and Homer climbed into the other.

'Why don't you come with us, Mundine, and see how it's done?'

Mundine thought he'd prefer just to wait on board, but he was embarrassed to decline the obvious challenge in the invitation. So, he stuffed his pistol in his belt and climbed into the longboat.

Five minutes later the two boats reached the palm fringed beach, and the men jumped ashore. Homer gave his orders: one seaman was to stay with the boats while the others were to advance into the bush in two groups. They were to scour the area until they found the village where the warriors came from and where the women and children would be hiding.

'We need to do this as quickly as we can,' Homer told his men. 'Before those warriors realize we're after their women and regain their courage.'

The two groups set off at a jog trot, Homer's group taking one end of the beach and the bosun's the other. A nimble-footed Malay ran ahead of Homer's group to scout the way. They hadn't gone far before he stopped and pointed to a narrow track leading into the rainforest. Homer urged his men into a run, and they followed the scout down the track.

'It won't be far,' Homer gasped as they jogged breathlessly behind the others. 'They always build their villages close to the lagoon.'

Mundine grunted his acknowledgement and was relieved to hear the scout call out that he'd found the village. It consisted of a motley collection of bamboo huts, thatched with palm leaves, standing around a much larger hut that clearly was the village meeting place. In the clearing between the lines of houses were several open fires with iron cooking pots hanging over them. They were still alight, and blue smoke was floating upwards between the canopy of trees. But the village was deserted.

'Looks like they've all made a run for it,' Mundine said.

''They can't be far away,' Homer snarled. 'They haven't had time to get too far away, not with kids and old people.' He gave orders for his men to start searching the bush around the village. The Malays cocked their rifles and began to advance cautiously into the undergrowth.

'Faster, you yellow dogs,' Homer roared.

He lashed out with his foot and caught one of them at the base of his tail bone. The man yelped with pain and quickly sprinted into the bush, the others following close behind. They spread out and began a systematic search of the undergrowth. Suddenly, Mundine stopped and gripped Homer's arm.

'Did you hear that?' he asked.

'What?'

'It sounded like a baby crying.'

'Where?'

'Over there,' Mundine pointed to a clump of palm trees to their left.

Homer, followed by the other seamen, started to run to the spot. The still morning air was suddenly filled with the sound of women's screams as mothers, hiding in the trees, grabbed their children and began to run. A few old men armed with spears bravely stood up to cover the women's escape. But Homer's men shot them down before a single spear could be thrown.

'Leave them,' Homer yelled. 'Get after the women.'

There were at least thirty of them, most of them younger women. They sprinted through the bush, urged on by terror, but burdened by the children they were carrying. Soon the women reached the beach only to find their path barred by the big bosun and his men. Caught between the two groups the women had nowhere to go and fell to their knees, wailing piteously and clutching their terrified children to their breasts. But even Mundine was appalled by what happened then.

Homer tore one of the children - a little boy barely able to walk - from his mother's arms and held him up high.

'You know what to do,' he roared to his crew.

Then, drawing his pistol, he tossed the screaming child to the ground and fired one shot into its tiny body. His mother shrieked hysterically, throwing herself onto the child's lifeless form, kissing and caressing his bloodied body, unable to comprehend the horror she had witnessed. The other women began to wail, desperately trying to protect their children from the merciless seamen, who were tearing children from their arms and slaughtering them.

Mundine watched in disbelief as this orgy of murderous savagery unfolded before him but said nothing; *Bulldog* Homer was not a man to be trifled with when his animal passions were aroused. It took less than three minutes for the crew to complete the slaughter, laughing as they sated their bloodlust on those poor innocents.

Homer turned to Mundine and grinned. 'Don't look so shocked, Mundine. They're only savages - little better than animals.' Then he signaled to his bosun. 'Get the irons on these women before they try to kill themselves.'

The bosun gave his orders and the seamen pulled the hysterical women to their feet and shackled them by their necks to long lengths of chain. Then, driving them forward with kicks and blows from their rifle butts, they marched them to the waiting boats and began to ferry them across the lagoon to the anchored barquentine.

As soon as they were aboard the ship Homer sent a seaman aloft to watch out for any sign of the warriors returning. But it wasn't until the last group was aboard and the boats secured that the first natives appeared on the beach.

Homer gave orders for the crew to get the ship under way. He looked back at the beach through his telescope and saw that the returning warriors had discovered the bodies of their slaughtered children and old men. The sound of their wailing carried across the lagoon and was taken up by their wives and daughters, now battened down in the ship's hold.

Mundine put his hands across his ears. 'I can't stand the sound of hysterical women,' he said.

'It won't be for long,' Homer smirked. 'They'll soon quieten down when the heat starts to build up down there. All we have to do is make sure they don't die before we reach our customers.'

He returned to his cabin, feeling well satisfied with the outcome of this latest venture, while Mundine began to wonder if he had made a big mistake in getting involved with such a man.

3 July 1886 – The Coral Sea

There weren't many things that would cause the patrons of the *Capricorn* Hotel to stop drinking, but the sound of hymn singing certainly did on the afternoon that Sele set sail for the Solomon Sea. They crowded onto the wide veranda and saw a group of twenty or more men and women standing on the town wharf, where a large ketch was preparing to cast off. A tall, slim man in a cream tropical suit was leading the singing, beating the time with his straw hat as the impromptu choir followed his lead.

The men at the pub strained their ears to catch the words of the tune.

'God be with you til we meet again,' a ruddy faced stockman announced. 'It used to be a favourite of my old mum. Quite a churchgoer she was.'

'Who's the bloke beatin' time?' his mate asked.

'It's Reverend Glaston,' the publican answered. 'He's the minister from the mission house up the hill. It looks like they're seeing off the missionary lady from Samoa; the one who got old Mason and his boat back after he got an arrow through him.'

'You mean the one who's a real looker?'

'Yeah; they say she's a princess back in Samoa. That's her over there.' He pointed to Sele, who was standing tearfully in the midst of the assembled group as Geoffrey committed her to the safekeeping of God. Her companions who had come with her from Samoa stood next to her, weeping, while Amelia did her best to maintain her composure.

One by one the women embraced Sele, followed by the male members of the little congregation who raised their hats as they shook her hand and wished her Godspeed. Last of all was Geoffrey who took both her hands in his as he tried, without success, to say what was in his heart.

'You don't have to say anything, Geoffrey. I know that you of all people understand what I'm doing.'

'I had quite a speech prepared,' he said. 'But now it all escapes me, except to say that our thoughts, our prayers and all our love go with you.'

'I know that,' she answered softly.

He looked deep into her eyes. 'There's a verse of scripture that keeps coming to my mind: *"Many are called, but few are chosen."* You are one of the chosen ones, Sele. God has given you something special. Sad as I am to see you go, and anxious though we may be about where you are going, I know that all will be well, and great things will come of it.'

She leaned forward and kissed his cheek. 'Goodbye, dear Geoffrey. Until we meet again.'

She turned around and walked across the gangplank onto the ketch, where Captain Mason took her hand to help her down onto the deck.

'No-one else but you could ever have persuaded me to go back to those islands, Miss Saena. But there's still time for you to reconsider.'

Sele smiled. 'There's nothing to reconsider, Captain. But let's be on our way before all this weeping breaks my heart.'

'And before the tide turns,' he muttered nervously. 'If it hadn't been for all that hymn singing, we'd have been on our way an hour ago like I intended.'

They crossed the sandbar at the mouth of the Endeavour River just after high tide. The ketch pitched and rolled violently as the depth of water decreased under her keel and she met the short, steep waves kicked up by the effects of wind and tide. The main boom began to swing dangerously as one larger wave caused the vessel to roll onto its starboard beam, spilling the wind from the sail.

'Secure that main sheet,' Mason roared to a crewman while wrestling with the ship's wheel. 'Miss Saena, watch your head. Please stay by the mast or go below.'

Sele ducked her head as the boom swung towards the centerline. A sailor pulled it up short, taking in the slack on the main sheet and throwing a hitch around the cleat to secure it. The ship continued to pitch and roll as she passed over the river bar, and then, as suddenly as it had started, the crazy motion ceased as the water began to deepen and the wind caught her sails again, powering her onward and outward towards the open sea.

'Ready to go about,' Mason called out as he prepared to bring the ketch around onto a new course. 'Helm's-a'lee.' Mason spun the wheel and then called out 'Lee-oh' as the wind began to fill the opposite side of the head-sail, and the crew hauled it across.

'Is it safe to come back on deck, Captain?' Sele asked

'Certainly, ma'am. Sorry if I sounded a bit sharp back there. It's always a bit tricky crossing a river bar, and if the boom starts to swing out of control it can do a lot of damage to someone's head.'

'Thank you for taking such good care of me, Captain. I know what you mean about a boom swinging out of control. That's what nearly brought us to grief when I tried to bring your ship into Refuge Bay.'

'When I was delirious down below and Captain Burns rescued you?'

She smiled and nodded. 'I wonder where he is now.'

'Could be anywhere between Melbourne and Brisbane, I'd guess. But we should be passing Refuge Bay in a couple of days. We could call in and visit Dr. Wakeley, if you like.'

'Thank you, Captain, but I'm anxious to reach our islands as soon as possible.'

'Anxious is a good word for it, ma'am. Do you really know what you're going to do when you get there? You don't even speak the language.'

'Neither did John Williams when he first went to Samoa. But don't worry, Captain. God will show me.'

'I hope He does,' Mason muttered to himself.

* * *

The sun was still low in the eastern sky as they approached the narrow gap through the reef fringing the lagoon.

'I don't like this,' Captain Mason said to Sele. 'I can't believe that I was stupid enough to get talked into coming back here.'

He swung the wheel to starboard, and the ketch began to make her final approach into the lagoon. Memories of his last visit filled his thoughts as he conned her through the gap in the coral and entered the calm, translucent waters beyond. Like all old *South Seas* hands, he knew the dangers of these islands and the fierce tribes that inhabited them. Apart from the savagery of European cutthroats like *Bulldog* Homer, Polynesia might have become civilized, and even the Fijians were now more interested in Christianity than cannibalism; but here things were as they'd been for centuries.

Pushed along by a light breeze blowing across the port quarter, the ketch glided through the narrow passage and entered the lagoon, whose turquoise water was as still as a millpond. Mason ordered the jib and mizzen sail taken in, then carefully picking his spot, spun the wheel and brought the ketch directly into the wind. The mainsail began to flog as the wind spilled from it, and the ketch came to a halt. A crewman let the anchor fall from the cathead into the still depths below, where it dug into the sandy bottom.

Sele walked to the bow and shielding her eyes against the sun, staring at the empty beach, now a mere two hundred yards away. She turned back to say something to Captain Mason and saw that he also was scanning the shoreline through his telescope.

'No sign of anyone,' he said. 'But that's how it was when we came here before. The natives didn't show themselves until we were ashore.'

'Do you think they're watching us?' Sele asked.

Mason nodded. 'Like I said, Miss Saena, I don't like it.'

'Have faith, Captain Mason. We're here at God's leading; of that I am certain.'

'That's probably what all those missionaries said before they ended up in cannibals' cooking pots,' Mason muttered to himself. He signaled to his mate who had just lowered the mainsail. 'You know what to do, Albert.'

Albert disappeared down the hatch and returned with rifles and a brace of pistols. Mason took one of the pistols and stuck it into his belt. 'Arm the crew,' he said.

Sele watched in horror as he handed a rifle to each member of the crew, keeping the other pistol for himself. 'Captain Mason,' she protested. 'We are here on God's business. Surely you don't think those firearms are appropriate.'

'You may believe you're on God's business, Miss Saena. But I saw my crew slaughtered by these savages last time we were here. This time I'm taking no chances.'

'Then please assure me that you will take no action unless we are attacked.'

'You have my word. But I won't be holding back if we are. My men have orders to shoot to kill.'

'Then I implore you, Captain. If the natives approach us, let me talk to them first.'

'Very well, ma'am. But you'd better make sure what you say works first time because I've no desire to have my head shrunk and hanging from their chief's belt.'

'I thought you said they were cannibals, Captain, not head-hunters.'

'It makes no difference what they are; one false move and my men start shooting.'

'Then I ask you to put me ashore alone, Captain. Your men can stay in the boat and watch. But I want the people of this island to know I come in peace.'

Mason shrugged his shoulders. 'As you wish, Miss Saena. But if things go wrong, don't say I didn't warn you.'

Thirty minutes later Sele stood alone on the narrow stretch of white sand that separated the rainforest from the lagoon. Mason and two of his men sat anxiously in the ship's boat, bobbing gently in the still waters of the lagoon thirty yards from the shore, their loaded guns ready in their hands. Further back, the others watched from the ship, their weapons also at the ready.

Sele began to walk along the beach calling out in Pidgin English to anyone who could hear that she had come as a friend. The only response was the sound of birds chirping in the trees overhead. She continued along the beach until she came to an opening in the palm trees from which a narrow track led off into the bush. Mason saw her stop and stare down the track. Then she turned and began to walk into the trees.

'Quick, row up to where she's gone,' he ordered.

The two seamen laid their rifles down and began to pull on the oars as Mason fingered his weapon nervously. They reached a spot just off the beach adjacent to where Sele had entered the bush and peered into the undergrowth. But she was nowhere to be seen.

'Miss Saena, come back to the beach where we can cover you,' Mason shouted. But there was no response.

He called out again, still with no response. He began to swear angrily, cursing all missionaries and do-gooders for refusing to just let things be.

'What you do now, boss?' one of his men - a tall Torres Strait Islander - asked.

Mason swore again. 'We can't leave her in there on her own. We'll have to go in after her.'

His crewmen looked decidedly nervous as they stepped ashore, but none more so than Mason himself. He ordered one man to stay with the boat while he and the other one went down the track they'd seen Sele take. They walked quickly but cautiously, anxiously scanning the undergrowth on either side, ready to open fire on anyone who might jump out at them.

They followed the track until it ended abruptly at a clearing, at the far end of which stood a semi-circle of palm thatched huts. At the centre of the semi-circle there was an open fire-pit, its glowing embers sending wisps of blue smoke into the air. A group of old men were sitting around it. Behind them were a few teenage boys, and further back stood thirty or so women and girls, with a number of naked children playing at their feet. And in the midst of the old men sat Sele, talking to a large, grey-haired Polynesian man, wearing a European style white shirt and black tie over the traditional Polynesian skirt and sandals.

'Miss Saena,' Mason called out with relief.

Sele and those around her looked up and saw the armed sailors standing at the edge of the clearing. The old men jumped to their feet and the women huddled together in alarm.

'Fata, tell them not to be alarmed,' she said to the Polynesian man at her side. 'These men are friends. They brought me here.'

The Polynesian spoke rapidly to the group in a language Mason couldn't understand. The old men seemed reassured and sat down as Sele walked across to greet the new arrivals.

'You had us worried ma'am, going off like that on your own.'

Sele smiled. 'I told you not to worry about me, Captain. God always looks after me as I do His work.'

'Like the missionaries in the cannibal stew pots,' Mason thought again.

She took him by the arm. 'Come with me. Let me introduce you to Fata. I haven't seen him since I was little girl.'

'You know this man?' Mason asked.

'Yes. He studied at the same Bible School I went to in Samoa. But Fata was there years before me. I remember when Fata left Samoa on a small ship just like yours. There were twelve of them, all young men sent out to take the Gospel of our Lord to the islands in the west. We didn't know where they would end up and neither did they. They just believed God would guide them to where he wanted them to go.'

'And this is where they ended up, right?'

Sele smiled. 'Yes. Fata told me that when they reached this part of the sea, they split up into groups of two and were left at different islands. Some of them were killed but the others, like Fata, have become trusted ministers and counsellors to the people of these parts.'

'But where are the men of this village? I only see old men and boys.'

'I'll leave Fata to tell you what he's told me.'

They greeted each other in the traditional Polynesian way, by rubbing their noses together. 'Greetings, Captain. Welcome to Vitu.'

'Thank you, sir. Is that the name of this island?'

'Yes.'

'You speak good English.'

'Thank you, Captain. I only get chance to speak it when ship come for water.'

Mason remembered his own earlier experience of trying to get water here. 'But you speak the local language.'

'Yes. I here many years.'

'Have you never returned to your home?'

'No, this my home, and these my people; these, and people on other islands nearby. Each year I go to each, teaching and preaching; then I go to next one.'

'But what's happened here? Where are all the men?'

'Come. I show you.'

He led them through the village to another narrow track that wound through the rainforest until it reached a clearing at the base of a hill. A large cross, made from two palm logs tied together by a length of vine, stood at the centre. The ground around its base was bare and surrounded by a large circle of rocks. Fata led them to the edge of the circle.

'They all here,' he said, pointing to the ground within the circle.

'You mean they're dead?'

'Yes. They buried here. But their heads far away.' He pointed to the south west. 'Over the sea, with Maaso.'

Mason turned to Sele. 'I don't understand. Who is Maaso?'

'He's a white man who lives on one of the islands to the south, close to Cape York. He's a powerful warrior who dominates those islands and is considered to be a god. Fata says that over the years he has gradually extended his influence to other islands, including this one. If anyone opposes him, he kills them and takes their heads as trophies.'

'Headhunters,' Mason shivered. 'I've often heard about 'em, but never encountered any, thank God.'

'Maaso very evil man,' Fata said. 'He do many bad thing. He attack white man ship too.'

Mason nodded. 'I've heard stories about ships sailing alone in those waters being attacked by war canoes, and about a big white man who seems to be the leader. They were from the ships that got away. No-one knows how many that have gone missing may have fallen foul of this renegade.'

Sele took up the story. 'According to Fata, Maaso came here some months ago with a large group of warriors in many canoes. He demanded that the local chief provide him with warriors and young women. When the chief refused there was a battle. The local men were heavily outnumbered and slaughtered. Their heads were cut off and taken away as trophies. A number of young women were also abducted. And now only a few old men and boys remain.'

'Maaso say he come back when boys grow up, they become his warriors,' Fata explained.

Mason looked puzzled. 'But what about when we were attacked here?'

'They Maaso's warriors who kill your men,' Fata said. 'He leave some warriors here after he go.'

'So, we were lucky to escape as we did. If we'd arrived a little earlier, we'd probably all have shared the same fate as those poor devils,' Mason said.

'Now do you believe what I say about God having a plan for us returning here?' Sele asked.

'Surely you're not thinking of staying here, Miss Saena. Not now you know this wild man is coming back?'

'Of course I'm going to stay here, Captain. There is a devil in these islands, and he has to be cast out.'

5 July 1886 – Cape York

Five luggers of the kind used by pearlers all across northern Australia were riding at anchor as the *Hoylake* entered a secluded bay near the tip of Cape York. She anchored a cable's length away and prepared to receive the skippers of the luggers, who were already climbing into small boats to be rowed across. Mundine joined Homer at the rail to welcome them aboard.

'Good afternoon, gentlemen. I don't believe you know my partner, Mr. Mundine.'

The five skippers, all of them villainous looking characters with grizzled features and wearing incongruous frock coats to denote their status, shook hands with Mundine and followed Homer to his cabin, where a bottle of Mundine's Jamaica rum and five extra glasses were waiting.

'You've got what we've been waitin' for?' a short, thickset man with an American accent, asked.

'We have indeed, Jethro,' Homer answered. 'And with them you are going to make a lot more money than you ever did as mate on that Yankee whaler.'

'I should durn well hope so!' He took a leather pouch from his pockets and poured a pile of pearls onto the table. 'Two pearls for each woman.'

Mundine picked a couple of pearls at random and examined them carefully. He turned to Homer, who was waiting for his reaction, and nodded.

'It appears that my partner is satisfied with the payment, gentlemen.'

'But first we need to be satisfied with the trade goods,' the American said, as he scooped the pearls up and replaced them in the pouch.

Homer got up, opened his cabin door, and called out to Harris. 'Get the women up on deck,' he ordered.

They finished their drinks and made their way back onto the deck just as two seamen were opening the hatch cover. The stench of unwashed bodies and waste was almost overpowering. Harris, holding a piece of cloth over his nose, went below and began pushing the captive women up onto the deck. After five days of being locked up, with little fresh air and temperatures which by midday were almost unbearable, the women were in bad shape. Some of them could barely crawl up the ladder.

'You'd better sit them down and give 'em some water,' Homer said to his mate. 'We don't want our friends here to think they're about to die.'

The pearling captains walked up and down the line of terrified women, stopping every now and then to pull one to her feet and examine her teeth and physique. 'They look half dead,' one said to Homer.

'Don't let appearances deceive you, captain. These native women are as tough as mules. In a day's time, with a decent feed and the threat of a flogging, they'll be scouring the seabed for pearl shells better than any Jap diver you've got. I've seen some of them stay down for almost three minutes.'

The pearlers stood in a group away from Homer and began to mutter to each other, occasionally casting furtive glances at him. Finally, they walked back and the American reported their decision.

'These women ain't worth more'n a decent pearl apiece. We'd be lucky if they lasted a month. We'll give you one pearl for every one of 'em.'

Mundine looked at Homer and saw the colour of his neck above his collar begin to turn a deep shade of crimson. He looked at Harris and noticed the anxious look on the mate's face. Harris had warned him about *Bulldog* Homer's rages. It seemed as though he was about to witness one.

'Gentlemen, gentlemen,' he intervened. 'Let's not quibble about this. I agree that these women look in poor shape, but that's because they've been locked up for five days. By the time you get them to your pearling grounds they'll be in tip-top shape. And your sailors, no doubt, will help get them back into shape as only sailors can.'

The pearlers guffawed, understanding perfectly well what Mundine was alluding to and the effect it would have on their crews' morale.

'O.K. We'll give you forty pearls for the thirty of them,' the American said.

Once again Mundine looked at Homer and saw his jaw tighten and his fists begin to clench. He could see the hoped-for deal about to disappear in a sudden squall of rage.

'Raise it to fifty pearls and you have a deal. What do you think, Captain Homer?'

He looked at his partner and wilted as Homer's savage gaze bored right through him. Then, to his intense relief, Homer unclenched his fists and muttered, 'I agree.'

The pearlers put their heads together and talked for a moment. 'It's a deal,' the American responded, holding out his hand. But only Mundine was there to shake on it. Homer had stalked back to his cabin.

By nightfall the transaction was completed, and the *Hoylake* was on her way, sailing north towards the islands of the Torres Strait. Harris walked over to where Mundine stood looking out to sea.

'I'd advise you to leave the cap'n alone tonight, Mr. Mundine. He's not in a good humour, and it's best to leave him to get over it.'

'How long will that take?'

'He'll probably get roaring drunk and then fall asleep. He'll be like a bear with a sore head tomorrow, but he'll soon be back to normal. All you need to do is stay out of his way.'

'You think he's angry at the deal I suggested?'

'Not the deal, as such. Just that you came up with it and put him in a position where he had to accept it or be stuck with thirty black women. He doesn't like to be seen to be beaten, does *Bulldog* Homer. And he's a dangerous man if he thinks someone has crossed him.'

Mundine watched the mate return to his position alongside the man at the ship's wheel. The deal he had negotiated was a good one as far as he was concerned. The fifty pearls they'd received included some that, even to his relatively inexperienced eye, were of excellent quality and, when sold in Sydney, would make the voyage a profitable one. But he began to wonder again if his partnership with Homer might not be more than he was able to handle.

* * *

Harris was right. By midday Homer was back to his old self, relishing the surge of his ship as it beat, close hauled, into a freshening breeze. Mundine remained in his cabin all morning. It was only after Harris had suggested he might like to step up on deck that he had ventured forth.

'Good morning, Mundine. Or should I say good afternoon,' Homer called out as Mundine poked his head through the hatch.

'Good afternoon, Captain. Sorry I wasn't able to join you for breakfast. With the ship pitching like this I was feeling seasick.'

'That's quite understandable. Now, come back here, I want to talk to you.'

Mundine felt a pang of anxiety grip his stomach. He made his way aft where Homer placed his huge brawny arm around his shoulder and led him to the windward rail.

'Have you ever heard of the Frenchman named Marcel?'

Mundine shook his head.

'He lives on an island at the northern end of the Torres Strait. The natives call it Mabi. They're all terrified of him and treat him as a great chief and war lord. The truth is that he was a convict in New Caledonia. He escaped more than twenty years ago and now lives like the blacks.'

'What about him?'

'We're going to make a deal with him. He's going to provide us with native women – this ain't the first time I've done business with him - and we're going to keep on collecting pearls. At a rate of fifty pearls to thirty women, we'll be rich within a year.'

Mundine felt relief flood over him. 'So, you're happy about the deal I struck yesterday?'

Homer smiled and nodded. Then his eyes hardened, and his voice fell to little more than a whisper – a whisper so full of menace that Mundine felt his knees turn to jelly. 'But if you ever do it again before you've talked to me, I'll make you curse the day you were born. Do you understand?'

Mundine nodded nervously. 'Of course, Captain. You can rest assured.'

Homer took his hand from around Mundine's shoulder and returned to his position near the ship's wheel. 'Mr. Harris,' he bawled. 'I want a reef put into those topsails before this wind gets any stronger.'

Mundine, still shaking, breathed a sigh of relief and returned to his cabin.

* * *

The journey to Mabi was swift and uneventful. Mundine, still nervous about his relationship with *Bulldog* Homer, watched his partner's moods carefully; he was anxious not to do anything that might upset him. Fortunately, a fair wind and the prospect of substantial profit had put the captain in a good mood. Each evening the two of them would gather in the large stern cabin where they would open another bottle of Mundine's rum, drinking and yarning until Homer fell asleep. It was at one of these sessions that he told Mundine the story of the Frenchman they were about to meet.

August 1866 - The Louisiade Archipelago

Marcel – no one knew his second name - had escaped from the French penal colony of New Caledonia more than twenty years earlier. He'd been convicted of armed robbery and sentenced to transportation for life, never to return to France.

Two years into his sentence, and with no prospect of ever being released from that living hell, Marcel saw his opportunity one morning when a brigantine put into their bay to make repairs to storm damage. Marcel watched its crew struggle to step a new mast, cut from timber given to them by a sympathetic camp commandant, and realized by the amount of effort involved that the brigantine was short-handed. That night, as they were about to set sail, he swam out, managing to avoid the sharks that the authorities encouraged to infest the bay by emptying blood and offal into it daily, and was taken aboard as an unpaid addition to the crew.

The brigantine's name was the *Dolphin,* and she was on her way from Sydney to Singapore. She was well into the Coral Sea before the authorities realized that one of their charges was missing. But even so they gave little consideration to the possibility that the escapee might be aboard her. The convicts lived in terror of the sharks that infested the bay. No one, the commandant assumed, would have risked swimming out to that ship. So, he concentrated his search on the thickly wooded interior of the island. But Marcel had been both desperate and lucky; and by the time the commandant was beginning to reconsider his previous assumption the *Dolphin* was too far away to pursue.

It was as they were approaching the Louisiade Archipelago and running before a storm that the *Dolphin's* captain, unsure about where he was in those uncharted waters, and aware of the dangers of coral reefs, doubled the watch. It was Marcel, clinging precariously to the foretop, who first spotted the breakers ahead. The captain immediately ordered the ship hove to and dropped both anchors, but they both ran to the ends of their cables without touching bottom.

The wind continued to scream through the rigging and the crew watched helplessly as the ship was driven on to one of the many coral reefs that abound in that area. Moments after she struck, she rolled over on to her beam ends. The captain ordered the tangle of broken mast and rigging to be cut away, hoping that by reducing the ship's weight she might right herself and float off the coral. But it was all to no avail. The ship was firmly stuck on the reef and was starting to break up in the constant pounding of the breakers.

Realizing their plight was hopeless, he then ordered the crew to launch the ship's boats. The two smaller ones survived less than five minutes, smashed to pieces on the coral, spilling their occupants into the fury of the waves, where they drowned or were dashed against the coral. The third was lucky. It remained afloat with its occupants, including Marcel, clinging to it, expecting any moment to be swamped like the other two. Then, a brief lull in the wind caused the waves to abate slightly. The men still aboard the

Dolphin managed to haul it back to the ship where, despite the captain's orders, there was a mad scramble to get into it.

Marcel, though, had had enough. He scrambled back onto the ship and watched the panic-filled sailors cut the line attaching the now heavily overloaded boat to the stricken ship and begin to pull away. Moments later, a man, standing in the bow, screamed a warning. Dead ahead was a jagged coral outcrop. The helmsman swung the tiller hard to starboard, but it was too late. A large wave caught the boat and dashed it onto the coral.

Marcel watched it sink as its screaming occupants tried desperately to cling to anything that might float. Within minutes their cries for help ceased as the pounding surf smashed them against the reef, or their heavy boots pulled them beneath the waves. Thankful that he had not stayed on the boat, he tore his gaze away and looked around to see who was left on the wrecked brigantine. There were six others apart from him, including the captain, his wife and their baby son, huddled together below deck. Exhaustion and a feeling of resignation caused by a sense of utter helplessness finally drove them all to sleep.

Marcel was the first to wake up. He was immediately aware of the stillness in the air and the absence of flying spray pouring down upon the sleeping figures huddled below the hatch. He realized the storm had finally blown itself out.

He climbed up on deck and saw the devastation the storm had caused – broken stumps where the masts had once been, shattered bulkheads open to the waves, the deck canting at a crazy angle, and all the boats lost. His tongue stuck to the roof of his mouth, and he realized he hadn't had a drink of water for nearly a day. He was also ravenously hungry. He made his way to the galley and found nearly everything had been washed away by the pounding waves.

Only one cask of fresh water had survived, and he broke into it, gulping down great mouthfuls until his thirst was satisfied. He found a sealed tin of ship's biscuit that also seemed untainted by sea water, prized off the lid and began to stuff his mouth full of the flat, unappetizing contents until his hunger began to subside. It was then that he felt a hand on his shoulder pulling him back.

'Get away from that. It's all we got left.'

Captain Jacobs was a short, burly man, but no match for Marcel, who stood well over six feet tall and was as strong as an ox. The Frenchman knew enough English to understand that Jacobs was confirming his fear that they had nothing left to eat or drink besides what now lay before him. His instinct for survival gave added strength to the blow that knocked the captain off his feet. Before the older man could recover Marcel had his right arm locked around his grizzled head and then drove it hard into the stump of the mainmast. The captain's body went limp, but to make sure he was dead, Marcel took the man's head between his huge hands and twisted it violently to the right, snapping his neck.

He heard a scream from behind and, turning round, saw Mrs. Jacobs looking at him over the rim of the hatch. He sprang at her, and she screamed again, darting back below deck. She scooped up her baby son and began to run along the sloping lower deck towards her cabin. Marcel let her go but turned his attention to three seamen who were the only other survivors. One of them, a small red-headed Cockney, held out his hands in a gesture of appeasement.

'Easy there, mate. We're all in this together.'

Marcel felled him with a vicious blow to his head.

The other two were Lascars who had learned long ago how to survive as members of the lowest order in the violent and racist world of seamen. One of them drew a razor-sharp panga from his waistband while the other tried to circle behind the Frenchman. But Marcel had grown up in the vicious underworld of the Marseilles dockland, where the use of knife and boot had been his major skills. The Lascar's attempt to slash at Marcel's throat came a split second too late as the huge Frenchman lunged forward, getting inside the swinging arm, which he seized with both his hands, snapping the man's forearm like a twig.

The Lascar screamed in agony, dropping the panga, which Marcel snatched up from the deck just as the other Lascar dived at him from behind. Marcel drove his left elbow into the little man's face then spun around with the panga now gripped firmly in his right hand. One lightning slash was all it took, and the seaman lay dead on the floor. A moment later his companion, still screaming from the pain of his shattered arm, lay dead next to him.

The little cockney sailor, who had watched in shocked silence as the escaped convict dispatched his two mates, took to his heels and made for the companionway leading up to the main deck. But Marcel, despite his size, was surprisingly quick on his feet. Before the little man could reach the top of the ladder Marcel grabbed him by the heel and hauled him down, sending him sprawling on the deck. His face white with terror, he held his hands out begging for mercy. But the Frenchman just grinned savagely as he swept the panga backhandedly across the sailor's throat, killing him instantly.

In an orgy of blood lust, Marcel dragged the three corpses together and, using the panga to chop and slash, severed the heads of his three victims. He laughed insanely as he took them by the hair and held them high above his head, staring at them as if they were trophies, while the blood continued to pour from their necks onto his hair, and chest. Then he went back to where the body of Captain Jacobs lay. Dropping the three severed heads he proceeded to hack at Jacob's head, chuckling gleefully to himself as he added a fourth to his collection.

Because Captain Jacobs had been bald there was no hair for Marcel to hold on to. So, he tied the other three heads to his belt with their strands of hair and carried the captain's head in his left hand, like an orb: its sightless eyes staring ahead as if to light the way. He then made his way to the captain's cabin, where Mrs. Jacobs had locked herself and her son inside. Even Marcel's strength could not break through the thick wooden door, so he returned to the open deck and walked aft to where he could look down on the cabin window below.

As he looked for a rope that he could use to swing down and break through the glass, he noticed something off towards the horizon. He climbed onto what was left of the ship's rail to get a better look. Moments later he was able to make out three large outrigger canoes with triangular sails made of latticed palm leaves, similar to the ones the Melanesians used in New Caledonia. Each of them had at least a dozen paddles, flashing in and out of the water in unison. As they drew closer Marcel could see the men wielding them – black skinned men with thick, curly hair; their faces painted with white ochre giving them a demonic look that would have terrified most men – but not this Frenchman.

By the time the canoes had reached the ship, Marcel, swinging down across the ship's stern from a piece of hanging rigging, had smashed feet first through the stern cabin windows to where Mrs. Jacobs cowered in a corner, whimpering and desperately trying to shield her child from the horror that approached. He snatched the little boy from her arms and, with two swift slashes of the panga, put an end to their terror, and their lives.

He unlocked the cabin door and went back on deck, now with two more severed heads attached to his belt. The three canoes by this time were alongside and the warriors in them were preparing to climb aboard. Their leader was a powerfully built man of middle age, naked, like all of them, except for a loincloth, and armed with a wicked looking club, mounted with a wild boar's tusk. He scrambled over the ship's side, followed by several others, and saw the Frenchman standing there before him. His stopped dead in his tracks and his eyes widened with horror. The other warriors likewise stopped and fell back from the apparition that confronted them.

And what a sight it was! A huge white man, his long hair, beard and matted chest coated with fresh blood, holding in one hand a large, bald, head with piercing blue eyes that stared right at them, and in his other a long, curved blade dripping with blood.

But it was the maniacal laughter that terrified them most as this giant of a man, much taller than any Melanesian, strode towards them, roaring at them in a language they could not understand. Their leader fell prostrate on the deck and the others followed in quick succession. Here before them was the terrible, white skinned god, whose coming the old men of the tribe had spoken of. Like them he was a headhunter, and never before had they seen such heads – the Lascars with their long black pigtails, the red-headed cockney, the woman with the long golden tresses and the child whose innocent blue eyes were identical to those piercing blue eyes that stared at them from the large, hairless head in the god's hand.

As silence fell all around him, Marcel's wild blood lust began to fade away, and sanity returned to his mind. He sensed immediately that the cowering natives before him were totally over-awed by his presence. He'd seen this before – in the back alleys of Marseilles when violent men had fled before his rage, and also in the convict dormitories of New Caledonia. But never before had he had quite this effect on savage, violent men. He began to laugh again; but this time it was a laugh of triumph.

* * *

As soon as the *Hoylake* had anchored in the lagoon, two war canoes put out from the beach. Homer and Marcel greeted each other with ill-disguised hostility as the renegade Frenchman, carrying a razor-sharp cutlass he had souvenired from a dead seaman, swung himself over the ship's rail. He was followed by a dozen half naked warriors, armed with vicious looking clubs. Homer beckoned to Mundine, who stepped forward from the throng of anxious but curious seamen to join him.

'Mr. Mundine, I would like you to meet Chief Marcel, or Maaso, as the natives call him; the most powerful chief and war lord in these islands.'

Mundine had never seen anyone so terrifying. Marcel, like Homer, was a huge man with fierce, piercing eyes. Unlike Homer he was naked, except for a loin cloth. His wrinkled, European skin, burnt nearly brown by years of exposure to the tropical sun, was covered with scars - mementos of many battles to the death. His hair, like his beard, was long, matted and streaked with grey, and around his neck he wore a necklace of hideous shrunken heads – victims of those battles.

'I am pleased to make your acquaintance, sir.' There was a slight tremble in Mundine's voice as he extended his hand.

Marcel looked at it with contempt and spat on the deck, causing Mundine to hastily withdraw it. Homer threw his head back and guffawed at his associate's discomfort.

'Chief Marcel doesn't care much for the niceties of European manners, Mundine. But he does care for gold sovereigns, ain't that so, m'sieur. '

Marcel eyed him warily. *'Q'est ce-que vous voulez.'*

'He's asking what we want,' Homer translated. 'We want some women, *m'sieur – des femmes*; young women; good divers.' He pinched his nose between his forefinger and thumb and with his other hand made out as if he were swimming under water. *'Jeunes femmes;* you understand – *vous comprenez?*

Marcel nodded. 'You show me gold.'

'Show him,' Homer said to Mundine.

Mundine thrust his hand into his jacket pocket and pulled out a large leather pouch. Bending down on one knee he poured its contents onto the deck. Thirty gold sovereigns rolled out towards Marcel's bare feet. A lustful gleam came into the renegade's eye as he bent down to scoop them up.

Homer stepped forward and placed his foot on the coins closest to Marcel's grasp, nearly stepping on the wild man's hand. 'Not so quick!'

Marcel sprang to his feet with a roar and drew the cutlass that hung from a leather belt – the only other item of clothing he wore besides the loin cloth. His warriors also raised their weapons and stepped forward. Mundine shrank back from the approaching onslaught, seeking refuge behind the *Hoylake's* crew who were lined up with loaded rifles at the ready. One thunderous volley over the approaching warriors' heads was all it took to check their advance. They fell to the deck, their eyes white with terror at the noise.

Marcel cursed them in a language none of Homer's crew could understand, kicking them to their feet and laying about them with the flat of his cutlass, until Homer managed to pacify his rage by scooping up half of the sovereigns and holding them out to him.

'Fifteen now and fifteen later - *Quinze maintenant, et quinze plus tard.*'

Marcel's rage disappeared as quickly as it had erupted. He took the handful of coins from Homer's huge paw, put one between his teeth and bit down on it. Convinced it was a genuine gold sovereign, he nodded.

'D'accord. Quinze maintenant et quinze plus tard.' He put the coins into pouch attached to his belt – another souvenir from a dead sailor.

Homer extended the fingers and thumbs of both hands in front of Marcel's face three times. 'Thirty women; thirty sovereigns. *Treize femmes.* Do you understand? *Vous comprenez?*'

Marcel gave him a dark, savage look, and nodded his head. *'Treize femmes.'*

He turned to his warriors and, pointing to the north, said one word: 'Vitu.'

10 July 1886 – Cape York Peninsula

Michael found it hard to contain his mounting excitement as the *Wahine* approached the mouth of the Endeavour River. It had been almost two months since he'd last seen Sele, and he'd not been able to get her out of his mind. He kept telling himself that he didn't want to get entangled with a missionary woman; especially one of mixed race. Even though people in those remote northern regions were accustomed to mixed-race marriages, they were still unacceptable in the colonial capitals to the south. And he didn't intend to spend the rest of his life as skipper of an island schooner. But no matter how much he cursed himself for acting like a love-sick schoolboy, he knew he was living for the moment when he would see her again.

They crossed the river bar shortly before high tide and anchored half an hour later. He told the mate that he'd be ashore until late afternoon when the flood tide would be high enough to get them safely across the bar again.

'Keep a lookout for when I get back to the wharf and send a boat for me,' he said. 'But don't let the boys ashore or we'll have the devil of a job getting them out of the pubs in time to get underway.'

By the time he reached the Glastons' house his heart was pounding, and the ends of his fingers were cold and clammy. He was desperate to meet her again, yet afraid that she wouldn't want to meet him. She was a God-fearing missionary and he - though not an unbeliever - was hardly what could be thought of as religious. But he still remembered how she used to look at him when they'd been together, and especially that moment at the *Wahine's* wheel when he had put his arms around her to keep the wheel from spinning.

It was Amelia Glaston who saw him first. She was sweeping the front veranda of the mission house with a long straw broom, humming to herself as she did so.

'Good afternoon, ma'am.'

'Why, Captain Burns, how lovely to see you again! We didn't expect you back here for ages.'

Michael raised his peaked cap and took her hand. 'And it's a pleasure to see you again, Mrs. Glaston. I hope you and the reverend are well.'

'Oh yes, indeed we are. I don't think we've ever been better.'

'Cooktown agrees with you, then?'

She took him by the arm and led him into the coolness of the house. 'Yes, we do like it here, even though the town is a very wild place. Both of us feel we're meant to be here; and we now have a small congregation.'

'You're not intending to move back to the islands, then?'

'No. The mission has asked Geoffrey to establish a base here from which we can reach out to the Torres Strait islands and beyond; perhaps even into New Guinea.'

'I remember Miss Saena telling me about that when I was here before.'

Amelia smiled to herself. She'd been wondering how long it would be before the subject of Sele Saena came up. 'Well, she's actually done something about it. She returned to that island where they were attacked by natives. Captain Mason has taken her there.'

Michael's face immediately revealed his shock. 'She's gone! What in God's name persuaded Mason to take her back there?'

'She believes it's what God wants her to do. And as for Captain Mason; well, Sele has a remarkable ability for getting people – especially men – to fit in with her plans.'

Michael shook his head in stunned disbelief. 'Forgive my language, Mrs. Glaston, but the people in those islands are savages. Nobody in his – or her – right mind would go there unless they were well protected and had something to gain.'

'Well, Captain. What Sele is doing is for the gain of God's kingdom, and both Geoffrey and I believe she will be well protected.'

'I suppose you're going to tell me she's being protected by God.'

'Yes. The Lord looks after His own as they do His will.'

'And what about all those who've been doing His will and have ended up as the main course for a cannibal feast!' Michael's face revealed his anger.

Amelia smiled and took his arm. 'Don't be anxious, Michael. I know how much she means to you. Now come into the parlour. Geoffrey will be home soon, and you can join us for lunch. He'll be able to give you more information.'

The *Wahine* did not sail on the afternoon tide as planned. She remained anchored in the Endeavour River as Michael, with Geoffey Glaston in tow, visited Cooktown's numerous pubs, looking for pearling skippers who were familiar with the uncharted waters around Warrior Reef. Geoffrey had only agreed to do this when he realized that Michael was deadly serious about finding the island where Sele had gone and ensuring that she really was safe.

He felt uncomfortable and out of place in those dens of vice, particularly when Michael plied the uncommunicative seamen with alcohol in order to get them talking. But by late that evening they were able to form a general idea of that fifty-mile-long reef system, lying north-east of Cape York at the approximate latitude of 9.5 degrees South, and 143 degrees East.

They returned to the mission house where Amelia served them cocoa as they talked about what to do next. Michael found it hard to relax. He paced up and down as he gave voice to the questions none of them could answer.

'If only we knew when Captain Mason might be back in Cooktown!'

'He's due to call in at Refuge Bay before the end of the month,' Amelia said, as she refilled their mugs of cocoa.

The two men looked at her. 'What did you say?' Geoffrey asked.

'I said he's due to call in at Refuge Bay before the end of the month.'

'How do you know that?'

'Dr. Wakeley said so in the letter that arrived on the supply vessel last week. He said that Captain Mason had called in and had left one of his men - a Kanaka named Jacob - at the infirmary when they were on their way to take Sele to wherever it is she wanted to go. It seems that Jacob had appendicitis and Captain Mason left him with Dr. Wakeley, telling him he'd pick him up on the way back south, which he expected would be before the end of this month.'

'My dear, why didn't you tell us this before? We've just spent the whole evening trying to find someone who could tell us what only Captain Mason knows.'

'I would have if you had told me that that was what the two of you were up to, of course! It's so typical of men!'

Geoffrey looked at Michael and rolled his eyes in disbelief. 'Well, there you have it, Michael. There are only a few days until the end of the month. If you leave for Refuge Bay right away, you might meet up with him.'

Michael got to his feet. 'I'll get back to my ship right away. We can't risk leaving in the dark, so I'll have to wait until the morning tide. But if the wind holds steady from the southeast, we should make Refuge Bay by late afternoon the day after tomorrow.'

'You're not going back to your ship tonight, Captain. You're going to stay here and get a proper night's sleep,' Amelia told him. 'I've already sent a message to them telling them you won't be back until dawn.'

'I don't think I will be able to sleep, Mrs. Glaston; not until I know Miss Saena is safe.'

Amelia placed a motherly hand on his shoulder. 'Sele will be all right, Michael. As long as she's doing what God wants her to do, God will take care of her.'

'I wish I had your faith,' Michael replied. 'Anyway, it's me that should be looking after her, not God.'

Amelia looked questioningly at her husband who just shook his head and looked away.

* * *

Unlike Captain Mason, Michael had never before ventured far into the Torres Strait. He'd sailed round Cape York and into the Gulf of Carpentaria several times, hugging the coast and staying away from the more hazardous waters to the north. But now, nothing would keep him away from them.

On the second day after leaving Cooktown the *Wahine* anchored in Refuge Bay, less than a cable's length from Mason's ketch. The crewman who had been left there was now fully recovered, and Mason was preparing to set sail. Michael immediately ordered his men to lower the ship's boat and row him across to the ketch.

'Good to see you again, Captain Burns. What can I do for you?'

'It's about Miss Saena, the missionary,' Michael said. 'I heard that she'd chartered your vessel to take her back to the island where you were attacked.'

'That's right, the island of Vitu. That's what the natives call it. It's up near Warrior Reef.'

'Can you show me where?'

Mason stood up and walked across the tiny cabin to a small desk bolted to a bulkhead. He pulled open a drawer and rummaged through a pile of charts until he found the one he wanted. Spreading it out on the desktop he pointed to a black blob that he had marked onto the Admiralty chart.

'It's here, in the Coral Sea, just nor'east of the reef.'

'And that's where you took her?'

'Yes.'

'But you didn't stay?'

'Of course not! Why should I?'

'I'm sorry, Captain. It's just that I'm concerned for her safety.'

'I didn't approve of it either. I tried to talk her out of it. But she wouldn't listen. You know what these missionaries are like, forever going on about being called by God to go here and do this and so on.'

Michael nodded. 'She is very determined.'

'And very persuasive,' Mason added.

'I know that too.'

'Anyway, when we got there, we met up with a bloke named Fata, whom she used to know. He's a Samoan; another God-botherer. Seems he's been there for years and got a lot of the locals converted.'

'Yet they tried to kill you when you were there before.'

'Ah, well that's the interesting thing. It wasn't the people of that island who attacked us. It turns out they were warriors left over from a raiding party from further south, down near Thursday Island.' Mason recounted the story of Marcel's raid and its aftermath.

'I see. So, who's there now – apart from Miss Saena and this other Samoan?'

'There's a few old men, some boys, about thirty younger women, plus some kids.'

'And are they able to survive alone?'

'They seem to. But I think they're scared that Maaso is going to come back.'

Michael looked alarmed. 'They told you that?'

'I don't speak their lingo, mate. But you don't need to be a genius to smell the fear in the place. You're not planning to go there, are you?'

'That I am, Captain Mason. And right away. If your suspicions are right, Miss Saena might be in great danger.'

'I tried to get her to come back with me. But like you said, she's a very determined woman.'

Michael nodded. 'That she is! So where are you going now?'

'South to Townsville. There's talk of a new gold discovery in the mountains inland from here. There'll be dozens of hopefuls lining up on the wharf, ready to pay handsomely for a one-way trip to Refuge Bay once the news gets out.'

'Yes, I heard about it from Bernie Matthews. He plans to come up here himself and try his luck.'

'Bernie's already here,' Mason said. 'I was talking to him last night. He's staying in the pub next to the creek. You'd better let him know you're here. I'm sure he'd want to go aboard his old ship again.'

'You're a fool, Michael, I thought you were taking supplies to Thursday Island.'

'I still am, Bernie. I didn't know about this Maaso character myself until Mason told me last night.'

'But you had an inkling something was up.'

'All right, I have to admit that once I learned Miss Saena had gone back to Vitu I began to feel worried. But not as worried as I am now.'

'Well, I'm not going to fight you over the decision to go there. You're the master of the *Wahini* now and get to say where she goes. But I'll tell you this: if anything happens to the ship because of this fool venture, the insurance company won't cover you if anything goes wrong up there.'

'I understand your concerns, Bernie. But I'm prepared to take full responsibility for my decision.'

'Well, that's not enough. I still have a half share in the *Wahini.*'

'Yes, and that's why I've come to see you. I want to buy your share, if you'll sell it to me.'

'You don't have the money to do that.'

'I was hoping you might consider a loan agreement. We could draw up a written agreement and have Dr. Wakeley witness it – he's a justice of the peace.'

Bernie sat silently for a while, then stood up and shook Michael's hand. 'Well. I wish you luck. You're goin' to need it.'

Michael gripped his hand. 'And good luck to you, Bernie. If there is gold up there, I hope you're the man who finds it.'

13

12 July 1886 – The Coral Sea

Fata stared at the pile of weapons before him and shook his head. 'These no good, Sele.'

Sele reached out and touched his arm. 'We know that Maaso and his warriors will return, Fata. And we also know that these people will be helpless against him if we don't do something to help them.'

'But Sele, if their men not beat Maaso, how we do it with old men and boys? We must go to safe place.'

'We could if we had canoes to take them there. But Maaso burnt them before he left. The only one we have is yours. Perhaps you should go to the other island near here and persuade the chiefs to form an alliance against him. He might be less inclined to raid these islands if he knew he'd be outnumbered.'

Fata shook his head. 'No. All islands frightened of Maaso. I try before, but they not listen.' He stooped down and picked up a heavy war club. 'When I young man, I was a warrior. Then I hear call of God to preach his word. So, I turn my back on fighting and follow Jesus words: "render evil to no man". Do I now go back to old ways?'

'I remember when you were a young warrior, Fata. I was a little girl then. I watched you change into a man of God, and I admired you even more. But I don't believe that means that people like you and I should not be prepared to use force to protect innocent people from evil men.'

Fata remained silent, pondering her words as he tested the weight of the war club in his hand. Then he looked up and nodded. 'You speak truth, Sele; we must defend women and children. Bible say Jesus take a whip and drive out evil men cheating people in House of God.'

'Then you will go for help, Fata?'

'No, Sele! It too late. I stay here with you and die with these people.' He swung the war club round and took up the warrior's stance he remembered from his youth. 'I no longer young man. It many years since I train for battle. But perhaps it come back to me.'

She smiled at him and placed her hand on his arm. 'You were a brave man then and you still are, my dear friend. But I'm not planning that you or any of these people should be killed.'

He looked at her inquiringly. 'They strong warriors. They spare no-one.'

'Do you remember the story of Gideon and his small band that defeated the mighty army of Midian?'

'Yes. God cause terror to fill hearts of Midianites, and they kill each other.'

'Well God has shown me that that is what He is going to do again.'

'How?'

'I don't know yet. But He will reveal it in due time.'

Fata looked at her and nodded slowly. 'You think you may be like Deborah, who call people of Israel to fight enemy.'

'Yes, and you, Fata, will be my Barak, the warrior who led them.'

* * *

For the next two weeks the people of Vitu worked tirelessly to prepare their island. Each morning Sele explained a little more of her plan to Fata, who listened in amazement that the little girl he had once known could possibly conceive of such things. He then called the villagers together and explained what was to be done.

He led them to the creek that spilled down the mountainside into the pool from which they drew their water. There, armed with fire-hardened digging sticks, they followed him along the creek to a shallow pool immediately below a rock ledge, into which a small waterfall poured steadily. It was a favourite spot for the children to play because of the flat, open area on each side of the pool and the shallowness of the water.

At the top of the waterfall was another pool, formed by a deep depression in the ground into which the creek flowed. Here Fata set them to work with their digging sticks, dislodging large rocks, which they carried to the pool and placed across its mouth. By midday they'd managed to construct a small dam which significantly increased the pool's volume of water.

Fata then had them strengthen the newly built wall with several short logs, laid horizontally behind the rocks, and braced by two other logs, driven deep into the soil on either side. Then, as they rested, he watched anxiously as the water gradually built up against the wall until it began to spill over the top and cascade down once more.

When they got back to the village, they found that Sele had sorted the pile of weapons into categories: war clubs into one pile, bows and arrows into another, and a third pile consisting of long lengths of bamboo, which, like the digging sticks, had been sharpened and fire-hardened at one end.

'What we do with these?' Fata asked.

'They are going to be our pikes – like soldiers in Europe used to have to protect themselves against men on horses. I remember how missionaries taught me about a man named Cromwell who trained ordinary farm workers to become the best soldiers in England by teaching them to stand firm, shoulder-to-shoulder. We will divide our people into groups. The women will have the bamboo pikes and will stand shoulder-to shoulder in a line. The old men will be with you and have the war clubs. They will stand between the women, and their job will be to attack any warriors that manage to get between the pikes. The boys will have bows and arrows. They will stand behind and pick off Maaso's warriors as they charge.

Fata's face broke into a broad grin. 'Ah! I understand. But now we train hard. Everyone must learn what they do. Tomorrow, we learn, become warriors.'

* * *

The teenage boys were excited. They skylarked around, showing off in front of each other until Fata ordered them to stand in a group. The women, though, were more subdued. They looked at the long bamboo poles in their hands with trepidation, not really knowing what lay ahead. But the old men understood. They stood quietly as Fata handed them short lengths of sharpened bamboo - ideal for stabbing at close quarters - and the heavy war clubs they knew so well. Each of them could remember times when they'd used them against warriors from other islands. But they'd been much younger then.

Fata called them to order and announced dramatically that God had sent a prophetess amongst them, and that she would now tell them what they were to do. He stood aside and asked Sele to address the people, who gathered anxiously around, while he translated her words into their language.

Sele's plan was quite simple. Fata had told her how the warriors of those islands fought. Tactics played little part in their battles, which were essentially deadly free-for-alls in which the side with the strongest warriors would usually prevail. But a free-for-all was not what she had in mind.

Her plan was to draw Maaso's warriors up to the ground of her choosing, where the women, standing shoulder to shoulder with their bamboo pikes, would form a defensive wall against Maaso's onslaught, protecting the boys behind them who, shooting arrows at close range, would pick off as many of Maaso's warriors as they could. The old men with the stabbing spears and war clubs would stand immediately behind and between the women, ready to jab and smash any warriors who managed to get inside the wall of bamboo pikes.

'How you know these things, Sele?' Fata asked in amazement.

She smiled. 'The missionaries made me read books about history as well as religion. I always liked the stories about battles where invading armies got beaten by people just defending themselves. Have you ever heard of Joan of Arc?'

'No. Was she a princess too?'

'No. She was a young French woman who believed she was led by God to lead her people against the English invaders.'

'Did she win?'

'Yes, Fata. God gave her victory, and God will give us victory too.'

Fata nodded in wonderment, which pleased Sele, especially since she omitted to tell him that Joan herself ended up being burnt at the stake. She tried not to think about the implications of this for her.

For the rest of that morning, she and Fata drilled their unlikely fighting force until everyone knew immediately where to stand and what to do when Sele sounded the signal by blowing a conch shell. One long blast would tell them to form their defensive position. Two blasts meant the boys were to start shooting. Three blasts were for the whole group to scatter into the bush, and a series of continuous blasts was the signal for the older men to advance in pursuit.

That afternoon she led them to the spot where they would make their stand. It was the ledge below the higher pool where they had built their dam wall. The track to it led past the clearing where their dead warriors lay buried beneath the large bamboo cross.

She then selected the two strongest men and led them to the upper pool, where she showed them the stakes that had been hammered into the ground.

'You are to stand here while the battle goes on below,' she said. 'When you see me wave both my hands above my head, you are to hit the sides of these stakes with your clubs until they fall flat. Then, the force of the water behind the dam wall will push the logs aside and pour down over the waterfall, bringing the rocks we placed there with them.'

Fata interpreted her message and the old men's toothless mouths broke into broad grins as they nodded their heads in understanding, jabbering excitedly to each other in words Sele could not understand.

'They say they will be warriors again, not feeble old men,' Fata interpreted.

Sele put her hands on their shoulders and smiled. 'You will be great warriors, and your grandchildren will tell of your deeds to their children.'

As they followed the crowd back to the village Fata said, 'We need lookout on hill to watch entrance to lagoon. If Maaso get through reef while we sleep, we be too late to get ready.'

'Yes. How should we do it?'

'I ask elders of village to send boys to take turns keep watch. Boys do as elders say. They stay awake and keep good lookout.'

They walked on in silence, each lost in thought until Fata said, 'But what happen if Maaso attack second time?'

'I hope that our defences will be effective enough to deter them from attacking more than once.'

'But they will. I know Maaso. Women and old men then have no more strength, and dam have no water.'

Sele looked at him with a strange smile on her face. 'That's where Gideon comes in.'

He looked at her quizzically.

'Come with me. I want to show you some things Captain Mason left with me.'

She led him to the hut they'd given her to use and showed him a small sea chest where she kept her few possessions. Rummaging through them, she pulled out four small oil lamps and a strange object made of iron. It was about the size of a meat grinder. It had a plunger-type handle on top and a small trumpet shaped mouth at the front.

Fata picked it up and looked at it with a puzzled expression on his face.

'Pull that handle up and then push it down hard,' she said.

He gripped the object firmly and pulled the plunger-like handle back to its fullest extent. Then he pushed it back down. It required some effort because the handle worked a screw mechanism inside. But it was not the effort that surprised him; it was the fearful sound that roared forth from the trumpet at the front. It so unnerved him that he dropped it in fright and stepped back as though he had been holding a poisonous snake. Nor was he the only one to react that way. All around the village old men looked up with shock, women screamed, and children hung on to their mother's knees, their eyes wide with fear.

Sele laughed as she picked it up from the ground.

'What that thing?' he whispered.

'It's called a klaxon,' Sele answered. 'A German trader gave it to Captain Mason in payment for some trade goods. It's what ships use when they're caught in fog. The noise lets other ships know they're there even when they can't see them.'

Fata took it from her and looked at it carefully. 'It like voice of God that speak to Israelites from Mount Sinai.'

'Well, I hope that's what it will sound like to Maaso's warriors, too. But now we'd better go outside and explain to our people that it's really just a white man's machine.'

* * *

They came just after the sun had passed its highest point in the sky. There were eight of them; long outrigger canoes, each with a short mast carrying a triangular sail and eight warriors, whose flashing paddles helped the sails propel them through the gap in the coral into the calm waters of the lagoon.

The boy on the hill saw them while they were still well out to sea. He picked up a stick and began to beat madly on a hollow log. Its sound reverberated over the village and down to the pool where some of the women were washing. Sele heard it and ran out of her hut to find Fata already running down the short track to the beach to view the approaching canoes.

A few minutes later he was back. 'They come into lagoon now,' he said. 'Eight canoes, maybe fifty warriors; maybe more. There is big man in first canoe. Must be Maaso.'

Sele picked up her conche shell and sounded a warning blast. The villagers gathered around her. She turned to Fata. 'Tell them to take their weapons and go to their places by the waterfall.'

Moments later they were off, grabbing bamboo pikes, war clubs, bows and arrows, all of which had been stacked under a low thatched shelter. Old men, women and boys ran up along the creek bank and climbed up to the clearing below the waterfall, while the old women scooped up the children and ran into the bush with them, away from the approaching danger.

Sele and Fata hurried down to the beach, where they could see the canoes rapidly approaching. They were now little more than a hundred yards away and presented a fearsome sight. The warriors' bodies were painted with ochre and their muscles rippled as they dug their paddles into the calm waters of the lagoon. They roared out a rhythmic war chant as they approached. To Sele and Fata the words were unintelligible. But the effect was terrifying, made doubly so by the sight of the huge, wild white man standing in the prow of the leading canoe. His long grey hair and beard was matted with thorns, giving him an almost devilish look; and round his neck he wore a necklace of shrunken heads whose sightless eyes stared straight ahead. In his left hand he carried a large club and, in his right, a razor-sharp cutlass, which he waved around his head as he uttered unearthly screams. But even more fearsome was the diabolical look in his eyes.

Even Fata was taken aback. 'It is Satan himself!' he whispered.

'No, Fata,' Sele replied. 'It is just one of his servants. But remember, we are the servants of God.'

Fata nodded. 'And "Greater is he that is in us than he that is in the world".'

14

16 July 1886 – The Coral Sea

Sele and Fata ran back to the village as the canoes reached the beach. The warriors poured out and began to run after the two figures they'd seen disappear into the trees. When they reached the village, they found it empty. Maaso then ordered half his men to continue the pursuit while the others searched for anyone who might be hiding.

Sele and Fata, running as hard as they could, reached the base of the mountain stream and began to scramble over the rocks up to the clearing where the others waited. The pursuing warriors arrived just in time to see them reach the ledge, where the villagers stood silent and afraid. They paused, unsure what to do; and then their leader decided to send one man back to report to Maaso.

Maaso immediately left the village and led his warriors up to the creek where the others waited. As they jogged through the bush, he saw the clearing where the large cross stood. He pointed to it with his club and laughed, recognizing it as the spot where he and his men had inflicted their previous devastating defeat on the men of this island. The warriors laughed with him, then followed him to the bottom of the creek, confident that the easiest of pickings lay ahead of them.

Still breathless from their run, Sele and Fata looked around and saw the terror on everyone's face. The women, as they had been drilled to do, were standing shoulder-to-shoulder in a semi-circle along the ledge below the waterfall. The only gap in their line was the spot where the pool spilled over the rocks to cascade down to the creek below. They held their long bamboo pikes almost horizontal with the blunt ends wedged into the ground behind them and the sharpened ends facing forward, presenting a barrier of spear points, each one no more than eighteen inches away from the next.

Behind and between them stood the old men with their war clubs in one hand and the short bamboo pikes in the other, ready to stab and club any warrior who managed to get between the outer wall of pikes. Immediately behind them, where the ground was higher, stood the boys with their bows and arrows, ready to pick off the warriors as they attempted to storm the perimeter.

The defenders allowed Sele and Fata through the barrier, then immediately closed up again. Sele looked up to the top of the waterfall and saw the two old men she had posted there, standing ready with their clubs on their shoulders.

'People need word of encouragement, Sele,' Fata said. 'They all terrified. Even old warriors are afraid.'

'So am I, Fata. But tell them this is the word God has given me to give to them: "*Stand still and see the salvation of the Lord*".'

Fata nodded. 'Moses say that to people of Israel when Pharoah about to attack.' In a deep booming voice, he called them all to attention and repeated Sele's words. Then he added his own instructions to the women, telling them that no-one was to move. They didn't have to jab or try to kill anyone. All they had to do was to keep their pikes levelled against the attackers.

Sele positioned herself amongst the boys on higher ground that afforded her a view of the whole area. She looked down and saw Maaso giving orders to his men and raising his cutlass over his head. She put the conch shell to her lips and blew one loud blast. The women immediately took up their positions, standing side by side, keeping their pikes at waist height – level with where the attackers' upper bodies would appear as they scrambled up the steep slope to the rocky ledge. The old men standing behind them gripped their clubs, ready to deal death and wounds to any who might break through, and the boys, shaking with fright, notched their arrows to their bowstrings and drew them back.

Maaso waved his cutlass over his head and gave a blood chilling cry, which the other warriors took up as they began their charge up the slope. The charge soon became a scramble as warriors slipped on the wet rocks and fought to regain their footing. But onward and upward they came, rending the stillness of the afternoon air with their fearsome war cries, while the defenders waited and trembled.

Moments later the first heads began to appear over the slope of the hill and Sele raised the conch shell again. She gave two short, sharp blasts - the signal for the boys to start shooting. Most of the arrows went wild as the terrified boys forgot to take proper aim or let their arrows go prematurely. But one lucky shot found its target. A warrior screamed as an arrow went through his throat. He fell to the ground, tugging hopelessly at the shaft.

Fata roared his encouragement to the boys who, seeing the effect of that one shot, notched more arrows to their bows and this time, taking steady aim, let another volley fly. Three more warriors went down; but by now the leading ranks of attackers had reached the perimeter, where they battered at the pikes with their clubs, trying to separate them enough to slide their bodies through. A couple succeeded and slid sideways between the shafts. But before they could continue their rush, the old warriors stepped forward and thrust their short stabbing pikes into bare flesh, followed by vicious blows of their clubs onto unprotected arms and shoulders.

The battle continued like this for what seemed an eternity but was in fact no more than a few minutes. Sele watched anxiously as the women held their ground and the old men made occasional quick dashes forward to jab and strike. The boys, by now, had recovered from their former debilitating fear. They kept up a regular rate of fire, scoring several hits until their quivers were nearly empty. Yet still the attackers pressed forward.

Maaso, who up to this point had been directing his warriors from below, suddenly emerged over the crest of the hill, roaring like a bull and swinging his war club from side to side as he tried to smash a way through the wall of pikes. The women standing immediately before him began to fall back in terror at the sight. Fata saw them and tried to check their retreat. But by now the wild renegade had managed to get his body between the pikes and, raising his cutlass high, swung it diagonally at one woman's head. She screamed and dropped her pike just as Fata stepped forward and parried the cutlass with his club. Another attacker, seeing the newly formed gap in the perimeter, rushed up behind Maaso and felled Fata with a swipe of his club, only to fall himself, speared in the belly by one of the old men.

Sele saw Fata fall and try to shield himself as Maaso raised his cutlass again. She realized she had left things too late. She blew three blasts on the conch shell and waved to the two old men at the top of the waterfall. With a few powerful blows they knocked the supporting logs over and stood back as the pent-up volume of water began to dislodge the log barrier. Below them the defenders, hearing the three blasts, dropped their weapons and took to their heels, scattering into the bush on either side.

Maaso, his cutlass raised over Fata's helpless body, was momentarily distracted by the sound of the blasts and the sudden retreat of the defenders. He looked up and saw the two old men hammering at the logs and suddenly realized what was about to happen. He was about to scream an order to his warriors when an agonizing blow to his knee brought him to the ground. Fata had recovered sufficiently to retrieve his club and, seeing Maaso standing over him, raised himself on one elbow and made a back-handed swing against the side of the renegade's knee. Maaso's leg collapsed beneath him, and he fell to the ground, roaring with pain. Fata took the opportunity to scramble to his feet and join the other defenders as they scattered into the bush.

He barely made it. A solid wall of water poured over the rim of the upper ledge, bringing with it the logs and rocks that had been holding it back. It fell into the pool below and swept on over the lower ledge, pouring in an unstoppable torrent down the creek bed. A few of Maaso's men managed to get out of its way, but most of them were knocked off their feet, bowled over as tons of water hurled them downstream, tearing flesh and skin and breaking bones.

On a patch of high ground to the right of the torrent, standing safely with a group of trembling women, Sele watched in shocked relief. Then she put the conch to her lips again and blew a series of short, sharp blasts. Hearing this, the old men, cheered by their sudden deliverance, raised a war cry they remembered from their youth and followed the wall of water down the slope, quickly silencing any fallen warriors who offered resistance.

Seeing them come, Maaso realized he was in peril of losing his force and his life. He staggered to his feet, his body torn and bleeding but his bones still intact, and, uttering fearful curses, led those of his men who could still walk back to the canoes. They quickly pushed them out into the lagoon and bent their backs to the paddles, heading for the opening in the coral from whence they'd come. A shower of arrows fell amongst them as the boys, having recovered some of the arrows that had missed their targets and fallen to the ground, stood on the beach and fired one final volley. They didn't hit anyone, but they cheered themselves hoarse, soon to be joined by the women and old men, who danced and shouted for joy.

Sele looked at Fata who had staggered wearily to her side. 'Oh Fata,' she said in their native Samoan. 'I thought he had killed you.'

'He nearly did, Sele, but God delivered me, like you have delivered these people.'

'I didn't deliver them, Fata. God did. And he used a Barak like you to do it.'

'Barak was no good without Deborah. You've won a great victory, Sele.'

She looked at him thoughtfully. 'Not yet, Fata. I think there may be more to come.'

15

16 July 1886 – The Coral Sea

Maaso had always been a fearsome character, but never more terrifying than when he flew into one of his rages. The warriors who had escaped with him eyed each other nervously as they paddled across the five miles of water that separated Vitu from the small atoll where they had spent the previous night. That tiny speck of land was uninhabited but had enough coconut palms and brackish water to replenish the supplies they'd consumed on the long passage from their home island. It provided a good base from which to mount their attack. Now it was a refuge for them to slink back to.

Maaso sat in the stern of his canoe brooding over the defeat he'd suffered, his mood growing blacker by the minute. By the time the canoes reached the atoll he was incandescent with rage. His warriors scattered as he began to lay about them with his club, cursing them with the most fearful oaths for their failure to subdue that pathetic group of defenders and vowing to put them to the most horrifying deaths he could think of if they should fail the next time.

Eventually, left on his own to brood and curse, he began to think back over the events of the day and ask himself how it could have turned out like that. Those old men couldn't have done it alone. He had easily defeated their young warriors previously. He remembered the man he had almost killed, but who had then brought him down with a blow to the knee. He was an older man, but well-built and courageous. He also handled his weapon like a warrior. He wasn't like the men from the island. He was bigger, heavier and had lighter skin. Maaso remembered having seen men like that when he'd been a convict in New Caledonia. They were Polynesians and came from the islands further out into the Pacific. Was this man the new war lord of those islands, he wondered?

Then he remembered the woman who had sounded the conch shell. Suddenly it all started to make sense. She was the one who had been giving the orders. It was at her signal that the defenders had scattered, and the torrent of water had descended on them. She wasn't a white woman, and she certainly wasn't Melanesian. In some ways she also looked Polynesian but was slimmer with slightly oriental features. He hadn't had time to get a good look at her but remembered that she had been quite beautiful.

He began to smile to himself and opened the leather pouch that held the gold sovereigns Captain Homer had given him – down payment on a cargo of native women. He was to get the same amount again as soon as he delivered them. But how much more, he wondered, would Homer be prepared to pay for a woman like that? It was then that he called his warriors together and began to give them their orders.

* * *

When it was clear that Maaso's warriors had left, the old men of the village, raising their war clubs high above their heads, began a low, sonorous chant that was taken up by the boys and then by the women.

'What are they chanting?' Sele asked.

'I'm not sure,' Fata replied. 'But I think we should watch them carefully.'

The chanting began to increase in volume as the people, now dancing as they sang, became increasingly agitated. Finally, it stopped and the old men, followed by the women and boys, began to run back to the scene of the battle.

'Where are they going?' Sele asked.

'Come quick! We'll follow,' Fata replied.

They set off and caught up with the crowd near the site of the bamboo cross. A little further on they could see some of the injured warriors struggling to get to their feet. Others were lying helplessly, unable to move because of broken limbs caused by the wild flood that had swept all before it.

The first people to reach the injured warriors were the two old men who had demolished the dam wall. They grabbed one man who was attempting to crawl into the shelter of the undergrowth, and hauled him by his long, frizzy hair back onto the track. Then, as the crowd raised their chant again, they raised their clubs and smashed the warrior's head into a bloody pulp. They looked around for the next closest victim, but before they could do anything, Fata roared out for them to stop, and Sele placed herself between them and the wounded man.

'You must tell them there is to be no more killing,' she said. 'Tell them that our Lord Jesus teaches us not to take vengeance on our enemies, but to forgive them and bind up their wounds.'

It took every ounce of authority that Fata could muster to hold the villagers back. The desire for revenge, justified by a culture of *payback,* nurtured over countless generations, as well as their own recent experience of seeing their menfolk slaughtered and young women abducted, had created an all-consuming bloodlust in the people of Vitu. But somehow Fata managed to restrain them, even while their anger continued to burn.

Sele stepped forward as the people watched and began to move amongst the bodies lying along the creek bed, assessing their injuries. Six of them were dead, including the man the old men had just clubbed to death. Another four had broken limbs, and the remaining eleven suffered from wounds caused by the boys' arrows. Fortunately for them, the arrows that the boys used to shoot birds did not have barbed heads and were easy to extract.

Throughout the battle Sele had carried her medical kit containing bandages, iodine and basic surgical instruments. With Fata's help, she began to cleanse and bind up the warriors' wounds, starting with the most serious, then moving on to the others. She then moved on to those with broken bones. Fata used his greater strength to reset the limbs, while the unfortunate victims roared in agony and Sele applied splints and bandages. The injured men watched her with apprehension and sometimes with fear; steeling themselves for what she might do to them. But their apprehension quickly turned to relief as she would lay a cool hand on their fevered brows and, in a language they didn't understand, speak softly and offer prayers for them. Seeing her, some of the village women began to do the same, bringing water to parched lips and easing broken bodies into more comfortable positions. The old men looked on disapprovingly, while the boys just watched in silence.

As evening approached, they carried the six dead bodies to a spot near the place where their own warriors had been buried, ready to dig a mass grave and bury them later. Then they returned to the deserted village and sat down for a meal, sharing their food and water with the injured warriors.

One of the wounded - the man whom Sele had shielded from the old men's vengeance - asked to speak to Fata. Fata went to him and they huddled together for a while, speaking quietly but with difficulty as they searched for words and phrases both could understand. Finally, Fata nodded his head and walked back to Sele, an anxious look on his face.

'What did he say to you?' Sele asked.

'He say Maaso will come back. He say they go to small island close. He think Maaso come back tonight and while we sleep and kill us. He say all other warriors think same.'

Sele nodded. 'That's what I've been thinking. So now it's time for us to be like Gideon and his small band. We must find a safe place and move the wounded and all the people, except for six of the boldest old men. Fata, you must call a council and find out where that safe place is and choose six volunteers - six steady men who will do exactly what I tell them.'

It was well past midnight when one of the boys, hiding in the palm trees behind the beach, saw them first and gave a long low whistle. This was taken up by another lad, hiding behind another tree, closer to the village. His signal set a third boy running along the track to where Sele, Fata and half a dozen of the old men were waiting behind a depression behind the fallen warriors' burial ground.

'He say they coming,' Fata warned her.

'Right. Tell everyone to get ready and wait until they hear the roar.'

The canoes were slithering onto the sandy beach even as she spoke. The boys hidden in the bush watched Maaso jump ashore followed by his warriors. They bunched together behind him, determined to avenge themselves for their humiliation of the previous day. The warriors fanned out and began to search the huts, looking for anyone who might be sleeping there. Maaso had given them strict instructions to kill everyone they found except for the younger women and boys. But most of all, they were to take the beautiful Eurasian woman alive. He had threatened the most fearful consequences for anyone who harmed her, even though it was she who had organized their defeat the previous day. But they found the village deserted.

Maaso began to curse and rage; but then a thought crossed his mind. He ordered his men to follow him back to the place where they had fought the battle. This time he told them to make as much noise as possible so as to terrify anyone who might be around and cause them to break cover and run, just as if they were hunting wild boar. So, the warriors began to shout and scream in a way that would make the boldest shake with fear. They leapt in the air, brandishing their war clubs and beating them against their wooden shields, making a sound like a steam train clattering along a railway track.

Sele and those with her heard them coming. She looked at the old men and saw the fear in their faces. Fata also looked tense and anxious as he tended the whale oil lamp at his feet, keeping the wick alight while ensuring that the lamp stayed out of sight of the approaching mob.

As the sound of the invaders grew louder, Sele told Fata to light the other lamps. Soon all five were burning. She peered over the top of the depression where they were hiding and saw the warriors approaching; the white clay on their naked torsos shining in the moonlight as they jumped and cavorted, giving the appearance of a mob of angry demons.

Sele looked again at Fata, who nodded that all was ready. Then she turned to the klaxon at her side and pressed the handle down with all the force she could muster. The unearthly roar that erupted from its trumpet mouth even frightened the old men who were with her and expecting it. But its effect on Maaso's men was astonishing. They stopped dead in their tracks and looked in the direction from which that awful sound had come. It was followed by another blood chilling roar, as Sele pressed the handle down again. Even Maaso seemed alarmed.

But if the sound of the klaxon struck fear into them, it was nothing compared with the terror they felt when right before their eyes, rising out of the mound where the village warriors had been buried, were five headless spectres with lights that burned within their bodies.

Nothing Maaso could do was able to stop the mad rush as his men dropped their weapons and ran screaming with terror back to their canoes. Maaso, still bewildered, but enraged by the flight of his men, ran after them, waving his cutlass madly and calling on them to stop. But their fear of him could not overcome the terror of those headless ghosts who, at that very moment, might be pursuing them down that track. When they reached the canoes, they didn't wait for anyone. Panic stricken, they pushed them into deeper water and began to paddle for their lives. The slower runners had to splash into the lagoon to catch and scramble aboard the last ones before they disappeared.

Back at the burial mound, the old men, holding poles on which the whale oil lamps hung, surmounted by warriors' feathered headdresses, began to dance for joy, soon to be joined by those women and children hidden in the bush close enough to have seen what happened. Fata joined them in their joy and relief, dancing and shouting verses of victory from the Bible.

Sele wanted to join in their celebrations, but first she needed to make sure that the attackers had really gone. She ran to the beach just in time to see the last canoe disappear into the darkness. She noticed there was still one canoe left there, abandoned in the mad rush to escape the ghosts of Vitu. As she went to look at it, some intuitive sense made her look around. Right behind her stood a huge man; his body daubed with red and white clay and his matted hair and beard festooned with thorns. His face was a mask of sheer evil; like nothing she had ever seen before. She barely had time to scream before his huge fist smashed into her face and everything went black.

17 July 1886 – The Coral Sea

Michael paced the *Wahine's* deck with mounting frustration. Based on what Captain Mason had told him, Michael considered they should now be close to the island of Vitu, but none of the islands they'd sighted matched Mason's description. The only sign of life they'd seen was a group of native canoes, spotted the day before, way off on the starboard beam and heading south. The canoes were under sail and moving quickly.

'Land ho!' The cry came from the masthead.

'Where away?' Michael shouted.

'Dead ahead. Three small islands.'

Michael cursed in disappointment. Three small islands couldn't be Vitu.

But then the lookout called out again. 'Deck there. It's not three islands. It's one small island and a larger one behind, with two peaks.'

Michael's disappointment turned to excitement. He grabbed his telescope and climbed into the rigging. Steadying himself against the roll of the ship, he trained the telescope on the low silhouette of land just appearing over the horizon and saw that it was indeed one small island – little more than a coral atoll – blending into a larger island surmounted by the twin peaks of an extinct volcano.

'That's it,' Michael said to the lookout. 'That's Vitu, exactly as Captain Mason described it.'

As the sun rose to its zenith the schooner passed the outlying island and began to cross the few miles that separated it from Vitu. The fringing reef was now clear to the naked eye and *Wahine* pushed on, weathering the western end of the island, when another cry from the masthead announced that the lookout had sighted the gap through the reef into the lagoon beyond.

Michael conned his ship carefully through the entrance and, minutes later, had the schooner brought up into the wind and the anchor dropped. Two hundred yards away the island seemed deserted, the white sand shimmering in the noonday heat. Suddenly, figures appeared on the beach, bursting out from among the trees and waving to them excitedly. Michael trained his telescope on them, anxiously hoping to see a slim Eurasian woman with raven hair and flashing eyes. But Sele was not amongst them.

He took another look at the group of people, which was growing larger by the moment, and saw that none of them was armed. Nevertheless, he stuffed a revolver into his belt and ordered the ship's boat to be lowered. An elderly man wearing a Polynesian skirt stepped forward to greet him as the boat crunched onto the beach.

'Welcome to Vitu. I Fata, missionary to these islands.'

Michael shook his hand. 'Thank you, sir. I am Captain Michael Burns, master of the *Wahine*.'

Fata's face lit up. 'Captain Burns. Sele Saena talk about you. I very glad you here.'

Michael's heart leaped as he heard her name mentioned. 'Sele? Is she here?'

'No, Captain. She save these people from devil name Maaso. But now she disappear. I think Maaso take her.'

Michael's face fell. 'Taken her where?'

'I think he take her back to island in south, five days in canoe.' He pointed to a young Melanesian whose head was swathed in bandages. 'This man Yauwii, he know where island is. We pray for ship to come and help us find her. Now God send you.'

'Oh my God! Sele is in the hands of that wild man?'

'Yes.'

'Then we have no time to waste. Your man will have to guide us to that island. How many canoes did he have?'

'Eight.'

'They must have been the canoes we passed a couple of days ago, heading south. If only I'd had the sense to go and investigate. You'd better tell me everything you know about this Maaso and the men with him.'

An old man who had traded with the islanders to the south and understood their language acted as Fata's interpreter as he passed on Michael's questions to the wounded warrior. It was a frustratingly slow process, but piece by piece Michael was able to work out that Maaso's base was one of a group of remote islands to the southwest. Yauwii also told them that he, like many of Maaso's warriors, had been forced to leave his home island to serve him. He agreed to go with Michael and guide him to the island if Michael promised not to kill him or let the people of Vitu kill him.

Michael turned to Fata. 'What will happen to these wounded warriors after we have gone? Will the locals kill them?'

'I not think so,' Fata replied. 'I speak God's word to them longtime. Now, their hearts made soft. Sele tell them not to take revenge. They listen to her. They say she great prophetess. She save them from death.'

Michael nodded. 'That sounds like Sele Saena.'

'She say we two like Deborah and Barak.'

'Well, I hope God keeps her safe like them. Let's get this man aboard my ship. The sooner we get on our way the better.'

'I come too, Captain. I pray for God to keep Sele safe but I have great fear in my heart for her.'

'It'll be dangerous, Fata. But I'll be glad to have you aboard.'

Thirty minutes later the *Wahine* passed through the reef once more and began to beat into a freshening southerly breeze.

20 July 1886 – The Coral Sea

Fifty nautical miles further east *Bulldog* Homer looked carefully at the needle of the barometer and said to Mundine, 'I don't like this. I think we're in for one hell of a gale.'

'Can't we run before it?' Mundine asked nervously.

'Run where?' Homer retorted testily. 'God alone knows how many reefs there are ahead of us. The last thing we want now is to find ourselves on a lee shore. If this wind strengthens much more, we'd never beat our way clear.'

'So, what are we goin' to do? There was a note of panic in Mundine's voice.

'The only thing we can do. We'll heave-to and hope for the best.'

Homer pushed past Mundine and shouted to the mate: 'Call all hands. And get the topsails and mizzen in before this wind rips 'em to shreds. We're gonna heave-to.'

The barquentine's deck suddenly came alive as men raced up the rigging and out onto the yards to furl the topsails, while others positioned themselves at the sheets and braces, waiting for the command to haul. Homer watched impatiently as the hands aloft struggled with the heavy canvas, bellowing at them through his speaking trumpet.

'Ready about,' Homer roared, then nodded to the helmsman: 'Helm's - a'lee.'

The helmsman began to spin the wheel, and the ship gradually turned into the wind. For a few anxious moments it seemed unable to decide whether to continue turning to starboard or fall back onto its previous tack. But finally, the forward edge of the jib began to shimmer and then filled from the opposite side.

'Lee - oh!' Homer roared, and the crew hauled the mainsail round while leaving the foresail and jib as they were, now sheeted on the opposite side. The effect of these sails working against each other brought the *Hoylake* to a standstill, and she began to toss and roll violently as the waves buffeted her mercilessly and the wind screamed through her rigging.

'Double the lookouts,' Homer ordered the mate. 'God only knows what we may be drifting onto.'

He left the deck and went below to his cabin. As he passed Mundine's cabin he bashed on the door. 'Mr. Mundine, join me in my cabin, if you please. There's not much for us to do for the next few hours. So, we may as well enjoy ourselves with some of your Jamaica rum.'

Mundine, who was lying on his bunk groaning with seasickness, dragged himself reluctantly to his feet and grabbed a new bottle. Contrary to his usual preferences, the last thing he wanted to do was to drink rum. But *Bulldog* Homer was not the sort of man whose invitations should be ignored.

The gale intensified overnight, and by the following morning Homer realized his ship was now fighting for survival against a major tropical storm. Fortunately, the *Hoylake,* though badly in need of a refit, was sturdily built, designed for the winter storms of the North Atlantic. Though tossing like a cork caught in a whirlpool, she was still riding with her bow to windward, taking the full force of the huge waves, while her backed storm jib counteracted the effect of her madly flogging mainsail.

Homer awoke to see Harris standing over him, furiously shaking his shoulder. Mundine lay unconscious at his feet, sprawled across the deck in a pool of his own vomit. The bottle of rum they had shared was empty and rolled back and forth across the deck in sequence with the ship's violent movements.

'What is it?' he snarled.

'The foresail's blown out, skipper. The storm jib's holding but I don't think we'll be able to keep her head to the wind for much longer. If we take one of these waves across the beam, she'll roll right over.'

Homer sprang to his feet and raced up on deck. As Harris had reported, the foresail had been torn to shreds and the ship was battling to stay hove-to. Every few seconds another huge wave would crash over the port bow, depositing tons of green water that surged across the deck and out through the scuppers.

Homer stared anxiously at the storm jib and wondered how long it would be before it also ripped to shreds and left the ship helpless before the force of the wind.

'We've got to get her 'round while we've still got a jib to do it, so we can run before the wind,' Homer shouted.

'She'll roll over, skipper.'

'Not if we get her onto a broad reach before the next wave hits her. How many men have you got on the pumps?'

'Every hand I could spare. They're working like demons down there. She's taking in water faster than we can pump it out.'

'Get half of 'em back up on deck and ready to haul the jib and mainsail. We'll need every bit of muscle we've got to get those sails trimmed to bring her 'round quickly. We've only got a few seconds to do it and there'll be no second chance.'

Harris went below and returned with a dozen exhausted seamen, whom he sent to the sheets and braces that controlled the mainsail and jib, while Homer called one of the lookouts back to assist the man at the ship's wheel.

He watched the waves continue to roll in and smash over his ship, counting the seconds between each one, while also gauging the strength of the wind, hoping for a momentary lull. But it never came. So, as another wave battered the ship's bow and poured across its deck, he gave the order: 'Lee-oh.'

The two helmsmen put their combined strength into turning the wheel while Harris's men hauled at the sheets, bringing the storm jib and mainsail round. Slowly at first, and then with increasing speed, the ship began to turn to starboard, bringing the wind back along her port beam. Homer watched the next approaching wave with mounting anxiety. It was vital that the ship should not meet this wave side on, or she would roll over and never rise again. Slowly, ever so slowly, she continued her turn as the wave approached.

'Faster,' he screamed at the men struggling with the helm.

The wave struck her side just abaft the main mast. Its force smashed the gunwales and swept the men at the sheets off their feet, sending two of them overboard, their screams lost in the roar of the elements, while the others clung desperately to whatever they could. She continued to roll helplessly to starboard until the end of her yardarm touched the sea's surface. But then, just as Homer thought she'd never rise again, the tough little vessel shook off the force of that last wave and began to right herself.

By the time the next wave hit her she was safely running before the wind. There was no time to get her sails in – it would have been suicidal to send men aloft. So, Homer ordered the helmsman to keep her stern to the oncoming sea while he left the remaining sails to flog themselves to pieces as the ship began to run before the roaring wind.

* * *

It was more by good luck rather than good planning that the *Wahine* managed to avoid the full force of the storm that savaged Homer's ship. Michael had shortened sail as the wind increased, beating into the wind with only a jib and double reefed foresail. It had been an uncomfortable journey since leaving Vitu, but the schooner, well suited to sailing close to the wind, had made good progress despite the heavy swell.

Michael's main problem was that neither he nor the native guiding him was really sure of where they were. Heavy cloud covered the sky, and he'd been unable to take a bearing on the sun to determine his position. By the middle of the afternoon watch he judged the wind strength to have dropped sufficiently to raise the mainsail but, like the foresail, he kept it double reefed. The wind blowing across the port beam filled the additional sail and the schooner picked up speed as she continued on her south westerly course.

Michael went back to his cabin where Charlie Grieve, the mate, was poring over the Admiralty chart upon which they had superimposed their penciled additions, based on what Captain Mason had told them.

'I estimate we're nor'east of the main Torres Strait islands, skipper.

'Then we should be close to Maaso's island, but we won't know for sure until we sight land that our native guide can identify.'

Their conversation was cut short by a shout from the masthead lookout telling them he'd sighted a ship. Michael and Charlie ran up on deck.

'Get up there and tell me what you see,' Michael said, handing his telescope to the mate.

Charlie climbed to the masthead and trained the telescope on a shape on the horizon. 'She's a barquentine,' he shouted down. 'Looks like she's runnin' under bare poles. What's left of her sails are in tatters.'

He continued to train the telescope on the ship and then called down again. 'It looks like they're trying to bend a new sail onto the yard. It'll be hard work with this wind still blowing.'

Michael wondered why they'd be trying to do that. Common sense told him it would be safer just to keep running before the wind and wait for it to drop before attempting to bend on a new sail. The only possible reason was if she was running onto a lee shore and needed sail power to work her way off it.

'Come back down, Charlie. They must be in trouble. We'll try to run up alongside her.'

He ordered the helm hard over and the sails trimmed to put *Wahine* on a direct course to the stricken vessel. Little by little the distance between the two vessels diminished until they were within hailing distance.

Michael was about to pick up his speaking trumpet when the barquentine hailed him.

'Ahoy there! I'm drifting towards a reef. Can you take me in tow?'

The voice came from a giant of a man, standing next to the ship's wheel. Michael grabbed his speaking trumpet and shouted back, 'Stand by to receive a line.'

Charlie already had three members of the crew racing down into the hold to bring up the heavy cable stored there for just such an emergency. By the time they returned he had a length of light line with a lead weight on the end spliced on to another length of regular sized cable, which he then attached to the loop at the end of the heavy cable.

Michael stood by the helmsman, waiting for the moment to give the order to bring the *Wahine* alongside the barquentine. Then, a shout came from the masthead, 'Breakers ahead.'

Michael strained his eyes and saw the flecks of white foam where the waves were passing over a submerged reef less than a nautical mile ahead. He swore quietly to himself and then called out to Charlie: 'We haven't got much time. We'll be on that reef before we know it.'

'Ready to go, skipper!' Charlie held up the end of the cable now firmly fastened to the smaller line.

As the *Wahine* drew alongside, Michael noticed a stocky man wearing civilian clothing standing near the hatch that led below deck. The man looked towards him and instantaneously they recognized each other.

'My God! It's Mundine! I said we'd meet again, but I never thought I'd be saving his neck. What the hell is he doing aboard her?' He began to have a bad feeling about what was emerging.

Mundine quickly scurried back below deck, hoping he hadn't been recognized, while Michael signaled for Charlie to take up his position at the schooner's stern. Holding the light line in his left hand, Charlie began to swing its weighted end in a large circle. It snaked out from the schooner's stern in a graceful arc, landing squarely across the barquentine's foredeck where a seaman grabbed it. Two others joined him and began to haul the line, followed by the heavier line, across the widening gap between the ships.

'Faster, you bastards,' Homer roared. 'We're nearly on the coral. Get that cable across.'

More men joined them as the heavier line came over the side, pulling the thick cable behind it. As soon as it was aboard Homer had the loop over a bollard and signaled to Michael that it was now secured.

Moments later the schooner gave a lurch as the cable went tight against the weight of the larger vessel. Charlie and the crew stood at the sheets and braces waiting for the order to start hauling.

'Hard a starboard,' Michael yelled. 'Haul away main and fore sheets.'

As the helmsman spun the wheel the crew hauled on the sheets and the *Wahine* began to turn to starboard with the *Hoylake* wallowing behind her. With the wind now coming across the schooner's starboard side, she started to pick up speed until she was jerked back as the cable became taut once more. But little by little she began to make progress, moving slowly parallel to the line of white water crashing over the reef.

Michael watched anxiously as his ship tried to claw her way out of danger, unable to do anything other than hope that the wind would be strong enough to pull the two ships away from the jagged coral that now lay less than a cable's length away. He told Charlie to be ready with an axe to cut the cable if they got dragged too close to the reef.

But then Charlie pointed to the barquentine's foremast. 'They've managed to bend a new sail on, skipper.'

Michael looked back and felt a surge of hope. Sure enough, a sail appeared below the *Hoylake's* lower yard, and the wind was beginning to fill it. He could feel the strain on his own ship easing as the *Hoylake* began to move under its own power.

'Look! They're getting a new mainsail bent onto the gaff. With luck, that might just give them enough headway to steer themselves off the reef.'

'And she's breaking out a jib, too,' Charlie added. 'I reckon she's going to gybe to starboard.'

Michael was in a quandary. 'Why the hell doesn't he signal his intention?'

The answer came as he saw a splash in the water just ahead of the *Hoylake*'s bow.

'They've cut the cable.' Charlie exclaimed. 'Why have they done that?'

'Breakers ahead, breakers ahead!'

The cry from the masthead tore Michael's attention from the *Hoylake* to his own ship. The long line of white water that marked the submerged reef they'd been trying to avoid came to an end a mere cable's length fine on their port bow. On their present course they would just miss it. But the lookout had failed to spot another outcrop of coral reef, dead ahead.

The same had not been true of the *Hoylake's* lookout, who, from his higher vantage point, had spotted the white water and warned Homer in time. It was lucky that by then she had enough sail up to be able to swing her stern across the wind and onto the opposite tack, where the wind began to drive her away from the disaster that now awaited the *Wahine.*

There was a grinding crunch, followed by the sound of tearing timber, as the schooner smashed into the jagged coral. Her bow lifted skyward and then over to port as her momentum carried her further onto the reef and left her stranded.

Michael knew immediately that his ship was done for. There was no way she would escape that reef until the waves broke her up and she slid, piece by piece, into the deep water beyond.

'Prepare to launch the boats,' he yelled. 'The barquentine will heave-to and wait to pick us up as soon as she's at a safe distance from the reef.'

'I don't think so, skipper.' Charlie pointed to the other ship, which now had its topsail set. 'It looks like she's high tailing it and leaving us behind.'

Michael trained his telescope on the *Hoylake* and could see her captain giving orders to the helmsman. There was no indication of him intending to heave-to. He could also see a stocky figure standing at the stern rail, waving goodbye.

'You swine, Mundine!' He cursed the figure who was still waving mockingly as the barquentine drew further away. He felt a violent rage rising within him that he knew would become uncontrollable if he allowed it to go unchecked. It was the sound of the schooner's mainmast toppling that pulled his attention back to his own safety and that of his crew.

21 July 1886 – The Coral Sea

Ernest Mundine, convinced that the ship was now out of danger and that the one man who might pose a threat to him was about to meet his maker, returned to his cabin for a celebratory glass of rum. Captain Homer joined him a little later.

'I imagine there's no way that schooner is going to get off that reef?'

'No way at all! Her bottom has been ripped out. In this sea she'll break up before the day is finished.'

'And what about the crew?'

'They'll need the Devil's own luck to get out of this one.'

'So, we can go and see our French friend to pick up the cargo of women he promised, and for which I've already given part payment?'

Homer put his arm around Mundine's shoulder. 'No, Mundine. I'm afraid you're going to have to write that off as a loss. This weather is developing into a full-blown tropical storm, and it's heading straight for Maasos's island.'

Mundine pulled away and stared at him. 'You can't do that! We have a deal! I agreed to give that mad Frenchman fifteen gold sovereigns on the understanding he'd have thirty women ready for us. He's probably got them there waiting for us; and now you want to run away just because the wind's too strong.'

He realized he'd made a mistake as soon as he'd uttered the words. Homer's face darkened, and his eyes turned hard and narrow. Mundine could feel his savage gaze boring through him. He grabbed Mundine by the front of his shirt and lifted him off his feet, drawing his face to within a few inches of his own. Mundine turned white with terror at what was about to happen. Then, when he spoke, his voice was quiet, but full of menace.

'I've killed men for insults less than that, Mundine,' he whispered. 'I've had men tied to a grating and flogged until their backbones appeared.'

'I'm sorry, Captain Homer. You must forgive my unseemly outburst.' Mundine barely croaked, his voice trembling as violently as his body.

Then, to his intense relief, he felt Homer's grip on him loosen and the savage gaze diminish as Homer's rage diminished. He dropped Mundine to the deck and stalked away, shouting an order to the mate to keep the ship running before the wind until the gale blew itself out. Then he disappeared below deck.

Harris helped Mundine to his feet. 'You're lucky,' he said. 'I thought he was goin' to throw you overboard. He's done it before, you know; and worse. He don't like havin' his courage called into question, does Cap'n Homer!'

Mundine, still shaking, brushed himself down. 'So where do you think he's goin' to take us, if not to Maaso's island?'

'Probably back to our old trade of takin' Kanakas home,' he answered.

'But why not just wait until the weather improves and then go back to the island?'

'It's too risky to spend time in these waters at this time of the year. Cyclones can come up outta nowhere and you never know what you are liable to run into. It's a lot safer to be back in the Coral Sea where the reefs and islands are clearly marked on the charts.'

'So, it looks like I've lost my money.'

'Looks like it, Mr. Mundine. Just think of it as an investment in stayin' alive.'

21 July 1886 – The Torres Strait

The exhausted warriors entered the sheltered waters of their home lagoon early the same day that the *Wahine* ran aground. Women and children, who for the past two days had feared for their safety in the violence of the tropical storm, ran to the water's edge to help them bring the canoes ashore. Maaso's canoe was the first to slide up onto the beach; but only the bolder women – or those keen to be noticed by the mighty war chief – rushed to grab its sides and hold it steady as the great man stepped unsteadily ashore, bowing their heads and uttering quiet words of thankful greeting for his safe return.

He ignored their disingenuous expressions of joy and, barking out a few words of command, pointed to the figure still seated in his canoe. The women looked at Sele in surprise. They'd expected the canoes to be filled with captive women, just as they had once been. But this one, with her flawless golden skin and almond shaped eyes, was unlike any they'd seen before.

Maaso shouted another order, and they ran to help her out of the canoe and onto the beach. Many long hours sitting in its confines had left Sele stiff and sore, and she nearly fell as she tried to get to her feet. Three sympathetic women took hold of her arms and helped her onto the beach. She turned to each of them and smiled with a kindness they hadn't known since the day they themselves had been torn from their families.

In response to Maaso's orders they led her to a large hut at the centre of the village and helped her climb the bamboo ladder into its dark interior. Another woman gave her a fresh coconut, pierced so that she could drink its milk, and a palm leaf filled with pieces of taro and fish. She smiled at them again and thanked them, gratefully accepting the food. Then she lay down on a mat and sank into a deep and dreamless sleep.

As soon as she was asleep the women began to talk among themselves, wondering who this strange and beautiful creature was and where she came from. They wondered if Maaso planned to sell her to the pearling skippers or to keep her for himself. Some of them - members of Maaso's private harem - began to see her as a threat to their own tenuous positions. But to the other women Sele was like a creature from another world.

'She a ghost,' one of them explained. 'Old women of my people say one day beautiful woman with golden skin and shining eyes come and teach us great mysteries.'

'Yes,' agreed another. 'Our old people tell same story.'

'No,' said a woman from the Torres Strait islands. 'She an angel, like white man missionaries tell my people. She come from Great Spirit chief of all spirits.'

Sele awoke to find two strange faces staring at her. They jumped back with alarm as she opened her eyes and saw them there. She sat up and smiled at them, telling them not to be afraid; but it was clear they couldn't understand her. So, she held out her hands and beckoned for them to come close. Slowly and nervously, they approached. Taking them by their hands she drew them closer to herself and said, 'Sele.'

They both looked at her with blank looks on their faces. So, she released their hands and pointed to herself, repeating her name.

'Sele,' she said. 'Me, Sele.'

Then she pointed inquiringly at each of them.

One of the women nodded and, pointing to herself, said, 'Sina.' Then, pointing to her companion, she said, 'Tala.'

Sele smiled at them again and repeated their names. Soon they were chatting excitedly to her, offering her pieces of fruit and bowls of coconut milk, while Sele, though not understanding a word they said, knew exactly what they meant.

From the corner of her eye, she caught a glimpse of movement and saw several women and children scurrying away. She called out to them, telling them not to be afraid, but to come back and talk to her. They, however, ran outside. She turned to her two new friends and made signs to them, indicating that they should bring the other women and children to meet her. The two women then disappeared outside and returned soon after, followed first by one woman, then another, and then by a small group of women and children. Before long the group had swelled into a crowd of thirty or more. But Maaso's favourites stayed outside, jealously watching what was happening.

The sun had already passed its highest point in the sky when Maaso finally arrived to take another look at his new captive. The women and children drew back in fear as he climbed the ladder into the hut. But this time he didn't order them away. He wanted them to stay and witness his display of authority over this woman, whom they seemed to view with awe. He was followed by another woman from the Torres Strait islands; one who understood a little English.

He strode up to where Sele sat and grabbed her by the arm, hauling her to her feet and then forcing her to her knees.

'Maaso come, you bow.'

She shook off his hand and stood up in front of him, staring directly into his eyes. The women stepped back in alarm, willing her not to arouse Maaso's anger.

'No!' she said. 'I am Sele Saena. I am of the royal family of Samoa. When I come, you will bow.'

Maaso's knowledge of English, though very basic, was sufficient for him to understand what she said - or perhaps it was her bearing and the fearless look in her eye that he understood. The other women watched in terror as his eyes began to blaze in the way they always did when he flew into one of his rages. He clenched his fist as if to strike her but then dropped it to his side. He tried to hold her gaze but found himself unable to stare her down. To the amazement of the other women, he turned on his heel and left as quickly as he had come.

Humiliated and confused, he stormed angrily back to his own hut – the largest in the village, decorated with the heads of many of his victims. He screamed at the serving women, ordering them to get out, while he sat staring at the trophies of his many victories and tried to come to terms with the strange power this woman seemed to have over him; a power that had nothing to do with physical strength, but seemed able to rob him of his.

The woman who had followed him into Sele's hut watched him go, wondering if she should follow him. But she decided to stay and give this strange woman the message Maaso had brought her along to help him interpret.

'Maaso, him great chief,' she said. 'Maaso like woman, Maaso take woman. Now, you Maaso woman. You go Maaso tonight.'

This message came as no shock to Sele. During the long hours in the canoe she'd had plenty of time to ponder her fate. Everything she'd heard about this evil man indicated that her future was not to be a pleasant one. Furthermore, she'd seen the way the other warriors had looked at her and knew that it was only their fear of Maaso that kept them away from her. The thought both terrified and disgusted her. The prospect of being the plaything of this ugly gorilla of a man, whose eyes bespoke madness, or something worse – something almost demonic – caused her to think about throwing herself overboard and drowning herself, rather than being made to submit to him.

Yet every time that despair had threatened to overwhelm her, something inside seemed to pull her back and calm her terror. She found herself repeating words of the Bible she'd learnt from the missionaries who had taught her: *"When you walk through the fire, I will be with you, and through the floods, they shall not overwhelm you.'*

But she also found herself praying: 'Dear God, bring Michael here.'

* * *

It had been more than a full day since Maaso's meeting with Sele, and his mood had steadily turned blacker, while her anxiety had grown higher. She realized that by defying him publicly she had humiliated him before the people over whom he had the most power – the women. She also knew that they had passed the news on to their men folk. The warriors also lived in fear of him; but it was they who provided the force that preserved his authority. It was only a matter of time, she thought, before he would return to break her or kill her. If he didn't, the warriors would begin to lose their fear of him.

As for Maaso, having spent the whole night in his hut drinking rum given to him by *Bulldog* Homer from Mundine's stock of inferior brands, the morning brought a new determination to avenge himself of the previous day's humiliation. He was also drunk enough to believe that he could do it. He staggered from his sleeping mat and called for his breakfast.

Lina, the undisputed leader of his private harem, had been waiting anxiously for him to wake up. She knew from experience that this was the moment when Maaso was at his most unpredictable, sometimes amenable to suggestions enticingly presented to him, and sometimes violently dismissive of them. But she also remembered her predecessor, whose skull Maaso had smashed with a club when she had objected to the attention he had been showing to Lina.

She entered his hut silently, bowing low as she did so, carrying pieces of taro, fish and a pierced coconut. She fed him gently as he leaned against the hut's centre pole and whispered words of admiration in his ear.

She watched his reaction carefully and was relieved to see that he seemed pleased to have his ego massaged even as his belly was filled. He finished the fish and taro, then picked up the coconut and began to drink its milk while she stroked his matted hair and continued to whisper endearments. Then, with a loud belch, he tossed the coconut aside and got to his feet.

'You woman know to honour great chief,' he said. 'Why that woman not know?'

'She bad woman. She witch,' Lina replied.

He looked down at her in surprise. 'How you know she witch?'

Lina kept her eyes to the ground as she knelt before him and said, 'My people have old story. One day woman with gold skin come. All men listen to her. All men obey her.'

Maaso nodded thoughtfully. What she said made sense. The woman was a witch! What other explanation could there be for the power she'd had over him the day before?

He picked up the string of shrunken heads and hung it around his neck. Then he chose his finest headdress, made from the feathers of birds of paradise. He grabbed his war club and strode out of the hut towards the place where Sele was confined. The other members of Maaso's harem watched him go, fearful as to what it would mean for them. But their fear turned to relief when Lina appeared at the entrance of the hut, smiling.

The women with Sele heard the sound of Maaso's voice as he bellowed orders to the warriors standing around, telling them to follow him. They shrank back into the dark recesses of the hut, while Sele, her heart pounding, sat up ready to meet him. Moments later his bulk filled the entrance, blocking most of the light as he entered.

He walked towards her, his war club resting on his shoulder and a savage look in his eye. She met his stare with the same steady gaze as before. Once again, he tried to stare her down but felt himself struggling desperately to keep from averting his eyes. It had never happened to him before. Even the strongest men always wilted before his savage gaze. Why didn't she? What was it about the look in her eye that was so disconcerting? It wasn't hatred, and it certainly wasn't fear. It was almost as if she considered his strength and authority to be of no account whatsoever. Lina was right. This woman was a witch.

Suddenly, it all became clear. He remembered his grandmother; the woman who had raised him after his own mother had died giving birth to him. People in his village said that she was a witch. They said that she had put a curse on his father, whom she hated. That's why he had died two weeks before Maaso's birth – gored by a bull that had escaped from its pen.

Maaso, then known by his real name, Marcel, had hated her and still cursed her memory because of the way she'd treated him, beating him mercilessly, even breaking his arms several times by forcing them back against his shoulder joints until the bones snapped. He remembered that it was when he had tried to stare defiantly into her eyes that she had done that to him. It used to drive her into a rage, and she would laugh at his screams until he begged for mercy.

Yes, she was a witch too. She was the only woman he'd ever been afraid of and the only one whose eyes were able to terrify him – until now. Yet this woman's eyes were different. There was no hatred or cruelty in them. But neither was there any fear. But he still couldn't hold her gaze, which meant that she had to be a witch too.

He also remembered stories about the way people in the old days used to deal with witches. They used to burn them alive. How many times he'd wanted to do that to his grandmother and set himself free from her power over him. Suddenly, it became clear to him what he had to do.

21 July 1886 – The Coral Sea

The *Wahine* carried a small gig and a twenty-foot longboat. Michael knew that the gig could never cope with the huge waves that were breaking over his stricken ship, so he gave orders for the crew to fill the longboat with whatever provisions they could and launch it across the leeward side. While they were doing it Michael ran below for his sextant and rifle.

They swung the boat over the side, waiting for the right moment to lower it, when, seemingly out of nowhere, a huge sea caught it and hurled it into the roiling surf. Miraculously it remained afloat, but all of their provisions were lost, swept away by the surging waves.

They pulled the swamped longboat close enough to the ship's side for the men on deck to scramble aboard. Michael jumped aboard, keeping an oilskin wrapped around his sextant and rifle. He took the tiller while the others threw themselves into the task of bailing the seawater out as fast as they could, using buckets, hats and even their bare hands. Eventually, they got the boat relatively free of water and began to make some progress, riding up across the tops of the waves before plunging into the troughs, and then up again to meet the next one.

A lull in the wind enabled them to step the stubby mast and raise the gaff- rigged sail stored in the boat's bilge. This gave the boat an added element of control and they were soon running before the wind as Michael fought to keep the boat surfing down the face of the following waves without broaching.

Throughout that day they held the same course, two men huddled at the front of the boat, anxiously watching the sea ahead for signs of coral, while the others just sat silently, wrapped in their own fear and misery. As nightfall came, they dropped the sail and continued to hold the same course, drifting along, pushed by wind and waves. They tried desperately to stay awake, fighting against an overwhelming desire for sleep, watching for any flash of white water, and straining their ears for the sound of waves breaking over coral. Though they said little, each of them was hoping and praying that the wind would die down and the waves diminish. They knew that a small boat like theirs couldn't survive too long in those conditions. Then, as daylight appeared, they realized that their prayers had been answered. The wind was now little more than a strong breeze.

'God answer my prayer,' Fata said. 'I pray for wind to stop.'

'We all did,' Michael answered. 'But what we need now is for Him to provide water and manna in the wilderness, like he did for the Israelites. Otherwise, we're done for.'

'I pray for that too,' Fata said gravely.

A voice from the bow interrupted them. 'There, skipper; fine on the port bow. It looks like a sandbank.'

Michael stood up and saw it for himself, less than half a mile away. Taking advantage of the easier conditions, he steered the longboat towards it and ran up onto the sand. His men jumped out and pulled the boat further up the sandbank, then collapsed exhausted until sleep released them from their fears.

The heat of the sun, beating down from a cloudless sky, woke Michael and brought him back to reality. He knew that they wouldn't last more than a couple of days without fresh water – not in that blazing heat. For the first time in his life, he began to feel close to despair. The long sandbank on which they rested was devoid of vegetation, and the surrounding waters offered nothing more than broken reefs and more sandbanks.

It was then that Billy, as he had done many times before, caused Michael to marvel at the way his people could survive in the most inhospitable environments, finding food where white men could only starve. He'd been awake for some time and had already reconnoitered the sandbank. As Michael stood surveying what seemed to be their hopeless position, Billy came trotting back with a grin on his face and his shirt full of eggs.

'These good tucker, boss.'

Then he was off again, jogging down to the far end of the sandbank where he scraped a hiding place for himself in the sand and lay down to watch and wait.

Observing through his telescope, Michael saw a few birds land at the far end of the sandbank where Billy lay hidden. They were boobies – the large seabirds that inhabit those tropical waters. With infinite skill and patience, Billy managed to creep up on them and kill two with well-aimed chunks of coral and then brought down another as it took to the air. The castaways shared the birds' raw flesh amongst themselves and drank their blood. It was not an appetizing meal, but it renewed their strength enough for them to push the boat off the sandbank later that day and continue on their way.

* * *

'Look, skipper! Over there!' Charlie Grieve pointed across the longboat's port quarter to a small dark cloud just above the horizon. 'It's a rain squall.'

Michael shaded his eyes against the sun and looked to where Charlie was pointing.

'You're right,' he said. 'And it's coming our way, thank God!'

After two days in an open boat, he and his crew were desperate for water. They were hungry too, but the pangs of hunger were nothing compared with the tortured agony of thirst.

'Get that sail down,' he ordered. 'We don't want to outrun this squall, and we'll need it to capture the rain.'

Moments later the small sail, still attached to the gaff and boom, was ready to act like a bowl to catch the rain they hoped would fall on them. The wind, meanwhile, pushed the squall closer and closer, and they could see the ripples coming towards them across the surface of the ocean. For several agonizing minutes it seemed as though it would pass astern of them, and they waited with mounting anxiety until suddenly they felt the wind hit them, followed soon after by large drops of water that quickly turned into sheets of driving rain.

The men in the boat began to cheer, throwing their heads back and opening their mouths wide to allow as much of the deluge as possible to trickle down their parched throats.

'Belay that,' Michael roared. 'Get that sail spread to catch the rain before it passes.'

Soaked to the skin, the men scrambled from one side of the boat to the other swinging the boom over one gunwale and the gaff over the other.

'Not too far,' Michael shouted. 'Let the sail bag in the middle.'

Within a minute the pelting rain had filled the sail with several gallons of fresh water, threatening to overbalance the delicately positioned rig and spill the trapped water into the ocean.

'Hold it steady, lads,' Michael shouted. 'Don't let it get lopsided. Those of you not holding the boom and gaff, fill every container you can find.'

They searched the boat for anything that could hold water, filling the containers and storing them under the thwarts. Then they plunged their hands into the pool, scooping up as much water as they could hold before pouring it down their parched throats.

The squall passed almost as quickly as it had come, but it lasted long enough to satisfy their thirst and lift their spirits. Furthermore, the water they'd managed to save would keep them going for a few more days. Michael realized he would have to strictly ration it because he was still unsure how far they were from land, and there was no guarantee of them encountering another rain squall. But deep inside he felt a surge of hope that all would be well. He had his men raise the sail and they continued on their way.

24 July 1886 – The Torres Strait

Yauwii stood up in the longboat's bow and pointed ahead, jabbering away excitedly in his own language. Fata, who had been drifting in and out of sleep, sat up suddenly and listened to what he said.

'What is it?' Michael asked.

'Yauwii know this place,' Fata replied. 'Over there.' He pointed dead ahead to where a break in the sea mist revealed a faint grey smudge, barely visible to the naked eye, emerging over the horizon.

Michael trained his telescope on it. 'It's land all right. But I don't know how he could recognize it from this distance or could have got us here with any certainty.'

'Island men sail sea here many lifetimes, like my people. They know stars and currents better than white man charts.'

Michael nodded. 'Well, I hope you're right, because all our food and most of our water is now gone.' He reached under the thwart and pulled out the long oilskin parcel wedged between the boat's ribs. He unwrapped his prized Winchester rifle and checked it carefully to ensure that it was still dry. If the land ahead really was Maaso's island, he needed it to be in good working order.

They continued to plough steadily on, pushed along by the same wind that had wrecked their ship, but had also brought the rain that had saved them from dying of thirst. As they drew closer to the approaching island Yauwii pointed excitedly to it.

'He say it Mabi,' Fata confirmed. 'Mabi where Maaso live.'

The longboat suddenly picked up speed as an unexpected wind gust filled the sail. Michael looked over his shoulder and saw another rain squall sweeping in from behind them. Moments later it hit them, drenching them thoroughly, then passing over them towards the island ahead.

* * *

The women screamed as Maaso, glassy eyed and full of rum, burst into the hut and dragged Sele to her feet. He barked an order to the men with him, and they pinioned her arms, binding them with a length of vine. They dragged her to the entrance and sent her sprawling down the ladder onto the ground below. They hauled her to her feet again and forced her to the centre of the village, where one long pole, supported at either end by small stumps dug into the soil, rested across the open fireplace. It was the place where the villagers roasted their slaughtered pigs. Fresh firewood had been laid in the trench below.

On Maaso's command, they laid her face down on the ground and placed the pole lengthwise along her back. She felt the vines bite into her flesh as they ran them under her body and legs, then over the top of the pole, pulling them tight and securing them with knots. She heard the other women begin to wail and scream, and suddenly she realized what they were about to do to her.

She wanted to scream herself, to beg for mercy, to plead with them not to do this. But somehow, she managed to hold her mounting panic in check. She closed her eyes and tried to pray, but no thoughts formed in her mind and no words came from her lips other than: 'Jesus, help me! Jesus, help me!'

She became aware of someone standing in front of her. Opening her eyes, she saw Maaso standing above her. His eyes were glazed. There was something almost maniacal about the way he looked at her.

'What are you doing?' she screamed at him. 'Let me go, let me go!'

He sensed the panic in her voice and for the first time began to feel that he now had mastery over her.

'She witch,' he shouted, so that all around could hear. 'She, witch, and witch die. Witch burn.'

He bent down so that his face was in front of her and leered jubilantly. 'You die, witch. You burn.'

Sheer terror drove Sele to the edge of uncontrollable panic. She tried to form the words of a prayer but was unable to do so, except to repeat: 'Jesus, Jesus.' Perhaps it was that moment of resignation when a person realizes there is nothing to do but accept the inevitable, or perhaps it was another presence standing with her; but Sele felt her terror disappear and a sense of calm flood her mind. Somewhere in the deep recesses of her memory, she recalled some words of Jesus, and responded to her tormentor as he once did by saying, "Fear not them which kill the body, but are not able to kill the soul: but rather fear him which is able to destroy both soul and body in hell."

Maaso stepped back, almost as if someone had struck him. His gloating look changed instantly to one of fear. It was what his grandmother used to say to him. She used to tell him he would burn in Hell for ever. He felt again the terror that used to come over him as a child, and all he wanted to do was run away. But he dared not show this to those around him. So, he turned away and signaled to a warrior standing close by, holding a lighted torch. The women screamed again as two burly men lifted Sele, now firmly tied to the pole, onto the supports and the warrior thrust the torch into the firewood stacked beneath.

Sele closed her eyes and began to pray again, 'Jesus, help me; Jesus, help me.'

The wood was still damp from having been soaked in the rainstorms of the past few days. Maaso had welcomed this, believing it would create a slower fire and consequently greater suffering for his victim. But this time it didn't work. The faggots refused to stay alight.

He roared with rage and seized the torch himself. He was about to thrust it deep into the piled logs when the air was filled with a long, loud rumbling sound. All the villagers standing around turned their eyes skyward as the rumbling turned into a crash of thunder and a simultaneous flash of lightning.

Maaso dropped the lighted torch and stared with disbelief. It seemed as if the very heavens themselves were conspiring against him. But for the Melanesians - already convinced that Sele was the prophetess whose arrival their ancient stories had foretold, and fearful lest their war lord be making them do something to anger the gods - the effect was terrifying.

The women began to scream, and the warriors looked to the heavens with fear in their eyes that quickly turned to terror. They began to run to their huts to hide themselves from the wrath that they believed was about to fall upon them, while Maaso, his face contorted with rage, raced around swinging his war club wildly at anyone within reach. Then the heavens opened, and the rain poured down upon them.

The intensity of the rain squall, as it moved across the surface of the ocean and then struck the island, had reduced visibility to little more than a hundred yards, which was why the *Wahine's* longboat was able to approach the island unseen.

'What the hell's goin' on up there?' Charlie asked. The sound of women screaming could be heard clearly, despite the deafening claps of thunder.

Michael unwrapped the oilskin bag and took out his Winchester. He opened the breech and inserted ten rounds into the cavity. 'You don't have to come with me, Charlie,' he said. 'You can stay here with the men and keep watch over the boat.'

'No fear, skipper. I'm comin' with you.'

The two of them, with Billy and Yauwii following, jogged to a spot where a dozen large canoes were resting on a grassy slope. A track led from there deeper into the bush, towards the sound of the screams and commotion.

Moments later they came across a slight rise and saw the village ahead of them. A collection of huts stood in a half circle around a large open clearing. The clearing itself was nearly empty except for a huge man racing around, yelling like a man gone berserk.

Then, through the pelting rain, Michael spotted something happening at the centre of the clearing. Three women dashed from a hut to something that looked like a bundle, tied to a pole. They began to cut the vines binding it, and it fell to the ground. Immediately, the bundle began to move, and he realized it was a person – another woman. The man with the club turned and saw the women. He let out a blood curdling shriek and began to run towards them.

'Sele,' Michael yelled. 'Sele! Over here, run this way!'

She looked up to where the cry had come from, thinking she must be dreaming. Then she began to sprint across the open ground, holding her long dress up above her knees. The native women scattered in different directions as Maaso came roaring across the clearing towards them. He ignored them as he saw Sele racing towards the beach. In his fury he failed to see the small group standing on the high ground, almost obscured by the sheets of rain. Nor did he notice one of them drop down on one knee and raise a rifle to his shoulder. All he could see was the red mist rising behind his eyes, just as it always did when he was in a rage. It had been like that ever since the day he'd set fire to his grandmother's bed while she was asleep in it. And now, as then, it blinded him to everything else except the need to kill.

His powerful legs taking huge strides soon had him almost within arm's length of the fleeing woman. He could feel her terror, and it filled him with a wild, almost sexual delight. He opened his mouth and let forth the most hideous shriek of maniacal joy as he reached forward with his free hand to grab her hair streaming behind her. She looked back and heard a terrified scream, which she suddenly realized was coming from her own mouth. Then she tripped and fell headlong to the ground. She turned to see Maaso's huge bulk standing over her, the grisly necklace of shrunken heads grinning down at her, and his face contorted with a look of diabolical glee as he raised his war club high. She closed her eyes and waited for the blow that would smash her head to pulp, hoping her death would be instant and painless. But it never came.

Instead, she heard the sharp crack of a rifle and the almost instantaneous thud of a high velocity bullet slamming into human flesh. She opened her eyes and saw Maaso staggering back, looking down in disbelief at the bloody mass at the centre of his stomach. He raised his eyes to look in the direction the shot had come from when another sharp crack cut through the rumbling of the thunder. This time a red blotch appeared on his forehead as another bullet smashed through his skull, splattering blood, bone and brain through the back of his head as he fell to the ground, dead. Then Sele fainted.

When she came to, she was back in the long hut, surrounded by the women of the village who were gently wiping her forehead with cold water. The anxiety on their faces quickly turned to relief as she opened her eyes. She turned her head and there was Fata - his face also betraying concern and then delight. For a moment she thought she might just have woken up in Heaven. Then she heard the voice she'd been secretly dreaming of for months.

'Sele, darling, you're all right now. You're safe.'

She turned her head to the other side and saw Michael bending over her, his eyes alive with joy.

'Michael, I knew you would come. I knew God would send you to me.' She reached up to him and took his face in her two hands and pulled it to her bosom, holding him tightly to herself as waves of relief and joy flooded over her. Charlie and Billy hooted with mirth and Fata looked the other way as Michael's face turned bright red with embarrassment, while the realization of her love filled him with a joy he'd never known before.

25 July 1886 – The Torres Strait

To celebrate their deliverance from the wild man who had held them in bondage, and to ensure that he would never return to torment them again, the warriors tossed Maaso's body into one of their canoes and, with the other canoes following, paddled out into deep water. They had been as much in his thrall for the past twenty years as the people they'd terrorized, and they were overjoyed to know he was now gone for good. They began to beat the surface of the sea and intone a deep rhythmic chant. Within minutes the first triangular fins appeared, soon to be followed by others.

The warriors ceased their chanting as the sharks circled round. Then, at a word of command from one of the elders of the tribe, three young men unceremoniously tipped Maaso's body over the side of the canoe, where it fell into the sea with a huge splash. They watched in horrified relief as a big bull shark led the others in a ferocious feeding frenzy, tearing the corpse apart as they fought one another to get to the body. It was all over in less than a minute. The black fins disappeared into the depths beneath and, apart from a widening pool of blood across the surface, Maaso was no more.

Michael and the others watched the warriors go out with Maaso's body. Sele, believing they intended just to bury Maaso at sea, had wanted to go with them in order to give her tormentor a proper Christian burial. But the warriors left before she could join them. So, she and Fata offered prayers for his soul as they stood with heads bowed at the water's edge. Michael did not join them. He guessed what was about to happen and preferred it that way.

* * *

They stayed on the island for another two weeks, replenishing their supplies and resting their weary bodies as the people of the island rejoiced in their deliverance. With Yauwii's help Fata was able to pick up enough of the local language to learn the story of the people who lived there. Many of them had been abducted by Maaso's war parties in the past and had been forced to stay on Mabi as his warriors or as workers. A couple of the old men had been present when their people had first encountered Maaso and succumbed to his brutal overlordship. They had been with him on his early expeditions to subdue the surrounding islands. They described how he had risen to be the great war chief who dominated the whole region, demanding tribute from the lesser chiefs in the form of young warriors for his raiding parties, and young women whom he sold to the pearling skippers.

They also talked about a black ship with three masts and a captain who was as big as Maaso and just as ferocious. They said he had two teeth that shone like the sun.

'That's got to be the barquentine we rescued,' Michael said with disgust. 'I remember her master was a giant of a man with gold teeth.'

'They say he Maaso's biggest customer for native women,' Fata added. 'Maaso want to sell Sele to him.'

'Thank God we got here in time. They must have been heading for this island to pick up more women. What else do they say?'

'They believe Sele is prophetess, sent to teach them. They want her to stay with them.'

'No, she can't stay here. She's been exposed to enough danger. She must return to Australia with me.'

'You try tell Sele that?' Fata asked with a slightly cynical look in his eye.

* * *

Eventually, Sele did agree to leave with Michael and his crew, but only for a time. It wasn't what Michael hoped for but, as Fata had indicated, Sele was not a woman who could be easily controlled. She promised to return to Mabi, and to the people of Vitu, bringing with her some of her former companions from Samoa who would join Fata in his work. Fata had already decided to stay on Mabi, believing that its dominance of the region provided the ideal base for his life work. He was overjoyed at the prospect that she and her companions were to join him.

As the two of them stood side by side, staring out across the sun-kissed waters of the lagoon, they reverted to their native Samoan tongue as Fata told her of his years of lonely isolation. 'I've served God here for a long time alone, Sele,' he told her. 'It's now many years since I last saw my own people. But now I am alone no more. I am very happy.'

That evening, the one before they were due to depart, the senior elder of the tribe came to Michael as he sat quietly staring into the burning embers of the communal fire pit. He made signs that he should follow him and then led Michael to the large hut where Maaso had lived and showed him

Maaso's treasures. Michael was not really interested in the collection of war clubs, cutlasses and trinkets taken from the vessels they'd raided over the years. He had already searched the hut for anything of value and had surreptitiously pocketed Mundine's fifteen gold sovereigns. But the old man insisted that he follow him further to the back of the pile.

He carefully removed a number of larger items until the bare floor beneath was exposed. Then he began to dig into the hardened soil, chipping away at the surface with a stone knife. Michael watched with growing curiosity until the old man finally stopped digging and began to scoop the soil out with his hands. Moments later he produced a leather bag, which he placed in Michael's hands.

Michael looked at him enquiringly, and the old man pointed to the pouch, indicating that he should open it. Taking the pouch back to the open doorway, where a ray of moonlight shone through into the darkness of the hut, he poured the contents onto the floor and gasped in amazement at a pile of the largest and most lustrous pearls he had ever seen. He was no expert in the value of pearls, but he'd seen enough to know that what lay before him was worth a small fortune.

He looked at the old man questioningly as if to say, what do you want me to do? The old man grinned a toothless grin and pointed first to the pearls and then to Michael.

Michael pointed to his own chest and said, 'For me? You want me to have them?'

Though not understanding the words, the old man clearly understood the question. He scooped the pearls up and put them back in the pouch, which he then placed in Michael's hand, closing it over the leather.

For a moment, Michael was dumbfounded, unable to really believe that this was happening. He could feel his heart beating faster as his mind began to grasp what this could mean. If he could get back safely to the mainland, those pearls would more than compensate for the loss of *the Wahine.* He put the pouch safely inside his shirt and smiled at the old man, 'Thank you.'

The old man grinned again.

Michael's first thought was to tell Sele what had happened, but on second thoughts he decided not to. Sele had little interest in material wealth. To her money was something to be used for the good of others. He suspected she'd probably see the pearls as blood money - the proceeds of unimaginable human misery. Or, if she could be persuaded to take them, she'd want to use them to pay for people like herself to come and bury themselves in God-forsaken holes like Mabi. So, he decided to keep the news to himself and make the most of this unexpected windfall, overjoyed that his luck had changed at last, while trying, with limited success, to stifle those inconvenient twinges of conscience that told him he was better than this.

* * *

There were only seven of them in the *Wahine's* longboat as it set sail this time. Fata and Yauwii, who had become Fata's first convert on Mabi and his devoted follower, stayed on the island. They were sad to see the others depart but were full of anticipation for what lay ahead when Sele would return with her missionary companions. The boat was now well stocked with fresh water stored in bags made of animal skins, piles of coconuts, taro and fresh meat left over from the pigs that had been roasted for the previous night's farewell feast.

'We don't have any charts,' Michael explained to Sele. 'But we do have the boat compass, my sextant and enough memory of these waters to get us to Cape York. Then we'll just follow the coast south until we get to Refuge Bay.'

'Just like I did when I first met you,' Sele smiled.

'I thank my lucky stars for that day,' he grinned.

'And I thank my God for it, too,' she replied quietly. But within herself she wondered if God felt the same way.

14 August 1886 – The Coral Sea

They departed early one morning just as the sun was rising. Fortunately, the storm had moved off into the Bismarck Sea, leaving them with a steady nor'westerly breeze that powered their passage eastwards towards Warrior Reef where they would enter the Coral Sea and turn south for Refuge Bay. They ran before that wind for two full days, Sele sitting close to Michael as he navigated the small boat through reefs and between sandbanks and snuggling up to him as they anchored at night under the brilliant canopy of the tropical sky. Michael had never known such happiness, and as he looked into Sele's eyes he knew she felt the same. He wished it would never end.

On the third day they sighted the southernmost point of Warrior Reef and turned south on a course that would take them safely past Cape York and down to Refuge Bay.

Two hours later, a sharp-eyed Kanaka seaman spotted white water ahead. Michael trained his telescope in the direction he was pointing.

'There must be a reef just below the surface,' he said. 'And it looks like there are others just beyond it.'

'I don't recall anything on the charts that warned of reefs round here, skipper,' Charlie said.

'Neither do I,' Michael replied. 'But that doesn't mean very much. Most of this area has never been properly surveyed.

Three days later the familiar outline of the large protective headland that gave Refuge Bay its name came into view. A pearling lugger, which had passed them a day before and hailed them to see if they needed help, had reported their presence to the settlement there, and Dr. Wakeley was standing on the beach to welcome them as they came ashore. He wasn't alone. Bernie Matthews was also there. Michael groaned inwardly at the sight. He'd been dreading the inevitable meeting with Bernie and having to tell him that the *Wahini* had been wrecked.

Much to Michael's embarrassment, Dr. Wakeley, after embracing Sele and pumping Michael's hand in joyful relief, called upon the little group to join him as he knelt on the beach to give thanks to Almighty God for their deliverance. Sele joined him on her knees, oblivious of the curious stares of the people who came out of the waterfront pub to see what was happening. Billy and the Kanakas, who felt no embarrassment about acknowledging the spiritual world that surrounded them, also fell to their knees. But Michael, Bernie and Charlie chose rather to just remove their hats and stand in embarrassed silence as Dr. Wakeley raised his voice in a fervent prayer of thanksgiving.

Having concluded his prayer, Wakeley got to his feet and invited them to the mission house where a good meal, a warm bath and a comfortable bed awaited them. He told them that they could relate what had happened as they ate. But Michael couldn't wait that long. He took Bernie by the arm and led him aside.

'I lost the *Wahine,* Bernie. I ran her onto an uncharted reef while trying to tow another vessel to safety. It was touch and go that we'd even get the longboat over the side.'

'Yeah; I know. I got the news from the pearling lugger that passed you the other day.'

'I suppose you're going to tell me I should have listened to you and not gone looking for Sele.'

'No. It's a grand thing you did. Pity about your money, though. The bank is still going to want its repayments on the loan you took out to buy your original share. But I won't be pushing you to repay me right away. I'll give you a chance to get back on your feet, but remember our written agreement was that you'd repay me within five years.'

'Thanks, Bernie. You'll get your money back.'

'Anyway,' Bernie continued. 'Things are looking good for me. I told you about the report of likely gold deposits up in the ranges. Well, I found them – or traces of them.'

'Have you started mining it?'

'No. I'm done with living in a tent and digging holes. I registered my claim and then sold it to a mining company from Victoria. There's a lot of interest in North Queensland down in Melbourne, and a lot of money too. Some of those geezers that struck it rich on the Victorian goldfields are looking for new places to invest their surplus cash now that they've paid for their fine mansions in Toorak. They think Cape York is where the next gold rush will be.'

'So, what'll you do now?'

'Like I told you, I plan to go back to Cooktown and open a store, filled with all the things people take for granted down south, but can't get up here. Then, when the gold rush starts, I'll build a wharf here at Refuge Bay and make this the port where the supplies come in and the gold goes out.'

Michael nodded admiringly. 'There's no doubt about you, Bernie. You know how to fall on your feet. I don't suppose you need a partner?'

'No offence, Michael. But this is a venture I'm going into on my own. But I'd advise you to give some thought to what you're going to do. The bank ain't gonna like it when they learn that your share of the *Wahini* wasn't covered by insurance.'

Michael touched the bulge beneath his shirt where a leather pouch rested secure. 'I realize that, Bernie; but I haven't played my last card yet.'

* * *

Sele remained at Refuge Bay for a few more days until Dr. Wakeley was able to arrange a passage for her to Cooktown on a trading ketch. Despite the ordeal she'd been through, she was determined to report all that happened and to keep her promise to return to the islands with her fellow Samoan missionaries. It was a prospect that filled Michael with gloom and apprehension. She was such an enigma: deeply religious, with an unshakable conviction that she'd been called to serve God in those islands, yet quietly passionate in a way that made his heart race.

Deep down inside he worried it was all too good to be true. Sele Saena was like something out of a dream. But the depth of her faith and her links to Polynesian royalty were so different from his impoverished and irreligious upbringing as to cause him to doubt she could really be interested in him. Nevertheless, as they spent those few days together, walking hand in hand along the white coral sands by day and in the evening sitting together on the wide veranda of the mission house, listening to the sound of the surf breaking on the distant reef, he started to hope that she wanted him as much as he wanted her.

As for Sele, she felt herself being torn in two. She knew that her life would be incomplete if she failed to carry her mission through. But could Michael Burns fit into it? He was a good man, and she loved him deeply . But she had to acknowledge that that he probably did not share her deep spiritual yearnings. She also knew that she had to broach this subject with him but didn't know how, which surprised her because she never felt the same reluctance with other people.

Early one morning, as the sun appeared over the eastern horizon and the bush seemed to erupt in a cacophony of birdcalls, she joined him on his regular morning walk along the beach that fringed the dense bushland surrounding Refuge Bay. It was that magical time of day that most people miss as they try to prolong their last few moments of rest before facing another day, and Sele, who was not accustomed to early rising, was enchanted by its freshness. She looked at Michael's face and saw that he loved it too.

'I wondered why you always got up so early,' she said. 'But now I know. The world seems so different.'

He smiled. 'When I first went to sea, I hated being kicked out of my hammock at 4 o'clock in the morning for the morning watch. But gradually I came to love it, and I've been doing it ever since – even though not quite so early when I'm on land.'

'What makes it so special, do you think?

'I suppose it's the silence and the stillness. I used to stand at my designated spot, all on my own, scanning the sea ahead, and the only time I would hear a word or utter a word was if something came up over the horizon.'

'Be still and know that I am God,' she mused.

'What's that?'

'It's a verse from the Psalms – in the Bible.'

'Oh! I haven't heard that one before.'

'It means you can sense God's presence when you really are still inside yourself. Did you ever feel that?'

He grinned shamefacedly. 'When I was that age, I was mostly thinking about other things.'

'What other things?'

'Things a lady would not want to know.'

She reddened slightly and fell silent as they continued their stroll along the coral sands. But she knew that this was the opportunity to raise the subject most dear to her heart, and if she didn't do it now, she probably never would.

'But you must have felt something, standing there in the silence.'

Michael stopped walking and gazed out to where the sun was now like a white ball hovering above the horizon. 'I remember how I used to look at the stars – thousands of 'em, maybe millions – sitting there in the vastness of space, and I used to say to myself: there's got to be more to all this than an endless series of accidents, like those smart-arse intellectuals keep tellin' us. And I used to hold my hand up in front of my face in the dark and think there's more to me than a bag of flesh and bones.'

Sele could hardly contain her joy. 'Then you do believe in God!'

'I suppose I do. Don't most people?'

'But you never go to church.'

Michael let out a sigh. 'I've never seen the value of it, Sele. Oh, I know it means everything to you. But I just find it all so…so boring! This is my church – out here, where it's all so beautiful and full of life.'

She nodded appreciatively and they continued their walk in companionable silence until they arrived back at the mission house, where Amelia had breakfast ready. And from that moment on, she began to do what countless numbers of women like her had done for centuries: she prayed for a miracle that would change this man she loved so deeply into a man who would also share her spiritual, as well as her emotional passion.

On the night prior to her departure, they sat quietly on the veranda of the mission house, watching the moonlight on the bay before them, cooled by a gentle breeze laced with the fragrance of frangipanis. Inside, all was dark and silent, everyone else having gone to bed. Michael plucked up his courage and began to slide over the bench closer to her. As his hip touched hers a thrill of excitement went through him, only to dissipate as quickly as it had arisen when she slid away from him. After a little while he slid closer to her again. This time there was no possibility of her sliding further from him because she was perched on the very edge of the bench. He half expected that she would stand up and leave: but she didn't.

He put his right hand behind her head and gently pulled her face towards him until their lips met in a long, lingering kiss. Her lips were soft, and the fragrance of her hair was almost intoxicating. She turned towards him and wrapped her arms around his neck, smothering his face with kisses.

But then, suddenly, she sat up straight and said, 'This is not appropriate, Michael.'

He quickly withdrew his hand, cursing himself for breaking the spell that had held them together. 'Sorry,' he said.

Then, from one of the open windows further along the veranda, they heard Dr. Wakeley's voice. 'Is someone out there?'

'It's all right, Dr. Wakeley. It's only me, Sele. I'm enjoying the evening air.'

'Oh, Sele. Sorry to disturb you. Good night!'

'Goodnight, Dr. Wakeley.'

She got to her feet and looked down at Michael, aware of the disappointment on his face. She reached down and took his hands in hers, kissing him gently again. 'And goodnight to you, my darling Michael.'

'Sele, I don't want you to go back to Mabi. I want you to stay here, with me.'

She turned back to him, her eyes filled with that same intensity he remembered so well from their first meeting. 'Please, Michael. This is breaking my heart. Please don't try to stop me, my love. I have to go back; it's what I was born to do.'

He looked away, trying not to show how devastated he felt, even though he knew there would be no possibility of changing her mind. Then, in one of those rare moments of insight, he realized how important it was that he should not try to deter her, and that for once in his life he should do something contrary to his own self-interest. As she turned to take her leave, he caught her hand. 'Sele, wait a moment. There's something I want to give you.'

'What is it?' she asked, surprised.

'Wait here. It's with my things from the boat.' He went into the darkened house and returned with a small package. 'This was among Maaso's things. The old man on Mabi – the elder of the tribe – he gave it to me.'

Sele took the leather pouch from his hand and looked at it with surprise and curiosity. She opened the drawstring at the top and poured some of the pearls out into her hand. She gasped at what she saw. 'Michael, they're beautiful. I've never seen such pearls. How did Maaso get them?'

'Stole them from pearlers he'd killed, I guess.'

'Thank you, Michael. But I could never accept these. They have the blood of island women on them - those poor girls taken from their homes and forced to dive until their lungs gave way or were taken by sharks - and the blood of the pearlers whom Maaso killed to get them. Perhaps you could sell them to help pay back the money you owe the bank.'

'No, Sele. You keep them. One day you'll find a use for them. If I keep them, I'll probably only add to the misery they've caused.'

She looked deeply into his eyes. 'Do you really mean that Michael?'

He hesitated for a moment, torn between the sudden urge to do something noble in her eyes, and his own instinct for survival. Then he nodded. 'Yes, I do.'

She looked at them again and said softly: 'You are a truly good man, Michael. This is costing you far more than you're telling me. But I know that God will reward you in his own way. I'll do what you say and keep these pearls for that day when they can do something to atone for all the evil surrounding them. Now, try not to be sad. If it's meant to be, I will come back to you.'

She kissed him again and went inside, while he watched her go and wondered what now was now left for him. But Sele couldn't help wondering if this was a sign that her prayers for him were being answered.

24

2 September 1886 – Cape York Peninsula

Sele left the following morning, a little after sunrise. They said goodbye on the beach, both of them aware of the emotional bond that now bound them to each other, but not knowing what to do about it. It seemed as though their lives were going in opposite directions. Michael could never see himself living on a mission station, helping run some sort of school or hospital. But neither could Sele reconcile herself to life as sea captain's wife.

He watched sadly as the small vessel slipped away into the channel and made its way out into the Coral Sea. He could see her standing at the stern, a tiny figure, growing ever smaller, waving to him until she was out of sight. Then, with a heavy heart, he turned back to the mission house, where Mrs. Wakeley had breakfast prepared. He and his crew ate in silence, each of them wondering what lay ahead. Their thoughts were interrupted by Bernie's arrival.

'I've got somethin' for you to think about, mate. Have you heard what people down south are prepared to pay for pearl shell these days?'

Michael shook his head.

'Well,' Bernie continued. 'A few years ago, a bloke named Banner was up in the Torres Strait, fishing for beche-de-mer. He got interested in the fancy pearl shell ornaments that the islanders were wearing, and they showed him where they got the shell from. It was that place called *Warrior Reef* that I've heard you talk about. Anyway, he filled his hold with the stuff and took it down to Sydney hoping to find a buyer. The experts there took one look at what he'd got and told him to forget about beche-de-mer and concentrate on this stuff. It's worth at least one hundred and eighty pounds a ton. He's made a fortune out of it.'

'Anyway, the pearl beds around Warrior Reef have been pretty well worked out by now, and the search is on for new sources. But in the pub last night I met a Kanaka who told me he'd worked with the pearlers up there and got shipwrecked in a cyclone. He and two others got away in a small boat and drifted south. He told me the other two died of thirst and he ended up stranded on a reef he reckoned was a coupla days south of Warrior Reef by canoe. And, like Warrior Reef, it's full of pearl shell.'

'So why he didn't he go back there himself?'

'He's a Kanaka. They ain't interested in pearl shell, except for hangin' it round their necks.'

'Then why haven't you gone looking for it?'

'Because there's more money in gold; and in them that wants to find it. But I'm prepared to finance an enterprising bloke who I trust and who might be interested in entering the pearl shell business.'

Michael sat forward on his seat. 'You mean you'd finance me?'

Bernie nodded.

'How much?'

'There's a lugger up for sale in Cooktown. They want sixty-five pounds for it. I reckon I could loan you that, plus a bit extra for supplies to keep you going for a month or two. You've already got a crew here, and your Kanakas are good divers. I reckon seven per cent interest on the loan, payable by the end of the year, sounds about right.'

'Are you serious, Bernie?'

'You know me, Michael. I always have my eye open for a good investment.'

Michael jumped to his feet and took Bernie by the hand. 'You've got yourself a deal, Bernie. And you blokes,' he turned to his crew, 'have got yourself a job.'

'Don't get too excited,' Bernie interjected. 'First, we need to book a passage to Cooktown so we can look at that lugger and get a loan contract drawn up for you to buy it.'

'So, when do we leave?'

'The supply ship arrives early next week and is due to return to Brisbane at the end of the week. We'll be able to take passage on her. So, let's get down to the pub and book ourselves a ride.'

As they walked back down the hill Michael remembered what Sele had said about God making it up to him for his gift of the pearls. Bernie's offer of a loan was a poor substitute for what those pearls would have provided. But it was better than nothing; and if that bed of pearl shell was really out there, it might turn out to be the best business decision he'd ever made.

* * *

The first thing Michael did after arriving in Cooktown was to walk up the hill to the mission house, hoping that Sele might still be there. The Glastons were overjoyed to see him and anxious to hear his account of the adventures Sele had already described to them. But Michael had no heart for storytelling. He wanted to know about Sele.

'She's gone back to Mabi, old chap.' Geoffrey could sense Michael's disappointment. 'She left two days ago with the other missionary teachers from Samoa who came here with her. We chartered Captain Mason's ketch again. Now that he knows the reason why he got attacked up there and that the troubles are over, he was much more amenable to the idea of a return visit. And as for Sele; after her experiences with that terrible wild man, she's even more convinced that Mabi is the place where God wants her to be.'

Amelia took Michael's hand in hers. 'We know how you feel about her, Michael; and we both think we know how she feels about you. But this is bigger than both of you. Sele is no ordinary young woman. She's one of those special people who've been called to do something most of us would never dream of. It's been with her all her life, and now she knows she's found what it is.'

'And it doesn't include me,' Michael said bitterly.

They said nothing, not knowing how to tell him that, in their opinion, there could never be a future for a woman like Sele and an adventurer like him, no matter how much they liked him. But Michael sensed it.

'You don't approve of us being together, do you?'

Geoffrey took his time in answering. He shook his head sadly. 'It wouldn't work, Michael. You come from such different backgrounds. And your lives are going in different directions.'

Michael shrugged his shoulders. 'Maybe you're right. But I hope to God you're not!'

Hearing him say this jolted Amelia's memory. She jumped to her feet with a start. 'Oh goodness, I forgot to tell you. Sele gave me a letter to give to you.' She hurried into her bedroom and returned with an envelope. 'She knew you'd call in here and made me promise to make sure you received it.'

Michael took the envelope from her hand. It was addressed to *My Darling Michael.* He opened it and began to read:

Dearest Michael. I had hoped to see you again before I returned to Mabi, but Captain Mason was back in Cooktown with his ship and able to take me and my sisters back to the islands. The mission, through Geoffrey, agreed to pay for our passage because it now recognizes that I have been called to serve those people whom we both know need it so much. My friends who came with me from Samoa have all agreed to join me.

I do not know when I shall be back. My heart is torn between you and the work I know I am meant to do. But I believe with all my heart that if I trust in God's leading, eventually all will be well – for both of us. But it is breaking my heart.

I will always love you, my darling Michael.

Sele.

Michael's eyes misted as he read the letter, though he made no sound. The Glastons sat quietly and pretended not to notice. Even though Sele had not told them what was in the letter, they guessed what it said.

Finally, Geoffrey said to Amelia, 'Why don't you go and make us some tea, my dear, while Michael and I talk.'

She nodded her agreement and went into the kitchen, patting Michael's shoulder in a motherly fashion as she passed him.

'What's ahead for you now, old chap?' Geoffrey asked.

'Bernie has offered to loan me enough money to buy a lugger that's up for sale here in Cooktown.'

'So, you plan to go into pearling. Is it still profitable around here?'

'It is if you can find pearl beds that haven't already been exploited.'

'And if you don't find it?'

Michael stood up and walked to the window. 'Then I'm done for.'

Geoffrey looked up as Amelia returned with a tray, loaded up with tea pot, cups, saucers and milk. 'You're just in time, my love. Michael was just telling me that he's about to go into the pearling business. We shall drink a toast to his success.'

'And to Sele's return,' Amelia said, quietly surprising herself that she should have openly admitted what she was feeling within.

* * *

Michael was pleased with his purchase. The *Jasmine* was only ten years old, sturdily built and capable of staying at sea for a couple of weeks at a time. Her previous owner had had little luck in the pearling business and was glad to accept Michael's offer of sixty-five pounds for his vessel. He promptly took passage on the next ship going south and returned to a less demanding occupation, glad to see the back of Cooktown.

The *Jasmine* was forty feet long. She had a single cabin aft containing two bunks and lockers, and a small forecastle which provided space for the crew. She could carry four tons of cargo in her hold, and her two lug sails enabled her to cope with most of what those tropical waters might throw at her.

As soon as she was provisioned and the loan agreement with Bernie signed, Michael and Charlie set sail for Refuge Bay. Two days later, with Billy and the two Kanakas on board, they were on their way again, heading northwest, searching for the reef they had spotted on their journey south in the *Wahine's* longboat, hoping that it might turn out to be the mysterious reef Bernie had told them about.

On the fifth day Billy spotted white water in a place where, according to the official chart, there was no reef. Michael took the lugger as close as he dared, carefully edging his way around the breakers – evidence of submerged coral beneath. Then he dropped anchor.

The Kanakas had already stripped off their clothes and were grinning at the prospect of doing something they hadn't done since they left their island homes.

'Don't dive too deep and don't stay down too long,' Michael warned. 'All we want is to find out what's down there and if this is the place Bernie told us about. Charlie and Billy, you post yourselves fore and aft with the rifles and keep watch for sharks.'

The divers stayed underwater for nearly two minutes. Michael and the others waited anxiously for their heads to break the surface, hoping for a good report. The first diver's head broke the surface slightly ahead of the lugger. Ten seconds later the other reappeared. They swam over and shook their heads.

'Nothin' down there, boss. We try again, further over.'

They hung onto the side of the vessel for a few minutes while they regained their strength. Then, gradually emptying and filling their lungs until they contained the maximum amount of air, they disappeared below the surface again. The heavy stones Billy had given them took them to the seabed where they searched some more until their lungs were about to burst.

By the end of the day, Michael's hopes had been dashed. They had moved the lugger several times and the Kanakas had searched every part of that reef, with no sight of pearl shell.

'I guess our assumptions were wrong, Charlie. If there really was a reef full of pearl shell, then it's not this one.'

'Where to now, skipper?'

'I reckon we keep on cruising around, searching for anything that looks like an uncharted reef. Then, when our supplies run out, we go home.'

15 October 1886 – The Torres Strait

The whole population of Mabi was there to welcome Sele and her companions. Fata was the first to greet her as she stepped out of the ship's boat. She looked around at the sea of welcoming faces - many of them women and children who, only months before, would have fled at the sight of a white man's ship.

'Oh, Fata, this is quite overwhelming,' she said excitedly. 'I never expected a welcome like this.'

'They believe you prophetess from beyond sea like old people tell them,' he replied. 'We tell them how you save people of Vitu from Maaso. They see how Maaso afraid of you. They see how you escape him. Now they sure you prophetess. They say you their saviour.'

'But, Fata, I don't want them to think of me as their saviour. I want them to think that of Jesus.'

Fata laid his hand on her shoulder. 'Ah, my little Sele! Even when you little child all you want is for people to love Jesus. Well, now you do it here; you and good sisters from Samoa. Please, you introduce me to them.'

The five teachers were already surrounded by smiling women and laughing children. Even the warriors seemed pleased. Sele introduced them to Fata, telling them again about how he had left their native Samoa so long ago and how he, all alone, had brought the Christian message to those islands.

'And what of Maaso? What do the people think now?' Sele asked.

Fata pointed to the large hut where Maaso had lived with his harem. There was a large bamboo cross outside it and another smaller one above the entrance. 'That once Maaso's house. Now it our chapel. Evil spirit gone. Holy Spirit now here.'

And what about that terrible man with his black ship – the one that left Captain Burns to die after he had stopped to help them. He was one of the people Maaso used to sell women to. Do you think he might come here again?'

'Yes. He not know Maaso dead.'

'And if he does come again, what will we do?'

'We tell him Maaso dead. We tell him go away and trouble us no more.'

'Will he believe us?'

'We must pray it be so.'

10 November 1886 – The Coral Sea

Four hundred nautical miles away, Michael's lugger lay wallowing in a choppy sea. She was at the end of her third trip in search of the mysterious reef with the promised deposits of pearl shell, and supplies were running low. So, Michael reluctantly decided to give up the search and set a course for Refuge Bay.

'We'll see if we can get credit for enough supplies to see us through another two weeks,' he told Charlie.

'And where are we going to look then?' Charlie said. 'We've already covered just about every square mile within the area Bernie Matthews told us to look.'

'That's what's got me puzzled. Maybe Bernie can tell us where to find the Kanaka who ended up on that reef. If we could talk to him, we might get a better idea of where to look.'

Charlie looked at Michael as though he were about to say something, and then looked away, as if he had changed his mind.

'What is it, Charlie? What do you want to say?'

Charlie shrugged his shoulders. 'Maybe there is no reef, skipper. Maybe the Kanaka was just spinning a yarn.'

Michael nodded. 'I've thought of that too. But I've got to give it another chance.'

Three days later they turned under the sheltering headland and entered the channel into Refuge Bay, dropping anchor just as the sun was setting. Charlie, Billy and the two Kanakas went ashore to spend the evening drinking at the shanty pub, while Michael called on the Wakeleys, hoping they might have some information about Sele.

He gladly accepted their invitation to stay for dinner, and they talked well into the evening about the state of things in Refuge Bay. Dr. Wakeley expressed his concerns about the deteriorating moral tone of the tiny community and how things would only get worse if there were to be another gold rush.

'Your friend Mr. Matthews seems convinced there's gold waiting to be found up there in the ranges,' he said.

Michael nodded. 'But Bernie's smart enough to leave the hard work to someone else. He's sold his claim to an investment group from Victoria. Bernie wants to be the man who provides supplies and port facilities when the rush begins.'

'Well, Michael. Much as I wish Mr. Matthews success in his business, I hope this one doesn't eventuate. What we need here is a more settled and responsible type of industry, one that will attract good, honest people prepared to raise their families and build a decent community.'

'Not like the pearlers and beche-de-mer men!'

Wakeley shook his head. 'It's not that I have anything against the pearling industry as such; it's just some of the people who get involved in it.'

'There are some pretty wild characters,' Michael agreed.

'And the way they treat their native divers – especially the women – is scandalous. I've written to the authorities in Brisbane about it. We need a police presence and a magistrate who's strong enough to enforce proper standards.' He looked directly into Michael's eyes. 'Someone like you, perhaps.'

'Like me?' Michael sounded surprised.

'Yes, like you. Would you be interested in such a position?'

'The thought has never crossed my mind. Maybe I would. But I can't see anybody in Brisbane offering it to the likes of me.'

'Why not? You are becoming a successful businessman and a respected member of this community.'

'I haven't always been! I grew up in some of the worst slums of the English Midlands, where my father was just an Irish navvy. That put us at the bottom of the pile that was bottom of the town. I ran away to sea when I was fourteen and have been a roamer ever since.'

Wakeley placed a fatherly hand on Michael's shoulder. 'In this country, Michael, and especially in this part of this country, they are the very things we admire most – men who prove their worth by their own achievements, not by their social connections.'

'And you think the bigwigs down in Brisbane would consider me?'

'It all depends on who makes the recommendation.'

'And you'd put my name forward?'

'Yes, and I'd have the support of other reputable people here and in Cooktown, including Geoffrey Glaston.'

They continued their conversation while sitting on the veranda, sipping cocoa. The conversation turned to Michael's newly formed pearling venture, and he confided in him that he was beginning to think he had made a mistake and might have to put his newly purchased lugger up for re-sale.

'Oh, I do hope not,' Wakeley said. 'It would be a blessing to this community to have someone like you running a successful pearling operation, instead of the scoundrels down there in that pub by the waterfront.'

Michael decided not to tell him that the members of his crew were also down there at that very moment, so he changed the subject. 'My former partner says there's a demand for pearl shell in Sydney. I was hoping I might discover some new pearl shell beds similar to those around Thursday Island.'

Wakeley nodded. 'Yes, I've heard talk about such beds. There was an islander who was picked up off an uncharted reef some time ago. He reported beds of pearl shell similar to the ones he had worked on around Warrior Reef.'

Michael sat forward on his chair. 'You wouldn't know where this man happens to be, would you?'

'No. I think he went back to the Solomon Islands. But I do know the man who rescued him.'

'You do?'

'Yes. It's Captain Ryall. He's the master of the schooner the mission recently purchased to service its mission stations up here.'

Michael felt a surge of excitement. 'When is he likely to return here?'

'I don't know. Why do you ask?'

'I'd like to ask him where it was that he found that man.'

'Oh, I can tell you that. I have it in my journal.'

'Your journal?'

'Yes. I've been keeping a journal ever since I came up here. I record all the interesting things that happen. I plan to write it all down in a book when I retire.'

Michael tried hard to hide his mounting impatience. 'Would you show me what you recorded?'

'Of course! Just stay here while I go and get it.'

Wakeley returned moments later with a leather-bound volume. He began to leaf through it, trying to find the record of his meeting with Captain Ryall. After much searching back and forth through the handwritten pages he gave an exclamation of triumph.

'Ah, here it is.' He scanned the report he had written down and finally found what he was looking for. He held it up for Michael to see.

'Approximately forty nautical miles northwest of Osprey Reef,' Michael read. For the first time in weeks, he began to feel a surge of hope.

* * *

The letter from the Cooktown branch of the Australasian Bank arrived the day before *Jasmine* was due to put to sea. It was addressed to Michael, but came care-of Dr. Wakeley, who had offered to keep an eye on Michael's affairs while he was at sea. He delivered it personally to him aboard the lugger.

'Bad news?' he asked, seeing the darkened look on Michael's face as he read the letter.

'I'm afraid so,' Michael replied. The bank has refused my application for a loan. And without that I can't buy supplies or pay my crew. Neither will Bernie Matthews loan me any more money. I've got enough for one more trip out to Warrior Reef but then I'm broke.'

'Do you have any other assets?'

'Only some shares in the Melbourne Omnibus Company.'

'How much are they worth?'

'Probably about fifty pounds; maybe a bit more. I have five hundred of them.'

'Why don't you leave them with me? I have to go to Cooktown on the steamer later this week. I know the bank manager. I performed an emergency operation to remove his young son's appendix when he first arrived here and I was working in Cooktown. Let me talk to him and see if he'll take those shares as collateral for a loan.'

'It's a kind offer. But the bank is going to want much more than what they're worth.'

'Well, let me try, anyway.'

'I suppose there's nothing to lose by trying. I'll get them for you.'

He pulled a sea chest from under his bunk and rummaged through it until he found a large envelope wrapped in a piece of oilskin.

'It was the only thing I had time to rescue from the *Wahine* when she went down – apart from my rifle. I hope you can do some good with it.'

'I shall certainly try, my boy; you can be assured of that. And now, good luck and God speed. I hope you find that bed of pearl shell this time.'

They shook hands and Wakeley returned to the mission house, while Michael busied himself with the final preparations for their departure next morning.

* * *

As the heat of the afternoon sun reflected mercilessly off the sea's surface, Michael stood silent and alone in the lugger's tiny wheelhouse. None of his crew, not even Billy, who had been with him through thick and thin for more than a decade, had ever seen him so dejected. It had been three weeks since the *Jasmine* had left Refuge Bay, but their efforts had, once again, proved fruitless. Now, pushed along by a freshening breeze, they barely had time to reach Refuge Bay before their supplies ran out.

For some time, Charlie had been watching a buildup of cloud behind them, hoping that it wouldn't affect their progress. By early afternoon his curiosity had turned to concern.

'I don't like the look of the weather building up behind us, skipper,' he said.

Michael grunted. 'I know. I've been watching it too.'

'Do you think we might be in for a cyclone?'

'Don't know, Charlie. It could be.'

'We need a plan, boss. We ought to change direction and head straight for the nearest spot on the mainland where we can find shelter.'

Michael shrugged his shoulders. 'It's no use, Charlie. If that buildup of cloud is the start of a cyclone, then we're better off trying to ride it out where we are. A ship this size wouldn't survive the sort of waves whipped up by hurricane force winds in shallow water. Anyway, you know what the pearlers around Thursday Island always say about cyclones around here.'

'You mean that they never come further north than Cooktown?'

Michael nodded.

'Well, I reckon we're about to find out.'

He'd hardly finished speaking when a gust of wind caught the lugger by surprise and swung her stern violently to starboard, causing the booms to swing erratically as Michael fought to bring the vessel under control. The shock of it woke him from his lethargy and he shouted for the crew to reduce sail before another gust hit them.

'I guess we've nothing to lose now, Charlie,' Michael said. 'I've lost the ship anyway. The bank will repossess it as soon as we get back.'

'By the look of what's coming up behind us, skipper, we could be about to lose it even sooner.'

Michael looked back over his shoulder and saw the white fleck on the waves behind them changing rapidly to flying spray as a strong wind swept towards them.

'Let's bring her around, Charlie. I'd sooner face into this than try to run before it. I should have been paying more attention to the weather instead of worrying about the bank. This is probably the start of something bigger, so let's take the weather on our strongest point.'

They brought the lugger around into the wind moments before another gust hit them, heeling the tough little ship over onto her starboard side as her bow took its full force. The waves, whipped up by the wind, grew larger, but *Jasmine* met every one of them, her solid hardwood bow unyielding as the rollers smashed against it.

Michael clung to the ship's wheel, trying to keep the bow as close to the wind as possible, fighting against the elemental forces that seemed determined to swing the vessel beam-on to the oncoming waves and roll her over. Charlie stood behind him, while the rest of the crew sheltered below deck, away from the tons of sea water already pouring over the sides and out through the scuppers.

All afternoon and well into the evening the tiny ship pitched and heaved as the wind - now at gale force – hurled its full fury at her. Undeterred, she maintained her slow, tortuous progress, keeping well away from the mainland. Every thirty minutes Charlie would replace Michael at the wheel or vice versa, while below deck even the Kanakas felt seasick and Billy lay groaning in his bunk.

Around midnight the wind seemed to ease slightly, causing Michael to hope that they might have seen the worst of it. He took the opportunity to call the Kanakas up to relieve him and Charlie, giving the two of them opportunity to get some sleep. It was one of them that spotted the faint outline of white water ahead, silhouetted against the blackness of the sky.

'It must be a reef,' Michael muttered. 'We'd better heave-to. We know there's nothing behind us, so there's no worry about us drifting onto another reef. Charlie, tell the boys to hold on, and then prepare to go about.'

He swung the wheel and the lugger turned up into the wind and then began to cross over onto the opposite tack. The trysail on the main boom swung across the deck, but the storm jib, still cleated into its same position and now backwinded, brought the lugger to a standstill, holding her steady as the power of one sail counteracted the effect of the other.

'OK, Charlie,' Michael sighed. 'Time for us to get some sleep while we still can.'

Dawn was breaking when Michael woke with a start and went up on deck, anxious to see the state of the weather. Billy was already there and greeted him with a grin. 'Storm, 'im gone, boss.'

Michael looked around and saw for himself that it was true. There was a heavy swell running, and *Jasmine* was still being thrown around quite heavily as the waves passed beneath her hull; but the wind had dropped to little more than a strong breeze, and the sky above appeared cloudless against the emerging dawn.

Charlie joined them on deck, rubbing the sleep from his eyes. 'Strewth,' he said. 'Looks like the big blow has passed us by.'

Michael nodded. 'I still reckon that was the build up for a cyclone, yesterday. But maybe we were lucky and just got the edge of it.'

'Do you think it may have crossed the coast further south?' Charlie asked.

'Could be,' Michael answered. 'But right now there's another little puzzle I'd like to have solved. Do you remember that white water we spotted before we hove-to last night? It might have been a reef. There's nothing on the chart about a reef in these parts, but I think we should go and check it out.'

'How far do you think we drifted last night?'

'Hard to say. It was after midnight when we hove-to. That was six hours ago. Maybe we've drifted ten or twelve miles, or maybe more. Let's go find out.'

They got the lugger under way again and began to retrace their course of the previous night. Michael had the wheel, and the other members of the crew positioned themselves around the ship and one at the mast head, straining their eyes for any sign of broken water. As the sun rose higher in the sky, its reflection on the sea's surface sparkled like millions of diamonds, but there was still no sign of the breakers they'd spotted in the darkness.

By nine o'clock Michael was beginning to wonder if they'd been mistaken in what they thought they'd seen. By ten o'clock he was convinced of it.

'We must have covered nearly twenty nautical miles by now,' he said to Charlie. 'There's nothing out here.'

'And I reckon we searched this area over a month ago,' Charlie replied. 'Where do you think we are on the chart?'

Michael pulled the chart out and pointed to an empty space. 'Somewhere around here. Take a look at the log and see if you can find the entry for these coordinates.'

Charlie went below, returning moments later with the ship's log in his hand. 'Here it is, skipper. 13th October. We covered this area during the afternoon and found nothing.'

'Then it seems we're wasting our time. Let's bring her around and head for Refuge Bay.'

One hour later a cry came from the mast head, 'Breakers ahead.'

Michael gave the wheel to Charlie and climbed up the ratlines to join the lookout. He pointed to a line of surf, now clearly visible, dead ahead.

'It can't be,' Michael said in amazement. 'We sailed through here a few hours ago and saw nothing.'

He returned to the wheelhouse and looked at the chart again. Then a thought crossed his mind. 'Charlie,' he shouted. 'Bring me the tide almanac.'

Charlie disappeared below deck and returned with a small volume that listed the dates and times of high and low tide all along the eastern Australian coastline. Michael found the right page and scanned the details recorded.

'Of course! Why didn't I see it before?'

'What is it, skipper?'

Michael pointed to the entry in front of him. 'We're nearly at the bottom of the tide. When we passed this way a few hours ago it was just after high tide. And the previous low tide was just after eleven, last night. It means the reef only appears at low tide.'

Charlie picked up the ship's log and turned back to the record of their previous visit to this area.

'You're right, skipper. It looks like we sailed through this area when the tide was full. We probably sailed right over that reef and never realized it was there.'

'Right! Get one of the lads up in the bow with a lead line. I want to know as soon as it starts shoaling. Have the others stand by to get the sails in and drop the anchor. Let's see if there's anything there for us.'

The two Kanakas broke the surface almost at the same time. They'd been down less than two minutes. They opened their mouths wide as they filled their lungs with air; then, their faces wreathed in grins, held up the canvas bags tied to their waists to reveal an abundance of pearl shell. Michael, assisted by Charlie and Billy, pulled them back into the lugger and poured the contents of their bags onto the open deck. They picked the pieces of shell up and examined them carefully.

'This is exactly what we've been looking for,' Michael whispered. 'Is there more down there?'

'Plenty shell, boss. Way out there and there,' the Kanaka pointed along the line of the breakers.

'Could this be the reef Bernie's Kanaka got stranded on?' Charlie asked.

'I reckon it must be,' Michael agreed. 'He must have run up on it at low tide; then floated off at high tide.'

'So, what now, skipper?'

'We get the boys working, and we fill our hold with shell.'

'And what are we going to eat and drink while they do it?'

'Billy managed to catch enough rainwater from the downpour last night to fill one cask. If we ration ourselves, it'll keep us going for a day or two. And Billy also knows how to catch fish better than anyone I've ever met. He can take the dinghy and go fishing while the boys are down below, and you and I watch out for sharks.'

'He put his arm round Charlie's shoulder. 'Charlie, I think our luck is about to change.'

22 November 1886 – The Coral Sea

Michael's assumption was correct. The gale force winds they'd encountered had been the outer rings of a cyclone that had moved westwards across the Coral Sea before crossing the Queensland coast near Cape Tribulation. Then, unexpectedly, it swung north, ripping through the rainforest between Cooktown and Refuge Bay, leaving a trail of destruction in its wake.

They were all relieved to see the familiar outline of the coast emerging from the horizon as *Jasmine* made her way steadily towards Refuge Bay. They rounded the familiar headland midway through the afternoon and began to head up the channel, looking forward to the prospect of a cold beer and a hot meal.

But this wasn't the only reason for their high spirits. The reef they'd discovered was a veritable treasure trove of pearl shell, and the lugger's hold was full of it. Moreover, no-one else knew of its existence - apart from a Kanaka who had disappeared back to his home somewhere in the vastness of the Pacific. Michael knew that one load wouldn't make him rich, but it might convince the bank to extend his loan and enable them to keep going back for more; and that would make him rich.

He opened his telescope to scan the bay ahead and gave a gasp of shock. Handing it to his mate he said: 'Charlie, take a look at this!'

'Bloody Hell! It was a cyclone, skipper. And Refuge Bay copped it.'

As *Jasmine* entered the bay, Michael and his crew looked round on a scene of devastation. Two small luggers were up on the beach, lying on their sides. The waterfront pub was a pile of timber and corrugated iron, and so were the jerry-built shanties nearby. Most of the other houses had sustained serious damage, and all of them had lost their roofs, including the mission house up the hill. On the higher ground they could see a ragged line of tents and lean-to huts. They also saw people walking around the ruins, clearing the debris and searching for anything worth salvaging. Michael's high spirits vanished at the sight.

Dr. Wakeley met them on the beach as they stepped ashore. 'Thank God you're all safe,' he said. 'We offered prayers for you. We didn't think a small vessel could survive that wind.'

'We were lucky,' Michael replied. 'It seems we only caught the edge of it. When did it hit you?'

'Four days ago. We were expecting strong winds but nothing like this. It came up from the south, you see; and we've always believed that cyclones never came north of Cooktown. But this one did!'

'Was anyone hurt?'

'Fortunately, no-one was killed. But I've had to treat a number of people for cuts and broken limbs.'

'What about the beche-de-mer boats and pearling luggers?'

Dr. Wakeley pointed to the vessels left high and dry on the beach. 'Apart from those two, the others put to sea when the wind began to build up. They went north, hoping to escape the worst of it. We don't know what happened to them, but we fear the worst. Did you see anything on your way in?'

'No. We haven't sighted another ship in the past two weeks.'

Wakeley invited them to the mission house for a meal and a bath. Despite having had most of its roof blown off, the building had survived the cyclone reasonably well, thanks to its solid construction and location, nestled just beneath the brow of a hill, which had given it some protection.

As they sat around the table, eating their first decent meal in days and drinking glasses of cool lemonade, Wakeley asked them about their voyage.

'If it hadn't been for what I've seen here since we arrived, you couldn't have kept me quiet about it,' Michael said.

'So, your search was successful?'

'Yes. We found the reef that Kanaka talked about. And we found out why no-one else has found it. It's only visible at low tide. There are at least two fathoms of water over it at high tide, so it's no wonder it's never been marked on any chart. We were lucky to have struck it at the right time, when the tide was low enough for it to appear.'

'But I'm not sure if that's going to be much use to me now. I was banking on using the facilities the other pearlers had set up here to prepare the shell for transport to Sydney. It would have helped me to convince the bank to extend my loan until I could start to turn a profit. But now, with everyone gone, it'll take time to get the process going again. I doubt the bank will want to give me that much time.'

Dr. Wakeley sat back with a smile on his face. 'Well, Captain Burns, I have some good news for you. You remember that I said I'd talk to the bank manager in Cooktown about your parcel of shares?'

'Yes, what about them?'

'Well, the manager was a little reluctant to extend your credit at first, but did agree, for my sake, to give you another month to meet your outstanding payments. But when I showed him your share portfolio his attitude changed considerably. He said he would be delighted to accept the shares as collateral.'

'But they'd be lucky to bring fifty pounds.'

'Not so, my dear chap. It seems that since your departure from the Colony of Victoria, the city of Melbourne has been experiencing a boom of unprecedented proportion, to the point where folk in London are calling it *Marvelous Melbourne* and see it as a good place to invest their money.'

'But why Melbourne? It's a fine city, but then so is Sydney, or Brisbane.'

Wakeley leaned forward and said: Melbourne is awash with money from the gold rush. Over the past forty years it has grown from a slab hut village to become the biggest city in Australia. People are still pouring into it, and, as a consequence, the city is experiencing a property boom that has seen prices go sky high. And this has led to the development of new villages all around the city to house the growing population. They're now calling these villages suburbs, and because the people in them are no longer able to walk to work, tramways have been spreading everywhere.'

'But my shares are in a company that runs horse drawn buses, not tramways.'

'Yes, I know. But the bank manager tells me that a couple of years ago the *Melbourne Omnibus Company* was bought out by a new amalgamation called the *Melbourne Tramway and Omnibus Company Limited.* And this new company has been given a thirty-two-year lease to operate cable trams to thirteen municipalities. Your shares were automatically transferred to this new company.'

'So, they've gone up in value?'

'My word they have! One share is now worth more than thirty-six shillings. That means that your five hundred shares are currently valued at close to one thousand pounds.'

'A thousand pounds!'

'Possibly more.'

'And the bank is prepared to hold them as collateral against my loan?'

'Exactly! Or you can sell them and just pay off the loan.'

Michael sat dumbfounded as his mind tried to grasp the sudden change in his fortunes. Then he gripped Wakeley by the hand and pumped it vigorously.

'Thank you, Dr. Wakeley. A couple of hours ago I thought I was finished. But you've given me new hope. As soon as my boys are rested, we'll head south to Cooktown and get my loan extended. Then I'll return to set up my new operation, right here in Refuge Bay. We'll bring prosperity back and make this place the little corner of paradise it was meant to be.'

Wakeley smiled beatifically. 'And my prayers will have been answered.'

* * *

The bank manager shook Michael's hand enthusiastically and wished him every success in his venture, assuring him of the bank's continuing support, which Michael, trying to appear grateful, knew was given solely because the bank had nothing to lose.

Nevertheless, it had been a successful meeting. The bank had agreed to hold Michael's shares as collateral against what he already owed, plus an additional amount that would enable him to purchase two more luggers that were up for sale in Cooktown. And so, it was with much satisfaction that he made his way up the now familiar hill to the Glaston's house.

Amelia met him at the front door and greeted him warmly. She was overjoyed to hear of his success. 'I am so sorry that Geoffrey is not here to hear your news, Michael. He'll be even more delighted than I am. He's in Sydney and won't be back until the end of the month. He went to tell the mission committee about the wonderful work that Sele has opened up and to seek support to expand it.'

'How is Sele, do you know?' he asked casually.

She looked at him and smiled softly. 'That's what you really came to talk about, isn't it?'

He nodded. 'I think you can read me like a book, Mrs. Glaston.'

'Please, call me Amelia.'

'All right, Amelia.'

She smiled again. 'The news is that Sele is very well and the work there is flourishing in a remarkable way. Her letters also speak about the dreadful exploitation of natives by evil men like that sea captain you spoke of.'

'*Bulldog* Homer.'

Yes, and others like him. She is determined to bring their trade in human misery to an end.'

'So, she's going to stay up there?'

Amelia laid her hand gently on Michael's. 'Yes, Michael. I think she will. She's torn within herself between wanting to come back here to be with you and her sense of call to those people.'

'Do you think she might ever change her mind?'

'I don't know. She may, but I doubt it. I think her love for God is even stronger than her love for you.'

He dropped his eyes and said: 'That's what I was afraid of. But tell me this: what sort of God is it that tears people apart who love each other.'

She remained silent for a while, lost for words. Then she walked to his side, taking his hand in hers. 'Perhaps it's the God who says: *"Delight in me and I will give you the desires of your heart."*'

'Is that in the Bible?'

'Yes. It's in the book of Psalms.'

'So, what do you think I should do?'

'I can't tell you that, Michael. You'll need to discover it for yourself.'

'How?'

'Just ask Him.'

'Ask God? Just like that?' Michael shook his head. 'I wish I had your faith, Amelia.'

'Faith is what it's all about, my dear,' she replied.

* * *

Michael spent the rest of the week in Cooktown, completing the sale of the two luggers and hiring crews for them. He also called on his former partner, Bernie Matthews, who was genuinely pleased to learn of Michael's change in fortunes.

Bernie's newly established store hadn't seen much business from the anticipated swarm of gold seekers. His hopes of a new gold rush hadn't eventuated, and he was feeling relieved that he'd sold his claims. But there was still a constant demand for supplies from the skippers of the small ships that put into Cooktown; and Michael's new venture seemed to offer even more.

By the end of the week, Michael had *Jasmine* and the other two luggers loaded with provisions purchased from Bernie's store and was anxious to get back to Refuge Bay. Charlie took command of the larger of the newly purchased vessels and Billy, by now an accomplished seaman in his own right, the other. They were about to get under way when Amelia arrived breathlessly at the town wharf, waving an envelope over her head.

'One more thing before you leave, Michael. This came for you today on the mail steamer from Brisbane. It's from Sele.'

'From Sele; for me?'

'Yes; who else?'

He took the small package from Amelia's outstretched hand and had to force himself not to tear it open in front of her.

'Well, aren't you going to open it?'

'I think I'd prefer to do it when I'm alone in my cabin.'

'Of course, you would. Silly me.'

He kissed her cheek then got into the dinghy to row out to the lugger; the envelope stuffed inside his pocket.

Amelia watched him sadly. She desperately wanted to know what Sele had to say. But in her heart, she knew that it might not be good news.

As soon as he was aboard the lugger Michael went below to open Sele's package. It contained a small, locked box and an envelope. He opened the envelope, took out the letter and began to read.

> My Darling Michael,
>
> Writing this letter is the hardest thing I have ever had to do in my life. I love you and miss you so much that it is like an ache always in my heart. I dream of you almost every night. But I know that I cannot be with you. Our lives are so different as to be incompatible. Ever since I was a small girl, I have known that God had a special plan for my life and that there was something I had to do for Him. I have now found it in the people of these islands. If I were to come back to be with you, I would betray my calling and the very meaning of my life. But it is a constant agony within me to have to admit it. I can only hope, my darling, that by following God's will both of us, despite our sadness, will eventually find peace and contentment.

I am returning the pearls to you that you gave me. I know that the loss of your beautiful ship has affected your fortunes terribly. Perhaps you can sell the pearls and buy another one.

Please continue to think of me as I will always think of you and never stop loving you. But, dearest Michael, for my sake, do not try to follow me. I could not bear to have to do this face to face.

My love always,
Sele.

ps. The pearls are locked in this box for extra security. You will have to find a way to force the lock open, but I know you will find a way to do that.

Michael pressed his face against the bulwark next to his bunk and, for the first time since his mother died, wept silently.

PART THREE

5 August 1889 – Cape York Peninsula

Three years after what had seemed to be the end of his dream, Michael stood on his newly constructed wharf and watched his pearl luggers put to sea, heading for the hidden reef, whose pearl shell deposit had far surpassed his expectations. Bernie Matthews' prediction had come true: the growing demand for pearl buttons in Europe and America had raised the value of pearl shell significantly, enabling Michael to gradually increase his fleet to fifteen vessels. His hard work and determination were beginning to bring rewards – they also helped ease the pain of a broken heart. But he still dreamt about Sele.

Dr. Wakeley joined him on the wharf. 'It's become quite an event now – watching your vessels put to sea.'

Michael nodded. 'Yes, but we waste so much time on these journeys out and back. Fifteen luggers taking four days for the round trip is a lot of time that could be better spent gathering more pearl shell.'

'What you need is a larger vessel to act as a mother ship for your fleet,' Wakeley said. 'It could take provisions to the luggers each week, pick up the pearl shell they've gathered and then return, while they gather more. That way your fleet would become twice as productive.'

'The *Wahine* would have been perfect for that,' Michael mused.

'Indeed, she would,' Wakeley added. 'Or a ship just like her.'

'Do you know of one?'

'I think I do. I've been told there's a vessel up for sale at Townsville. It might serve your needs admirably. Do you think the bank in Cooktown might loan you the money?'

Michael thought for a moment. 'I think I have something they might be prepared to take as collateral.'

* * *

The valuation on Sele's pearls was more than enough to convince the bank manager. With them as collateral he agreed to a large increase in Michael's overdraft, enabling him to take passage to Townsville, two hundred and fifty nautical miles south, to look at the schooner that was up for sale. Two weeks later he returned to Refuge Bay with *Wahine 2* and just enough hands to crew her.

'She's a beautiful vessel,' Wakeley beamed as he welcomed Michael back. 'And now, with your jetty completed, you're well on your way to making our little community the pearling centre of North Queensland.'

'Thanks to your advice. It's also time now to make Refuge Bay a decent place for working families.'

'My sentiments exactly, which is why I want to talk to you about the police magistrate position. You remember me telling you about it?'

'Yes, but I didn't take it seriously.'

'Well, you can take it seriously now, old chap. Word about your role in restoring hope in this little community has reached the Legislative

Assembly in Brisbane, and I've been asked to enquire about your willingness to take the position. It isn't a full-time job, of course, but it does have a small stipend. There'll also be a police presence established here. You'll be responsible for the administration of the law while the police enforce it. We need to get rid of the cutthroats who've brought so much misery to these parts. Why, only last week I received a letter from Geoffrey Glaston giving an account of the things Miss Saena put in her last report: dreadful stories of native villages pillaged, men and women abducted and sold to German planters and pearling skippers. The plight of the women is particularly appalling.'

Michael looked up enquiringly, 'Miss Saena, you say ? Has Reverend Glaston been to see her?'

'Yes. The mission committee in Sydney has instructed him to give whatever support he can in her attempts to bring an end to this trade. They were appalled by the stories of abuse by villains like that one you encountered - the one who abandoned you after you'd rescued his ship.'

'*Bulldog* Homer. I wonder where he is now?'

'Well, nobody seems to have seen him or his ship for ages. But Miss Saena believes he is still involved.'

'Maybe she's heard something that the authorities don't know.'

'Well, I think she'd be overjoyed to know that Refuge Bay, at least, will offer no safe haven for the likes of Captain Homer, as it has in the past. Anyway, can I write to Brisbane and tell them you'd be willing to accept an offer of the police magistrate's position?'

Michael held out his right hand. 'Please tell them I would be honoured.'

* * *

Bulldog Homer had no intention of returning to North Queensland. He and his ship were off the west coast of Bougainville. After another three years of battling tropical storms, torrential rains and blistering heat, the barquentine *Hoylake* was well overdue for a refit. Her sails were patched and threadbare, and some of her standing rigging was rotten. Her hull also needed recaulking to stop the inflow of water through the gaps in her seams, keeping men at the pumps almost continuously.

'We're headin' back to Sydney,' Homer announced after they'd dropped off their last load of returning Kanakas. 'The trade in native women is gettin' too dangerous, and there's no real money in takin' natives home like we did this last trip.'

'Well, I suppose we can't complain too much, Captain,' Mundine replied. 'We've made a nice profit in the past few years. But what are we goin' to do in Sydney?'

'We're goin' to mount an expedition.'

'What sort of expedition?'

'An expedition to find gold over there in New Guinea.' He pointed to the west.

'I've never heard of any gold there!'

'Well, you're about to learn somethin', so shut up and listen. I went to a public lecture last time I was in Sydney. The town has been awash with interest in New Guinea. Henry Chester – he used to be the magistrate on Cape York – went exploring up there and came back with reports of having found specimens of gold. There's talk about a new gold rush. It hasn't happened yet because all the attention has been on North Queensland. But I reckon now's the right time to spark some renewed interest in New Guinea.'

'And I suppose you want me to finance it?'

'Of course! That's how this partnership works. I provide the ship and the muscle, and you provide the cash.' He put his arm around Mundine's shoulder. 'We'll return to Sydney and spread the word that we've found traces of gold around the Fly River. There are enough people who believe it's there already to ensure plenty of interest. Then, you'll finance the formation of an association for prospecting for gold up there. You'll charter the *Hoylake* and offer passages to all who are prepared to invest in your association. But these passages won't come cheap. Neither will the supplies that you'll provide when they get there.'

'But who's going to believe me? Do you think people are going to just take my word for it?'

'I know they will. You've seen the crowds who go to horse races every Saturday and stake their wages on nags that can never win. Gold fever is like gambling. It's a disease that with a bit of help can become an epidemic. It makes the few people who run it rich by takin' the money off hundreds of fools who get infected. You should know that.'

Mundine nodded. 'But we'll need more than just my say so.'

Homer gave an evil grin. 'Just follow me.'

He led Mundine back to his cabin. In one corner there was an iron safe which Homer opened. He reached inside and pulled out a small jar. Inside it were several gold nuggets, the size of peas.

'I won these in a card game, last year,' he said. 'I decided to keep 'em for when I might need something for a special project. I realized what the project was goin' to be when I heard that bloke in Sydney talking about gold in the Fly River. We are going to be the first to benefit from the latest gold rush.'

'And if there's no gold to be found?'

'Then by that time we'll be well away from there with our profits.'

Mundine thought for a moment. 'All right; you can count me in.'

Homer gave him that same hard-eyed stare as before. 'I wasn't asking whether you *wanted* to come in, Mundine.'

6 September 1889 - Sydney

One month later the ballroom of the Sydney Masonic Temple was filling fast. Ernest Mundine stood slightly off stage and peered through the corner of the curtain.

'It's gonna be a full house,' he whispered.

'Isn't that what I told you?' Homer replied.

'But what do these jokers know about New Guinea?'

'What they know doesn't matter. What matters is what they want to believe. And they want to believe that there's a fortune in gold waiting for them. Now, get out there and do your stuff.'

Mundine straightened his bow tie, took a deep breath and walked to the centre of the stage. The chatter died down as he stepped up to the lectern.

'Gentlemen,' he boomed forth in his most stentorian voice; then, in a lower tone adding, 'and ladies; for I see that there are several members of the fair sex who are also here tonight to hear of the opportunities that lie undiscovered along the banks of the Fly River - true daughters of Brittania, ready to urge their menfolk to go forth with boldness and enterprise to seize them.'

It was good start. Mundine knew the tricks of the trade. For the next sixty minutes he described the lush banks of the Fly River, unknown and untouched by the outside world until recent years, and the riches that were continually washed down from the highlands beyond. Holding up a glass jar, he allowed the crowd to see the very thing he was referring to. Homer's gold nuggets sparkled like small chunks of sunlight as the operator at the back of the gallery moved the solitary spotlight from Mundine's face to the jar he held aloft.

A low murmur of awe swept through the auditorium as people craned their necks to see the very thing that over the past thirty years had brought so much wealth into the Australian colonies.

'These gold nuggets were discovered by my associate, Captain Homer, master of the barquentine *Hoylake.*'

The spotlight moved again, this time to the right of the stage where Homer appeared, dressed in a newly purchased uniform - one befitting a master mariner who had found gold.

'Captain Homer has sailed the waters to the north of Australia for more than twenty years. No man knows them better than he. He studied the report written by that valiant explorer and former magistrate at Cape York, Henry Chester, of whom you have all heard. That report spoke of gold deposits - known only by the primitive savages who live there, and who have no use for them. Well Captain Homer has found it, and the evidence is here before you.'

Another murmur of excitement went round the auditorium, only dying when a man at the back stood to his feet and shouted, 'Then what's he doing back here? Why isn't he up there making his fortune?'

Homer's brow darkened with anger, but Mundine was ready for interjectors.

'A fair question, my good sir. Captain Homer was under contract to transport natives to the Queensland cane fields. He was compelled to go ashore on the southern coast of New Guinea when blown off course by a violent storm. His supply of fresh water was running low due to the violence of the storm that battered his vessel and smashed many of the casks. It was while searching for fresh water that he found what you now see before you. But the plight of those poor natives aboard his ship was such that his first responsibility was to see them safely to their destination.'

'So, he was a blackbirder, then!' Another interjector at the back joined the fray as Homer's rage began to rise again. But once again Mundine rose to the occasion.

'That, sir, is a scandalous insult. A slur on the good name of a brave and honourable mariner. The natives were all properly indentured labourers who chose to go to Queensland to serve the period of their contracts and to return to their native islands with money jingling in their purses and trade goods that would make them wealthy in their villages.'

The crowd, apart from a handful of skeptics, rose to its feet in support of Mundine's words, clapping enthusiastically, while the more vociferous among them called on the interjectors to be silent or leave the gathering. About twenty people, including the two who had spoken out, did get to their feet and leave; one of them reminding those left behind in a loud voice of the old saying that a fool and his money are soon parted.

Undeterred, Mundine pressed on, painting a picture of solid Sydney citizens - true sons of Albion - returning home to purchase harbourside mansions as a result of their bold decision to seize the opportunity given to them this night. The crowd loved it, their excitement growing by the minute. Cries of 'Hear, hear.' began to be heard around the auditorium as he explained what would be required of those enterprising gentlemen prepared to invest their capital and efforts in the *Fly River Gold Prospecting Association.*

His clinching argument was to hold up an official certificate, duly signed and sealed, proving that he, Ernest Mundine, had already put his money where his mouth was, and had invested five thousand pounds in this venture. He called on all present to join him, either by purchasing shares in the company, or by investing in the price of a ticket to the Fly River aboard the *Hoylake.*

By the end of the evening even *Bulldog* Homer found it difficult to believe there could be so many gullible fools in one place.

Over a hundred people stayed behind that evening to register their intention to invest in the *Fly River Gold Prospecting Association.* Within a week they had all purchased their share certificates and seventy-six of them had also paid for tickets to be taken to the Fly River aboard the *Hoylake.* Mundine gave them a list of the things they would need on the goldfield and informed them that all of these items could be purchased from a store in Goulburn Street, which specialized in equipping gold prospectors and adventurers bound for remote and unexplored regions.

Grateful for his advice they made a run on that establishment, cleaning it out of its stock of picks, shovels, gold pans and tent canvas. They also provided a nice profit for Mundine, who had rented the store for a month and had filled it with goods purchased elsewhere at a fraction of the price.

Even the rumour that Harris, the ship's mate, had refused to sail with them could not dampen their enthusiasm. They judged the officer to be a coward and a fool and welcomed his replacement by a former 2nd mate of a wool clipper, who had jumped ship in Melbourne some years earlier to join other gold seekers.

One of the investors, however, did take the time to question Harris about his concerns. Cecil Barnes was a solicitor, who was bored with life in Sydney, surrounded by wearisome legal documents. His craving for adventure had attracted him to the meeting at the Masonic Temple and he, like most of the people there, had been swept up in the euphoria of the moment. It was only later that he began to wonder if he'd made a mistake. He met Harris in a dockside pub and plied him with enough beer to loosen his tongue.

'What made you decide not to sail with us?' Barnes asked.

'Because that ship is a death trap. It won't survive another tropical storm, and you're heading off into the cyclone season. She's been overdue for a refit for years. Three years ago, we nearly didn't make it back. We were heading for an island north of Cape York to pick up some native women and we ran into a tropical storm that blew out our sails and was pushing us onto a reef. We were lucky that a schooner took us in tow just in time. We got some new sails up and managed to work our way off the reef. The schooner didn't, though.'

'What happened to it?'

'It ran up onto a reef.'

'Did you rescue its crew?'

'No. Homer ordered us to sail on.'

'You left them there to drown, even though they tried to rescue you?'

Harris nodded. 'Now you know what sort of man Homer is.'

The lawyer shook his head in disbelief. 'And you say your purpose was to pick up native women. Were they indentured workers?'

'Indentured workers! That's a joke. *Bulldog* Homer don't waste his time on natives with contracts.'

'So, he was a blackbirder.'

'Yeah! He was probably the worst of 'em. I could tell you stories about what he did to those natives that would make your skin crawl.'

'Women too?'

'Oh, he treated the women worst of all. The ones we were to pick up were to be sold to pearling skippers who'd use them as divers during the day, and entertainment for the crew at night.'

Barnes looked away in disgust. He returned to his office a worried man. He found it hard to believe that he had allowed himself to get caught up in the euphoria of gold fever without having done his homework on the people involved. He sat at his desk with his head in his hands as a battle raged within him between his conscience and his desire to protect his investment.

Eventually, it was his conscience that won, and he wrote to the Maritime Board raising concerns about the seaworthiness of the *Hoylake* and asking them to conduct their own survey before allowing it to leave Sydney.

7 October 1889 - Sydney

The Maritime Board's inspectors lost no time in carrying out the survey. Their report was damning. The vessel's hull leaked beyond the capacity of the pumps to cope in heavy weather; the rigging was rotten and unable to cope with a tropical storm; and, most serious of all, there weren't enough lifeboats for the number of passengers.

Their superiors studied the report and agreed to issue a notice that would prevent the *Hoylake* from leaving its mooring in Wooloomooloo Bay until the Board was satisfied that the ship was sufficiently seaworthy to carry passengers.

Homer and Mundine received the notice next morning. They were sitting in Homer's cabin, celebrating the handsome profit they had already made. Mundine was surprised that Homer seemed to take the news quite calmly.

'You don't seem too worried about this, Captain?'

'A temporary setback, Ernie; that's all.'

'A temporary setback! But they say the ship's not seaworthy.'

'Stop worrying, Mundine! One more voyage is all we need from this ship. The cyclone season is still a coupla months away. We'll have taken those mugs to their Eldorado and be back before the big blows start.'

'But they won't let us sail with passengers. So, it's all over.'

Homer laid the Maritime Board notice before Mundine and pointed to the section that gave the Board's main reason for preventing the ship from sailing.

'They 'ain't worried about the likes of you and me riskin' our necks aboard a leaky ship, Mundine. It's the passengers they're concerned about.'

'But we can't sail without the passengers. That's what this venture is all about.'

'I know that you fool. So, we don't take 'em as passengers. We sign 'em on as crew. After all, we are shorthanded.'

Mundine thought for a moment. 'Do you think that will really change the Maritime Board's decision?'

'Mundine, I've been at sea long enough to know that lily-livered dogs like the Maritime Board are only concerned about covering their own arses. If the record shows that the *Hoylake* isn't carrying passengers, then they'll clear us to sail – especially if a bit of pressure is put on them.'

'What sort of pressure? You're not thinking of threatening them, are you?'

'Of course not, you fool. I'm talking about political pressure. What's the name of that young bloke on your list whose old man is in the colonial government?'

'Stanwell. Lawrence Stanwell.'

'That's the one. Well, Mundine. I suggest you get young Mr. Lawrence Stanwell to talk to his dad about putting pressure on the Maritime Board to withdraw that notice.'

'Shall I tell him about your plan to sign them on as crew?'

'Naturally. And tell him that he and his mates will be signed on as ship's officers. That should appeal to him. And if it doesn't, remind him how much money he has already invested in this project. Spin a yarn about how most of it has already been used in overheads and can't be returned to him.'

'And what about you, Captain? Do you want to come with me?'

'No, Mundine. I want to find out who put the Maritime Board onto us.'

'How will you do that?'

'I'm meeting one of the inspectors for a drink at the Wooloomooloo hotel this afternoon. A small investment in good quality whiskey will loosen his tongue. So, you'd better dip into that war chest underneath your bunk and advance me a bit of drinkin' money.'

* * *

Sir Randolph McKay was a short, round man with a bald head and expansive mutton chop whiskers. As one of the longest serving members of the Legislative Council, and a close friend of Lawrence Stanwell's father, he had no trouble arranging a private meeting with the members of the Maritime Board.

'Gentlemen, where would this great land be if it were not for brave young men prepared to risk life and limb in a noble endeavour? We all know that the colony of Victoria has now surpassed New South Wales in wealth due to the vast quantity of gold discovered there. Sydney, Australia's oldest city is now lagging behind Melbourne, which forty years ago was nothing more than a scattering of slab huts. And why? It is because of gold, gentlemen. Gold - the very thing that these young adventurers are determined to find. There is nothing that is better able to restore the fortunes of this noble city, and indeed the whole colony, and cause us to hold up our heads in pride against the pretensions of Melbourne's *nouveaux riche.*'

'That is true, Sir Randolph,' the board chairman interjected. 'But our concerns are for the safety of these young adventurers. We don't consider the *Hoylake* to be in a fit condition to stand up to the tropical storms she's likely to encounter.'

'But what if they were to sign on as members of the crew, not as passengers? And what if the ship were to depart immediately, before the start of the cyclone season? With a fair wind she'll reach the Fly River within three weeks. The members of the expedition will be put ashore with their provisions, and the ship will return. Surely you must see that the level of risk is small.'

The discussion continued for nearly an hour until the chairman finally called a halt, indicating that all that could be said had been said, and that it was now time for the board to make a decision. He put the motion that the notice preventing the barquentine *Hoylake* from sailing should be withdrawn on condition that the vessel carried no passengers. The result was a tie, with an equal number of ayes as nays.

'This means that I, as chairman, have the casting vote,' he announced. 'I vote for the motion that the notice be withdrawn and therefore declare that to be the decision of the board.' He pounded the table with his wooden gavel.

The other members sat back in their seats, some of them glad to have the matter settled, and others shaking their heads resignedly, while the chairman rose from his seat to escort Sir Randolph to the door.

'Thank you for presenting your arguments so cogently, Sir Randolph,' he said as they shook hands.

'And thank you for your wise decision,' Sir Randolph replied. Then he whispered: 'I look forward to being able to recommend your re-appointment as chairman of the Maritime Board.'

They smiled knowingly to each other and Sir Randolph departed.

* * *

The meeting between *Bulldog* Homer and Cecil Barnes, however, was far less cordial. The young lawyer was about to leave his office when his exit was blocked by a huge man who pushed him back inside and closed the door behind them.

'What on earth are you doing!' he expostulated. 'You can't just burst in here like this! Get out right now before I call the police.'

His words ended in a gasp of pain as he felt Homer's left hand grip his throat and his right hand fasten onto his groin.

'Have you ever wondered what it would be like to be a eunuch, Mr. Barnes?' Homer whispered menacingly. 'Because that's what you're about to become. The only question is whether you'll be a live eunuch or a dead one.'

The pain shooting through his groin became excruciating as Homer increased the pressure of his vice-like grip. 'I hear you've been spreading rumours about me and my ship,' he snarled.

Homer then began to lift Barnes off his feet, causing the lawyer to scream in agony. He withdrew his hand from his victim's throat and clamped it over his mouth, stifling the scream. Then he gave one last squeeze with his right hand before dropping him to the ground, where the young man lay doubled up, moaning with pain and terror.

Homer squatted down beside him and grabbed him by the hair, turning his face upward and thrusting his own face towards him. 'This is just a taste of what you'll get if you say one more word to anyone about our little enterprise. Do you understand?'

Barnes, white faced with terror, whispered: 'Yes.'

Homer stood up and reached into his coat pocket. He pulled out a wad of bank notes and dropped them on Barnes' chest. 'My partner, Mr. Mundine, is far more generous than I am. He insisted that we should refund some of the money you invested. So, there it is – less the cost of various overheads. Now pick it up and say thank you.'

Barnes scrambled to his feet and bent over to retrieve the scattered banknotes. 'Thank you,' he said, unable to lift his eyes and look at Homer's face.

Homer took him by the throat again once more and whispered in a voice full of menace: 'Remember that I know where you live, Barnes. Don't make me want to come and visit you again.'

He stared once more into the young man's terror-filled eyes, then turned and left the office as suddenly as he had arrived, while Cecil Barnes collapsed into his office chair and remained there until he had finished trembling.

19 October 1889 – The Arafura Sea

The adventurers put to sea five days later, waving farewell to the comforting sight of Sydney Harbour as their ship turned north-east and began to track up along the east coast of Australia towards the new El Dorado. For three weeks they ploughed steadily north, taking the safer, but longer passage outside the Great Barrier Reef, pushed steadily onward by the prevailing south-easterly trade winds until they reached a point due east of Cape York, then turned west into the Torres Strait.

The barquentine had barely settled on its new heading when Jarvis, the new mate, knocked on Homer's door and reported an ominous-looking cloud formation just above the horizon dead ahead.

'I don't like the look of the sky, Cap'n,' he said. 'And the glass is falling too.'

Homer, who had been taking an after-lunch nap, struggled to his feet and looked at the barometer mounted on the bulkhead. He grunted angrily and then shoved Jarvis aside as he hurried up on deck. The mate was correct; the sky was turning dark green.

Homer swore violently. 'It's too bloody early in the season for tropical storms! Call all hands. I want a reef in those topsails now.'

'We'll need more than just reefs in the tops'ls, Captain. We need to get them in.'

'Don't question my orders, Jarvis,' Homer roared. 'Call the hands!'

Jarvis touched the peak of his cap and did as he was told. The sound of his voice bawling orders and the noise of seamen running on the deck above also woke Mundine from his afternoon nap. He joined Homer on the quarterdeck.

'Is there a problem?' he asked.

Homer pointed to the darkening sky. 'We're in for a blow, Mr. Mundine.'

'How bad, do you think?'

'Don't know. But with luck we may get across the strait before it hits us.'

'And if we don't?'

'Then it'll push us back the way we've come, and we'll lose days – maybe even weeks. I advise you to go to your cabin. You'll only be in the way up here.'

The crew had barely finished reefing the topsails when the wind began to strengthen and blow from the north-west, making it impossible for the helmsman to keep *Hoylake's* bow into the wind. With the additional strain on her rigging, she began to lose way.

Despite Homer's assurance that they would sight the coast of New Guinea within a day, the weather got worse, and no land was in sight. The heavy overcast and driving rain prevented him from taking a bearing with his sextant, and all he was left was dead reckoning and guesswork. The ship was also beginning to take in water through seams where the caulking had rotted away. So, he forced his unwilling passengers below to man the pumps, while keeping his few experienced seamen ready to go aloft to shorten sail if necessary.

Later that afternoon a sudden squall hit them. It snapped the rotten main top gallant yard, bringing it crashing down onto the deck, followed by a tangle of rigging. Fortunately, no one was injured, but even Homer began to grow anxious.

He turned to Jarvis, both of them red-eyed from lack of sleep, and barked his orders. 'There's nothing left for us to do but to turn and run before the wind. Get everybody you can on deck; seamen aloft and passengers on deck ready to haul on the sheets and braces. As soon as there's a lull, we'll bring her about.'

As luck would have it the wind did drop slightly for long enough to bring the ship around so that it was now blowing across the stern, pushing them back in the direction they'd come from. They ran before the wind all that day and throughout the following night, the pumps clanking continuously as the exhausted gold seekers toiled for two hours at a stretch, then sank into their hammocks asking themselves repeatedly what insanity had persuaded them to do this to themselves.

* * *

By daybreak, the *Hoylake* was in trouble. Her topsails had blown out and were hanging in rags from the yards. The wind by now had reached gale force and the heavy overcast, flying spray and absence of landmarks made it impossible to estimate their position with any degree of certainty. Jarvis was becoming increasingly anxious about what might be lying ahead of them. He made one last attempt to appeal to Homer.

'We gotta go south, skipper. If we can get under the lee of the mainland, we might have a chance. But if we keep running like this, we're as likely as not to run up on a reef.'

'Shut yer trap,' Homer snarled. 'I haven't come this far to give up yet. I've got too much invested in it! By my reckoning we should reach the southeast corner of New Guinea today if we stay on this course.'

'We could also be running directly for Warrior Reef!'

'So, double the watch, you fool. I've been sailing these waters for twenty years. Do you think I don't know about Warrior Reef?'

Jarvis touched his cap and ordered another seaman to the masthead to join the lookout already there. As soon as he had gone Mundine, green with seasickness, joined Homer on deck.

'I heard you tell Jarvis we're heading for the coast of New Guinea. What are we going to do there?'

'Put our passengers ashore and let them start panning for gold.'

'I thought the Fly River was in the direction we came from?'

'It is. But I can't risk the ship by turning beam on to this wind. Anyway, these fools haven't a clue where we are. The first river we find we'll tell 'em is the Fly River.'

'What if they twig to what we're doing?'

'They won't; not until we're long gone.'

'So, you intend to leave them there?'

'What the hell do you think I intended to do? We've got their money. We take them to El Dorado. Then we sail away into the sunrise.'

'But what happens when they wake up to what's happened and get back to Australia? Every copper in the colonies will be lookin' for us.'

'We 'aint goin' to Australia. You remember our friend Marcel, or Maaso, as he likes to be called by his associates with bones through their noses. He owes us thirty women. By now he's probably got even more ready for us.

He might even have some boys as well. The German planters love the boys. They can train them more easily and they can get more years out of them.'

'We'll drop our passengers on the coast, sail for Marcel's island, then on to those plantations up in the Bismarck Sea, like we did before. After that we'll make for Manila and divide the profits. I'll sell the *Hoylake,* buy myself a decent house, find a nice Philippino girl or two, and settle down.'

'And what about me? What do I do?'

'I've no idea, Mundine. And neither do I care.'

* * *

Perhaps it was the relief that comes after being delivered from days of gut-wrenching seasickness; or perhaps it was the blind optimism of the inveterate fortune hunter. Whatever it was, the decreasing strength of the wind and the sight of an emerging land mass, backed by jungle clad mountains brought cheers of excitement from dozens of throats as *Hoylake* made her way steadily towards the south eastern corner of New Guinea.

'There you are, lads,' Homer boomed from the quarterdeck. 'Didn't I tell you we'd sight New Guinea within a day or so?'

Lawrence Stanwell called out to Homer, asking the question that was on everyone's mind. 'How long before we sight the Fly River, Captain?'

'Not too long now, I suspect, Mr. Stanwell. By my reckoning we should be within twenty miles of the position reported by Captain Blackwood.'

The young gentleman hardly had time to return to the ship's rail before a cry was heard from the lookout; 'River mouth ahead, fine on the port bow.'

'Well, there you are, gentlemen. Before you is the Fly River, just as I promised.'

A spontaneous burst of cheering erupted from the excited passengers, who were now shaking hands and slapping each other's backs, all their previous regrets having vanished like mist in the morning sun.

Mundine sidled up to Homer and whispered: 'Which river is it, really?'

'Who cares?' Homer replied. 'But as long as they think it's the Fly River, we've nothing to worry about.'

* * *

By late afternoon the gold-seekers were ashore and had selected a site for the base camp. They were somewhat surprised that the river was smaller than they'd assumed. However, as none of them had ever taken the time to read Captain Blackwood's report, they just accepted Homer's assurance that this was indeed the place.

They chose a flat, grassy area on the western bank as their site. It was close enough to the river to enable easy access, but far enough away to minimize the danger of lurking crocodiles, and high enough to keep them safe from an unexpected flash flood. Lawrence Stanwell took charge of a dozen armed men and positioned them around the camp site to guard against any possible attack by natives, while the others carried stores from the boats and set up their tents.

It was an excited body of men who gathered around the campfire that night to listen to the leaders of the expedition detail how things were to proceed, starting the following day. It was then that Captain Homer surprised them by announcing that the *Hoylake* would return to Sydney on the morning tide. This brought forth a barrage of angry objections from the prospectors, who had assumed that the ship would remain anchored in the river mouth, ready to carry them away should disaster strike.

Stanwell led the attack. 'You cannot be serious, Captain. When we put our money into this venture, we naturally assumed that you and Mundine were to be part of it equally with us. Your ship is our lifeline to civilization.'

The prospectors roared their support and some of them began to express more than mere arguments for the ship and her crew to stay. Mundine began to feel increasingly anxious, especially as he saw signs of one of Homer's rages developing. He could also see that the mood of the prospectors was growing uglier, and the fact that many of them were armed caused him great alarm. So, he stood to his feet and called for calm.

'Gentlemen, gentlemen. Let us not become unduly alarmed by this. You saw for yourselves how sorely Captain Homer's ship was battered by that gale a couple of days ago. You yourselves spent hours manning the pumps just to keep her afloat. If she's to be your lifeline to civilization, then she has to return to it for long enough to get her rigging replaced and hull re-caulked. You need have no fear that she'll return as soon as those repairs have been completed. After all, both Captain Homer and I have considerable sums of money invested in this expedition. We want it to succeed every bit as much as you do.'

He was relieved to see Homer calming down and the murmuring begin to diminish. He was almost ready to breathe a sigh of relief when a man from the back of the group stood up and pushed his way to the front. He was a big man – as big as Homer – and not easily intimidated.

'Then you stay with us until the ship returns,' he said.

A roar of approval burst from the assembled gold-seekers. Mundine felt himself going pale. He looked to Homer for support but found his partner nodding his agreement too.

'If you leave me here, I'll tell them what you intend to do,' he whispered in the captain's ear.

Homer's face blackened and his eyes hardened. Mundine felt panic rising within him as Homer reached for him, then slid his huge paw down onto Mundine's shoulder. He leaned towards him and whispered in his ear.

'Be on the beach at four o'clock tomorrow morning. Don't let anyone see you. I'll have you picked up in one of the ship's boats. We'll be away before they know what's happened.'

Mundine breathed a sigh of relief. He held his hands up to signal for quiet and then announced to the crowd that, as evidence of their *bona fides*, he would gladly stay with them until the *Hoylake* returned.

'Then all is well, gentlemen,' young Mr. Stanwell reassured them. 'We have our assurance. Tomorrow Captain Homer can depart to refit his ship and return as soon as he can to learn of his share in what we will have discovered.'

The gold seekers, reassured, drifted off to their tents to get a good night's rest, ready for the big day ahead. Homer winked slyly to Mundine before walking back to the beach, where a small boat waited to take him back to his ship. As soon as he was aboard, he ordered Jarvis to have the vessel ready to sail on the early morning tide.

Mundine went to his tent, relieved, but still anxious. He had no way of being sure that he would wake up in time to be on the beach at the time Homer had indicated. So, he lay on his camp bed all night, looking at his pocket watch by the light of a spluttering candle, smoking and worrying.

Just before four o'clock next morning he slipped silently out of his tent, carefully avoiding the armed guards, whose positions he had carefully noted the night before, and made his way down to the beach, where he waited with mounting anxiety for Homer's boat to come out of the darkness to pick him up. The blackness of the night only served to accentuate his fears, and his ears became super-sensitive to every sound. His over-active imagination turned every animal screech from the jungle behind him into a party of head-hunting natives, and every ripple in the water into a crocodile. But it was the latter that terrified him most. The estuarine crocodiles that infest the rivers and coastal waters of New Guinea - living links with the dinosaurs of pre-historic times, sometimes growing to twenty feet in length – like those of northern Australia are amongst the most terrifying of predators. Mundine remembered how Captain Homer had regaled him with stories of how they would lie silently in the water for hours with only their eyes above the surface, waiting for the moment to pounce on an unsuspecting victim.

And so, he waited, and waited, praying for the sound of approaching oars which never came. The *Hoylake* - its anchor chain and capstan muffled to reduce noise - had departed an hour earlier and was well out to sea when the huge reptile shot out of the river, where it had been watching him for an hour, and grabbed Mundine before he even had time to react. Its enormous jaws clamped on to his legs with a vice-like grip and dragged him back into deep water, where it rolled him over and under the surface until his pitiful struggles finally ceased and he drowned, his mouth still open as he tried unsuccessfully to scream his terror.

22 November 1889 – The Torres Strait

Fata looked up and saw an outrigger canoe skimming across the lagoon, heading for the beach as fast as the three men aboard could paddle. As it slid up onto the sand two of them pulled it up onto the beach while the third ran to the village, shouting a warning as he went.

Sele heard the noise and joined Fata. 'What is it? What are they saying?'

Yauwii suddenly appeared carrying Maaso's cutlass. He said something to Fata, pointing out to sea.

'He say black ship come.'

'What is the black ship?'

'He say it ship belong white devil with shining teeth. He say him white devil who buy women from Maaso. He man Maaso want sell you to.'

'Captain Homer!'

'Yes.

'That's the man Michael saved from being wrecked and then left him to drown.'

'Yes, Sele. He very evil man.'

'Do you think he's expecting to find Maaso here with more women for him?'

'Yes.'

'Then we must take all the women and children to the caves in the hills.

The villagers usually avoided those caves, believing them to be the home of spirits. But their fear of the black ship was greater. So, at Sele's word, they climbed the steep hillside, carrying their small children and whatever food they had in their huts.

With Fata interpreting, she told them: 'This is the place that God has provided for us. There are no evil spirits here; only God's Spirit who has led me to bring you here.'

They dropped their loads to the ground and looked nervously at the promised refuge. Then, one of the women, scooping up her baby and basket of taro, said something Sele couldn't understand, and went into the cave. Another woman followed her, and then another, and another. Soon, they were all inside; men, women and children, completely hidden from the view of anyone at sea level.

'What you want we do now, Sele?' Fata asked.

'I want you to go down to the bottom of the hillside and watch for Homer and his men. Watch what they do, then come back and tell me.'

'And what you do?'

'I will pray for deliverance. Now, tell the people what I have just told you, and tell them that they must all remain completely silent - even the children. Tell the mothers to put their hands over the children's mouths if they have to.'

In the lagoon below a boatload of armed seamen was pulling towards the shoreline. *Bulldog* Homer was the first to step ashore, a brace of revolvers stuck in his belt and a puzzled look in his eye. Jarvis joined him as the boat was pulled up onto the shingle.

'Where are they?' he asked.

'Maybe Marcel is off on another raid,' Homer replied. 'But there ought to be someone here to meet us. The canoe we spotted must have seen the ship approaching. Leave one man here to guard the boats and the rest will follow me to the village.'

They set off at a jog trot and soon entered the deserted village. He ordered his men to search the houses while he looked inside the one where he knew Marcel lived, but he found it empty.

Jarvis made his report. 'There's nobody 'ere, Cap'n,'

'What's this?' he asked, pointing to the wooden cross outside Marcel's former dwelling.

'Looks like a church,' the mate replied.

'Yeah; and what's more, there's nothin' inside except a table and another cross, like you see at the front of a church.'

'Do you think Marcel's got religion, skipper?'

'I've seen stranger things happen in these islands,' Homer muttered. 'But I doubt it. Somethin's happened here. I think Marcel's gone. But the natives are around somewhere; their canoes are still on the beach. But where the hell are they?'

'These ashes are still hot, skipper,' Jarvis said poking into the smouldering remains of the communal fire trench.

'Then they can't be far away. Tell the men to spread out. We'll pull the jungle apart if we have to.'

With Homer and Jarvis at the centre of the line, they began to comb the bush, looking for traces of the missing villagers. When this produced no result, Homer ordered his men to return to the village to start another sweep; this time heading inland towards the high ground leading up to the peak that towered above them.

From his hiding place behind a rocky outcrop Fata saw them approaching. He counted nine men, all of them armed and led by a huge white man brandishing two revolvers. They kept coming closer and closer until Fata realized he had left it too late to change his position. So, he crouched lower behind the rock and peered through a crack.

Then he saw the big man order the advancing line to stop while he opened a brass telescope and began to scan the slope above.

'They must have gone up there,' Fata heard him say. 'There's nowhere else they could have gone.'

Suddenly, the silence of the afternoon was broken by the distant sound of a baby's cry, which stopped almost as quickly as it began.

Jarvis pointed to the hilltop. 'Up there, skipper. It came from up there.'

An evil grin came across Homer's face. 'That was a kid. That means there's women up there; and women is what we've come for.'

'There might be warriors up there too, skipper. We could be walking into a trap. We'd be crawlin' up there on our hands and knees. They could be on us before we knew it.'

Homer nodded then called out to the men. 'Back to the ship, lads. If they're hiding up there waiting to pounce on us, we're going to need more guns than we've got here. Let's give 'em a couple of volleys to let 'em know what they're in for. Then we'll give 'em a night to worry about it and come back tomorrow with the rest of the lads.'

He drew his pistols and, pointing them up the hillside, began to shoot into the bush. The rest of his men cocked their rifles and did the same. Fata pressed his face into the ground as bullets sprayed in all directions over his head. The unaccustomed noise and the sharp twang of bullets cutting through the trees and ricocheting off rocks shocked and temporarily disoriented him. He covered his ears with his hands and curled himself into a ball as the firing and yelling continued. Then, as the echoes reverberated around the crags above, the seamen turned around and made their way back to their boat.

Fata remained as he was for several minutes, then peered over the lip of the rock and saw that they'd all gone. He scrambled back to where Sele and the others lay hidden, to tell them the worst.

23 November 1889 – The Torres Strait

Lieutenant Commander Morton, captain of Her Majesty's Ship *Seraph*, looked up wearily as a knock on his cabin door interrupted his breakfast.

'What is it?' he bawled.

The door opened to reveal the anxious face of *Seraph's* only midshipman.

'Mr. Farmer's compliments, sir. He says to report a ship anchored off an island dead ahead. He thinks it may be the *Hoylake*, sir.'

'Tell Mr. Farmer I shall come up on deck.'

The midshipman scurried back to the first lieutenant, while Moreton drained his coffee and followed him. There had been a signal about the *Hoylake* waiting for him two weeks earlier when the *Seraph* had made her scheduled call into Darwin, ordering him to watch out for the barquentine and ensure that its activities remained strictly in accordance with the law.

Lieutenant Farmer touched the peak of his cap and pointed to the island dead ahead.

'She fits the description of the *Hoylake,* sir; a three masted barquentine with a black hull.'

'Take her in, Mr. Farmer; and have an armed party ready to board her.'

'Aye, aye, sir.'

The lookout on the *Hoylake* had also spotted the approaching warship and reported this to the mate, who ran below deck to alert Homer. Homer followed him back up on deck and trained his telescope on the *Seraph.* A string of profanities erupted from his mouth as he spied the White Ensign flying from the stern of the ungainly looking vessel that belched black smoke from her single funnel as she made for the entrance to the lagoon.

'Get all the firearms out of sight,' Homer yelled. 'Put 'em down in the hold somewhere where a boarding party won't find 'em. Then get the men working on the rigging. Make it look like we're here to repair storm damage.'

Jarvis called all hands and got them to work on repairs, while Homer watched anxiously as the gunboat approached. Though the *Seraph* was small – steam driven with two masts for auxiliary wind power – she packed enough punch in her single four-inch gun and four six pounders to deter aggressive action by ships like the *Hoylake.* So *Bulldog* Homer, contrary to his usual, aggressive nature, decided that acquiescence would be his best defence.

Thirty minutes later *Seraph* hove to, a cable's length to windward of the anchored barquentine. By this time *Hoylake* was a hive of activity. Some of her crew were working on repairs to broken rigging while others were attempting to re-attach the collapsed yard to the mast.

'She's the *Hoylake* right enough, sir.'

Morton nodded and raised his speaking trumpet. 'Ahoy there. This is Her Majesty's Ship *Seraph.* I'm sending a boarding party to you. Do not make any attempt to resist them.'

Homer picked up his own speaking trumpet and replied. 'Ahoy *Seraph*. I have no intention of resisting you. I'm here to make repairs to my ship.'

Even as they spoke the warship's longboat was filling up with armed sailors. The young midshipman, with a holstered revolver that seemed too large for his body, climbed down into the stern sheets, ready to order them to cast off.

'I've put Niven in charge of the boarding party, sir,' Farmer reported. 'His orders are to check the ship's manifest and log, and to search for natives or any other suspicious items on board.'

'Very well. Tell him he can cast off.'

Lieutenant Farmer ordered the longboat away and six seamen bent their backs to the oars, sending the longboat skimming across the gently lapping waters. The cox'n brought her alongside to where a rope ladder hung from *Hoylake's* side, and Midshipman Niven led his sailors up onto her deck.

Bulldog Homer was standing by the main mast ready to meet him, towering over the diminutive midshipman as he approached with eight armed sailors behind him.

'I am Midshipman Niven of Her Majesty's Ship *Seraph*,' the young man's voice trembled slightly as he looked up at the huge bulk of the man standing before him, legs apart and hands clasped behind his back. 'I have orders to examine your ship's manifest and log, and to search for any illegal items or persons. My captain also wants to know what you are doing here.'

Homer stared directly into the young officer's eyes for a couple of seconds before answering. 'My ship has sustained storm damage. I have anchored here in the lee of this island so that I can conduct emergency repairs. My papers will show that the *Hoylake* has been chartered by the *Fly River Gold Prospecting Association* to transport an expeditionary party to the Fly River. This I have done, and I am now en route to Sydney where I will have my ship properly refitted.'

'If your destination is Sydney, Captain, what are you doing this far north?' Niven asked, growing bolder by the moment.

Homer bent forward so that his face was only inches away from the young man. 'Because a great big wind blew me here.'

Niven's face turned red with embarrassment as he saw the barquentine's crew laughing and heard sniggers coming from his own men standing behind him. He tried to recover his dignity by ordering two of the sailors to follow him while the others kept watch on deck. Unfortunately, his voice broke as he gave the order, making his attempt to speak with authority sound more like a squeak, which raised even louder guffaws from *Hoylake's* crew. Finally, he managed to compose himself and order Homer to show him the ship's log.

Five minutes later he was back on deck and ordered a petty officer to take four men and search the ship. He tried to maintain an appearance of being in charge but found himself increasingly anxious for the petty officer to return and report that all was well, so that he could escape back to the *Seraph* with whatever vestiges of his dignity still remained intact.

After what seemed an eternity, the petty officer reappeared and reported that all seemed to be in order. Relieved, Midshipman Niven thanked Captain Homer and climbed back into the longboat, followed by his men. Five minutes later he made his report to Lieutenant Commander Moreton.

'Well, it seems that we have nothing to be concerned about, then.'

'No, sir,' the younger man said. 'But…'

'But what? Speak up man if there's something on your mind.'

Niven blushed again. 'I…I just didn't like the look of the man, sir.'

'What do you mean; you didn't like the look of him?'

'Well, I really don't know how to describe it, sir. But Captain Homer is a very…well, very aggressive and rather brutal looking character.'

'Sounds like most of the senior officers I've served with,' Moreton snorted. 'Come on, snotty. Half the sea captains alive are rough looking rascals. You've got to have more than the fact you didn't like his face.'

'Well, sir. It was just something about him...like the way he winked at his mate when he told me to go ahead and search his ship. It was almost as though he was prepared for it.'

Moreton turned to Lieutenant Farmer. 'What do you think, Number One?'

'Don't know, sir. I've been trying to recall if *Hoylake* and Homer were among the names I've heard before. They seem familiar, somehow. But I can't be sure.'

'You think they may have been blackbirders?'

'Could be, sir. There are a lot of seemingly respectable ships' masters in these parts that used to be blackbirders but got out of the trade once the authorities tightened up the laws.'

'Well, I think we will let Captain Homer know that we'll remain here until he completes his repairs and sets sail. We'll also tell him that we'll be cruising these waters for some time to come and will be keeping an eye on him. Niven, pass me my speaking trumpet.'

* * *

High above the shoreline, Sele, Fata and the people of Mabi sat in anxious silence as they ate their scanty breakfast. Despite Sele's exhortations for them to trust in God and Fata's whispered Bible stories of divine deliverance, the villagers' fear was palpable.

'What are they doing, Fata. Why haven't they come back. I've prayed all night for God to send an angel to deliver us. But nothing has happened.'

Fata placed his hand gently on Sele's shoulder. 'If God want send angel, then He do it. We go see.'

They scrambled down the rocky slope to the grassy area above the beach, then cautiously moved onto the beach, where Fata stopped dead in his tracks and pointed out to sea.

'There, Sele. There is answer.' An ugly white ship with smoke belching from its funnel was beginning to move away from the island. Beyond it was the black hulled barquentine, all sails set, heading towards the horizon.'

'What ship is that?' Sele asked.

'It warship, Sele. I see it before. Look, see guns.'

'But why is it here?'

'It hunts ships that steal people from islands.'

'Oh Fata, how wonderful! How wonderful! Our prayers have been answered. I wonder what its name is?'

'I know name, Sele. I remember from when I see it before. It name *Seraph*.'

Sele put her hand to her mouth and gasped in wonder. '*Seraph,*' she said. 'A seraph is an angel.'

'Yes,' Fata replied, pointing to the ship. 'You ask God to send angel. God, He send that angel.'

November 25 – The Solomon Sea

Two days later, as the *Hoylake* sailed into the maze of reefs at the northern end of the Torres Strait, Jarvis knocked on Homer's cabin door.

'We need to go easy on the crew, skipper. They haven't had a rest for weeks and they're exhausted.'

'I don't give a damn if they're nearly dead,' Homer snarled. 'I want to get this ship to Manila before we strike any more storms. They can rest for as long as they like then. They'll have plenty of money to do it with. So, you can get back up top and keep them at it. I'll flog any man who refuses to obey. You can tell 'em that's a promise; and *Bulldog* Homer always keeps his word.'

'I'll tell 'em, skipper. But they're starting to look mutinous to me, and there's only two of us against fifteen of them.'

Homer went to his locked cupboard and took out two revolvers. He gave one to Jarvis and the other he stuck in his own belt. 'Then make sure they see you've got this and that you are ready to use it. Now, get back up on deck and do as I said.'

Jarvis was right. The Malays were in an ugly mood. Days spent working the pumps whenever they weren't aloft had brought them to the limits of their endurance. So, Homer and Jarvis began to drive them mercilessly, enforcing their orders with fists and boots as they tried to put as much distance as possible between themselves and the Australian mainland.

Unfortunately, the wind began to increase in strength again and Homer had to tack his ship time and again to maintain any headway. It meant that the exhausted sailors who had been replaced at the pumps were constantly going aloft to shorten sail, or haul on the braces to bring the ship onto a new tack.

The mutiny, when it broke out, was unplanned and spontaneous. One unusually large wave washed over the starboard bow, tore off one of the hatches and poured into the decks below, sweeping the weary men at the pumps from their feet and leaving them standing in sea water up to their waists. It was an isolated event and in itself posed no great threat to the ship, but for the bone-weary sailors it was the last straw.

Panic took hold of them, and they dragged themselves up through the broken hatch and onto the main deck. Homer saw them and drew his pistol, threatening to kill any man who refused to return to the pumps. But the Malays were past caring. They charged at him in a solid mass. His first shot took one of them in the chest, killing him instantly, and the second went through another man's shoulder. But instead of intimidating them, it enraged them further; and before he had chance to pull the trigger again, they were on him, punching, kicking and gouging at his eyes with savagery born of terror and months of abuse.

Jarvis saw what was happening and drew his revolver. Then he saw more seamen coming down from the rigging to join the mutineers. He immediately changed his mind and ran below to lock himself in his cabin. Homer saw him go and uttered a stream of profanities. But before he had chance to join him, half a dozen Malays were on him, beating him unconscious.

The crew, seeing Homer lying motionless, left him there as they made a mad rush for the ship's boats. Despite the ferocity of the wind and the state of the sea, they managed to launch the cutter and the jolly boat, scrambling aboard and pulling at the oars with all their might to get away from the foundering ship. But *Hoylake* refused to sink. Half full of water and buffeted around like a cork in a whirlpool, she drifted helplessly until the gale blew itself out as quickly as it had arisen.

For the next two days Homer and Jarvis struggled in vain to maintain steerage and to keep the ship running before the wind, hoping that it would not push them onto a reef. Homer tried hard to keep a lid on the rage boiling inside him over his mate's cowardly run for safety, leaving him alone to face the mutinous crew. He realized that his survival depended as much on Jarvis as it did on his own efforts. So, he consoled himself with thoughts of how he would exact a brutal and bloody revenge if they managed to survive this ordeal.

But that moment never came. After two punishing days of taking turns at the ship's wheel, they were both so exhausted that they just gave up. They retreated below deck and, fortified by what was left of Mundine's Jamaica rum, awaited whatever was to come.

It came first in the form of two large tiger sharks that had been following them for days. It was Jarvis who saw them. 'My God, skipper! Look at the size of 'em.'

Homer dragged himself to his feet and followed Jarvis' outstretched arm pointing through the cabin's stern window. 'Bloody hell! I'm glad we didn't take to the boats with those buggers following.'

'I've heard some of the old South Sea hands talk about sharks having a sixth sense about boats in trouble and following them for days, hoping the survivors throw the dead bodies overboard.'

'Or maybe they just learn by experience that ships chuck food scraps overboard. Anyway, do you think the sharks then leave a boat alone if they get a dead body to feed on?'

'Dunno, skipper.'

'Then let's find out.'

He pulled his revolver out of his waistband and pointed it at Jarvis. 'You thought I'd forgotten about you runnin' away and leaving me to face those mutinous dogs on my own, didn't you.'

'No, skipper. I thought you was right behind me.'

'You lying bastard. Let's see if those sharks like you better than I do.' He aimed the pistol at the terrified mate's head and pulled the trigger. There was the sound of a click but nothing else. Homer cocked the revolver again and pulled the trigger, but with the same result. He threw the empty firearm aside in disgust and with a wild roar launched himself at Jarvis, determined to beat the smaller man to a pulp. But the terrified mate had already drawn his own revolver from his belt and managed to get off one wild shot before Homer was on him.

It didn't go where he'd intended and pierce Homer's heart; the gun was pointing too far down for that. Even so, a .45 calibre round, fired at close range, will bring down even the largest of men, and when it strikes the victim's belly, it causes a terrible wound that few ultimately survive. But the hours of agony that precede death usually cause the victim to wish their assailant's aim had been better, and *Bulldog* Homer, for the first time he could remember, found himself begging for mercy – this time for a clean shot through the head that would put him out of his misery.

But Jarvis could not oblige him. The bullet lodged in Homer's enormous belly had been his last. So, when he finally realized that his fearsome captain was no longer able to defend himself, Jarvis settled down to terrorize him as he'd seen Homer do so many times before. He refused Homer's requests for rum to deaden his senses and tormented him further by taking his own swigs from a newly opened bottle. When Homer begged for water, he filled a mug and deliberately left it on the cabin floor where Homer could see it but just beyond his reach. Finally, as Homer weakened further, he announced that he was now going to feed him to the sharks, whose dorsal fins, cutting through the water in the ship's wake, were clearly visible through the stern window.

He began to drag Homer across the cabin floor and then tried to lift the screaming giant up high enough to rest his bulk on the window ledge, where shards of broken glass from the shattered window lacerated his body. But before he could maneuver this dead weight high enough to tip him over into the depths below, he looked out towards the horizon and saw ten large war canoes from one of the islands of the Louisiade Archipelago, where their black hulled ship was well-known and feared, manned by warriors, some of whom had lost wives and daughters to what they called the *devil ship*.

'Oh my God!' Jarvis whispered. Homer turned his head towards the sea and saw them too. For the first time in his miserable life, he realized that he was now totally helpless against people who were as cruel as he was. And like all bullies, it terrified him, and he began to tremble uncontrollably. He was still shaking when the headhunters came aboard.

12 May 1890 – Cape York Peninsula

On his way back from Cairns after delivering another load of pearl shell to the steamer bound for Sydney, Michael called in to Cooktown to see the manager of his bank. Then he made his way up to the mission house where Amelia and Geoffrey were waiting for him on the veranda.

'I saw a trim schooner enter the river through my telescope,' Geoffrey said, shaking his hand, 'And I knew it had to be you, didn't I, my love.'

'You did indeed, dear,' Amelia answered, standing on tiptoe to kiss Michael's cheek. 'But tell me, Michael; don't you think it's time you got yourself a proper house to live in?' A successful businessman and police magistrate shouldn't be living on a boat.'

'*Wahine 2* is a ship, Mrs. Glaston. Boats have oars.'

'Alright, ship then. But you are a man of some importance now, not just the captain of a schooner.'

'Well actually, I have my eye on a house overlooking Refuge Bay. It used to belong to the man whose luggers were wrecked in the cyclone.

The house got damaged too. It lost its roof and some of its walls. But its basic structure is still sound, and its location is glorious. The bloke who lived there lost everything in that cyclone and couldn't meet his mortgage payments. So, the bank repossessed it and is prepared to sell it for what is owed to them.'

'You've talked to them about this? Geoffrey asked.

'Yes. This very morning. The manager is more than happy to extend my credit so that I can buy it and return it to its former glory.'

'Well, that is marvelous. Now come inside and you can tell us all about it.'

'I will. But first I have to do something I've been wanting to do for years.'

'And what's that, old chap?' Geoffrey asked.

'To give you this.' Michael took a bank cheque from his pocket and gave it to Geoffrey, whose eyes opened wide with astonishment as he looked at it.

'My dear fellow. This is for five hundred pounds.' He showed it to Amelia who put her hand to her mouth, unable to find the right words to say.

'I promised that one day I'd repay your generosity for sending me those fifty guineas that had been given to you, and now I've been able to do it.'

'But…but it's far too much.'

'And we never expected you to have to repay that money,' Amelia added. 'After all you did save our lives.'

'No, I want you to have it.' Michael insisted. 'I know that clergymen don't earn much money, and those fifty guineas could have made a lot of difference to you.'

Geoffrey smiled. 'We believe that God always provides for our needs as long as we remained in the centre of his will.'

Michael shrugged his shoulders. 'Well, that's as may be. But now maybe He wants me to help Him do it. So, just take it, it's yours.'

'But, my dear chap, five hundred pounds! We've never even seen that much money, let alone possess it!'

'I insist, and that's my final word. I'm sure you'll find a good use for it.'

There was a knock at the door, and Geoffrey went to answer it, leaving Michael and Amelia alone.

'This is so generous of you, Michael,' she said. 'Perhaps we could use it to help Sele and Fata in their work. They've not only been preaching the gospel, they are also trying to stop the dreadful abuse of natives by devils like Captain Homer.'

'And if he ever comes back to these waters, I'll track him down myself, now that I represent the law. But tell me, what else have you heard about Sele?'

'She's in Sydney now, speaking at public meetings.'

'Sele is in Sydney?'

'Yes. Her health has broken down. She's had malaria – it's endemic in those islands, you know.'

'Yes, I know. But how bad is she?'

'Her last letter indicated she was much improved. But she won't be able to return.'

'What will she do?'

'Probably stay in Sydney and work with the mission committee down there. She's much in demand as a speaker you know. She's a great asset in raising support for the work in the islands.'

'Why didn't Geoffrey tell me she was there?'

'Because she asked Geoffrey not to tell you. She knew you would go looking for her.'

'So, she still doesn't want to see me.'

'Of course she wants to see you, you silly man. She just doesn't want you to know it.'

Michael looked puzzled. 'If she wants to see me and she knows I want to see her, why doesn't she want me to know?'

'Oh Michael, why can't men understand what is so clearly obvious?'

Somehow, the logic of Amelia's argument escaped him. But he was glad to accept the slip of paper she pressed into his hand. It was the address of a house in Sydney.

She put her finger to her lips and said, 'Don't tell Geoffrey I told you this.'

8 August 1890 - Sydney

Sydney's mild winter days tend to take a turn for the worse in the first weeks of August. Grey skies and strong westerly winds, blowing down from the Blue Mountains, bring an uncharacteristic bleakness to a city usually known for its warm, sunny climate. It certainly was so the afternoon that Michael knocked on the door of a small suburban villa in the suburb of Annandale, a few miles west of the city centre. He could feel his heart pounding as he rapped the brass knocker.

Moments later it opened to reveal an elderly woman with a heavy shawl around her shoulders.

Michael raised his cap. 'Good afternoon, ma'am. I was told that Miss Sele Saena lives here.'

'She did until this morning,' the woman replied. 'She's gone away on a speaking tour for the mission.'

Michael's face fell. 'When will she be back?'

'She's not coming back here. Now she's recovered from her illness she's thinking about going home to Samoa as soon as her speaking engagements are over.'

Michael was devastated by the news. 'Do you know where her first speaking engagement is to be held?'

'Yes. It's in the city, at the Morrison Street Congregational Church. She's addressing the Christian Women's Temperance Union.'

'At what time?'

'Three o'clock. But you'll never make it now.'

Michael was already hurrying back through the front gate as he raised his cap and thanked her. She watched him run down the street towards the tram stop, wondering what business a sea captain would have with a lady missionary - and a coloured one at that.

The meeting had concluded by the time Michael found the church. Most of the people had departed, but there were still a few ladies cleaning up and putting chairs away. He approached one of them.

'Good afternoon, ma'am. I understand Miss Saena spoke at your meeting this afternoon.'

'Oh yes,' she answered. 'She was so inspiring. I don't think I've ever heard such a challenging and uplifting message. And they tell us that women can't be ministers!'

'And she's so beautiful,' one of the others joined in. 'Not exactly like a European woman; more exotic and eastern looking.'

'And she doesn't wear any cosmetics or jewellery,' added a third.

Michael felt his impatience rising. 'Sele Saena doesn't need cosmetics and jewellery,' he snapped. 'Is she still here?'

They looked a little startled and began to shake their heads in unison.

'N...no, she left about half an hour ago.'

'Where did she go to?' Michael's exasperation was very evident.

'Central Railway Station. She has to catch a train to somewhere. Do you remember which one it was, Gladys? Was it to Bathurst?'

'No, I think it was to Goulburn,' Gladys replied.

'No, that was last week. I think it was Bathurst; or was it Maitland...?'

Michael left them to their debate and rushed out of the church hall. They turned and watched him go.

'What a rude man!' said Gladys.

'Yes, indeed!' her friend replied. 'But a rather handsome one, don't you think?'

The three of them began to giggle and returned to stacking the chairs.

Sydney's Central Railway Station was a handsome sandstone building that housed the terminus of a network of railway lines that spread across New South Wales. Michael arrived there breathlessly twenty minutes later. He searched the departures board and saw that the only train due to depart in the next thirty minutes was abound for the town of Bathurst. He hurried to the platform and scanned the faces of those preparing to board, but Sele was not amongst them.

An elderly man was standing at the barrier, searching through his pockets for his railway ticket while the station assistant waited patiently for him to produce it. Michael saw his opportunity. He took his used tram ticket from his pocket, flashed it briefly in the direction of the station assistant, who was busy concentrating on the other man, then hurried to the waiting train. He strode along the platform, looking through the carriage windows, scanning the faces of those already on board.

Each carriage had several compartments with two rows of bench seats facing each other. Some, already full, had their doors shut. It was in one of these, three quarters of the way along the length of the train, that he saw her, sitting next to the window on the far side of the compartment, her head buried in a book.

Michael felt his heart surge within him. It had troubled him greatly that he'd been unable to picture her face in his mind. But now it was as though he had awoken from a bad dream to discover that everything he longed for was right before his eyes.

She looked different somehow; perhaps because he'd never seen her wearing a heavy coat, or perhaps because her face seemed tired and pale. But her loveliness still took his breath away. Her long raven hair fell down over her shoulders from beneath a tartan bonnet, and her eyelashes flickered gently as she concentrated on her book.

He rapped on the window and some of the people in the compartment looked up to see who or what it was; but she seemed too engrossed in her book to notice. He rapped again, this time harder, causing the large woman next to the window to look up in alarm and then whisper some words of disapproval to the man sitting next to her. Sele looked up and turned to see what the commotion was about. Her large, almond eyes opened wide in surprise, then disbelief, and finally joy. He saw her lips move and realized that she was saying his name, over and over again. Moments later she was out of the carriage and in his arms, standing on the station platform, her arms around his neck, smothering his face with kisses in a way not usually associated with missionary ladies.

10

8 September 1890 – The Tasman Sea

Sele returned from her speaking tour four weeks later. She had addressed gatherings in regional centres all over New South Wales, telling the story of her experiences amongst the people of Torres Strait and beyond. It had been physically exhausting, weakened as she was by the aftereffects of malaria, but emotionally invigorating as she witnessed a developing groundswell of public opinion against the abuses of the trade in native labour. But the thing that thrilled her most was the knowledge that the man she'd inwardly loved for the past five years was waiting for her in Sydney.

Michael was waiting for her at Sydney's Central Railway Station when her overnight train from Wagga Wagga arrived. They greeted each other with that special joy known only to those whose broken dreams have been restored to life. They had breakfast together in the station dining room, then took a hansom cab to Walsh Bay where Michael's schooner was loading cargo for the far north of Queensland.

'Oh Michael, she's beautiful!' Sele exclaimed as she stepped onto the wharf and gazed up at the graceful, white-hulled ship, with its long bowsprit and tall, raked masts. *Wahine 2* was 150 feet long and 24 feet across her beam. The bust of a Polynesian maiden – a wahine – surmounted her bow. Everything about her evoked thoughts of coral seas and balmy trade winds.

'She is indeed, but not as beautiful as you, my love,' Michael said.

Sele smiled happily. 'I can't wait to go aboard. Do I have your permission, Captain?'

'You do indeed, ma'am.'

The ship's Chinese cook served them lunch under a canvas awning, rigged across the mainmast's boom. He'd set up a table and chairs near the taff rail on the afterdeck, from where they could gaze out over the shimmering water of Sydney Harbour, its surface gently ruffled by a soft nor'easterly breeze.

'You really do mean it when you say that you want to be part of my work?' she said.

'Of course. You'll establish your school there in Refuge Bay, and I'll get on with running my business and being the police magistrate.'

'But are you sure you won't resent my work and the need for me to be seen to be *"beyond reproach"* as the Bible puts it?'

Michael threw his head back and laughed. 'I think you think that I'm too much of a rogue to change my ways.'

'Of course not, Michael! I've never thought of you as a rogue.'

'But you haven't exactly thought of me as a missionary, have you?'

'Well…no. But you wouldn't be a missionary. You'd just be married to one.'

'But I'd be the only husband of a lady missionary who isn't one himself. Are you sure you won't mind that?'

She turned to him, tears in her eyes as she took his face in her hands. 'Oh, my darling Michael. I love you so much. I want so much for God to approve of us getting married.'

He looked deeply into her eyes and said, 'Sele, I will never willingly cause you pain. I've not been the most religious man, but I've seen what you do and what you are, and I admire and respect you more than anyone I've ever known. I may be a poor excuse for a God-fearing man, but if anybody could make me want to be one, it's you.'

'Oh, Michael! Do you really mean that?'

'I do. And I'm determined to use my position to help rid the north of those blackguards who've brought so much misery to the people you're trying to help.'

'Oh, Michael, darling. But I want you to follow Christ because you want to – not just to please me.'

'Sele, my love, that's exactly what I'm trying to tell you.'

She laid her head happily on his shoulder.

'Now' he said. 'Let's speak no more about these things; just accept what we've been given.'

She smiled. 'Yes, we'll speak of it no more.'

And they didn't.

A week later, *Wahine 2,* with Michael at the helm, sailed from Walsh Bay, bound for Cape York. Sele, her speaking engagements now completed, stood at the taffrail waving to the members of the mission committee who had come to see her off. At Geoffrey Glaston's suggestion, both she and the committee had agreed that she would return to North Queensland and establish a school for promising young people from the islands who wished to further their education.

Once past Fort Denison the schooner heeled slightly to port under the pressure of the south easterly breeze and began to pick up speed. Michael spun the wheel and brought her closer to the wind until the jib began to shimmer. Then, bearing away slightly, he gave the order to sheet in the mainsail and foresail as she began to cut through the calm waters of the harbour towards the Heads - the two sandstone headlands that form the entrance to Sydney Harbour.

Soon they were in the open sea with that same south easterly wind blowing across the starboard quarter. Michael ordered the mainsail and foresail swung further out to port, maximizing the effect of the wind as they followed the north easterly set of the coast. Sele stood beside him, her arms around his waist, watching the great sandstone mass of North Head fall astern.

'You'll be getting cold, darling,' Michael said. 'Wouldn't you prefer to go below?'

Sele smiled and shook her head. 'It's such a beautiful morning; I don't want to miss anything.'

'May there be many more like it,' he said.

She smiled and kissed his cheek. 'Oh, yes; many, many more.'

For the next few days *Wahine 2*, powered by that same south easterly, made her way steadily north. After four days the air seemed to have lost its winter bite and began to feel almost balmy. They passed Stradbroke and Moreton Islands, beyond which lay the city of Brisbane, and a few days later, having passed Fraser Island, they entered the sheltered waters of the Great Barrier Reef.

They were now in that part of Australia dominated by the south easterly trade winds - balmy breezes that last from March until September and make sailing the Queensland coast a joy. Each evening after dinner, Sele and Michael would sit together on deck, their arms around each other, looking up at the myriad stars in the tropical night sky, dreaming of their future together.

* * *

One sun-kissed day they sailed through the Whitsunday Passage - a hundred miles of azure sea and verdant islands, which Captain Cook had navigated on Whitsunday in 1770. They passed Scawfell Island and entered its vibrant blue waters, where islands rise majestically from the deep, and the whiteness of the sandy beaches merges with the aquamarine of the fringing waters before blending into the deep blue of the ocean beyond.

They continued on past Townsville, lying sleepily beneath Castle Hill, and on to Trinity Bay and the town of Cairns, before setting out again for the run to Cooktown. With a steady breeze behind them they finally entered the Endeavour River, coming alongside the town wharf just before noon, where the Glastons were standing ready to greet them.

'We've been waiting for you for days,' Geoffrey said. 'The mission committee sent us a telegram telling us to expect you.'

'We've been watching every ship that crosses the river bar through our telescope,' Amelia added. 'Hoping it would be you. And now, here you are. And you look so well, Sele!'

'Yes. I'm quite recovered from the malaria, thank God. But the doctors say I shouldn't return to the islands because I could probably get it again.'

'And now you're going to set up a school at Refuge Bay,' Geoffrey said.

Sele looked at him with surprise. 'How do you know? It was only decided a few days before we left Sydney.'

'We received a letter three days ago. It came on the steamer that probably left Sydney about the same time that you did. It gave us all the news. We were so delighted, weren't we Amelia?'

'Oh, yes,' she replied. 'And that's not all. You tell them, Geoffrey.'

'I've been asked if we would be prepared to go back to Sydney where I would take up the role of General Secretary of the mission.'

'Oh, Geoffrey,' Sele exclaimed. 'That's wonderful! Are you going to do it?'

'We've decided to say yes. We'll return south in a couple of months. You and Dr. Wakeley will be the mainstay of our work up here then. I'm sorry we won't be around to see you as much as we would have if we'd stayed here. But we'll be back from time to time.'

She threw her arms around him and hugged him. 'Then you'll still be here long enough to do the wedding.'

'What wedding?' he asked.

She took hold of Michael's arm. 'Ours,' she said happily.

Amelia squealed with delight, while Geoffrey simply smiled as he shook Michael's hand and said: 'I am so glad for you both.'

* * *

While in Cooktown, Michael took the opportunity to visit his bank. The manager was delighted to receive the man who was now one of his most prosperous clients.

'It's good of you to take the time to drop in, Mr. Burns. What can I do for you?'

'Well, it's not an increase in my overdraft, this time. What I want is to redeem those pearls you're holding as collateral against my loan.'

The manager, not wanting to offend one of his largest account holders, cleared his throat nervously and said, 'Well, it would be necessary for you to consider selling some of your assets in order to do so, Captain Burns.'

Michael enjoyed watching his embarrassment. He remembered the times when he had squirmed before bank managers – back in the days when he had little money, and they didn't want to know him.

He pushed a folded newspaper across the table. 'Here, take a look at this.'

The banker opened the newspaper and saw that it was the financial section of the Sydney Morning Herald. There was an article that Michael had outlined in blue ink. It was headed, *'Shares in Melbourne Tramway Company Skyrocket.'*

He read the article carefully then looked up in astonishment. 'It says that those shares of yours are now worth nine pounds each.'

'That's correct,' Michael said. 'And it also says that the company has declared a twenty percent dividend, as well as giving a bonus of three new shares to every five held.'

'Which means that your portfolio of shares is now worth …' he paused to do a quick mental calculation… 'Around eight thousand pounds.'

'Quite sufficient for me to redeem my pearls, don't you think?'

The bank manager stood up and extended his hand across the desk. 'More than sufficient, my dear sir; more than sufficient.'

* *

Wahine 2 entered the channel to Refuge Bay two days later, anchoring close to the palm-fringed beach that shimmered in the morning sunshine. Most of Michael's luggers were still at sea, but Billy was there to meet them.

'Thought you forgot where you live, boss!'

Michael slapped him on the shoulder. 'I've got a surprise for you, Billy. Miss Saena and I are getting married.'

Billy began to cackle with laughter, dancing from one foot to the other.

'What are you laughing at, you silly bugger?' Michael asked.

'Thought you'd never get courage to do it, boss!' He continued to shriek with mirth.

'You cheeky sod,' Michael replied. Here, make yourself useful. Pick up these bags while I show Sele to her new home.'

Shaking with merriment, Billy led them up a path of crushed coral to the spacious bungalow atop the hill. It was, without doubt, the finest house in the settlement - made of red cedar taken from the rainforest behind the town and set high on hardwood posts that allowed the cooling sea breezes to flow up into the rooms above. Louvred windows opened out to a wide veranda running around all four sides and provided exquisite views of the palm-fringed bay and the turquoise waters beyond. The garden was filled with magnolias, bougainvillea, hibiscus and a brilliant, red flowered poinciana whose branches covered the front veranda.

'Welcome to Athlone, Sele,' Michael smiled.

Her eyes wide with wonder, Sele walked up to the house, overwhelmed by the heady perfume of the plants and the brilliance of the colours.

'Oh Michael,' she whispered. 'Is this really your house?'

'No,' he said. 'It's yours. I bought it and rebuilt it for you.'

He pulled aside the long strands of beads hanging from the beam above the doorway, allowing her to pass through. She stepped into a large, high-ceilinged room that felt deliciously cool after the heat of the noonday sun. As her eyes adjusted to the darkened interior, she saw that it was simply, but tastefully furnished, mainly with rattan furniture and a few heavier pieces of oriental design. Exotic flowers were everywhere, in vases, large seashells and coconut husks that hung from the rafters.

'Athlone; is that the name of the house?' she asked.

Michael nodded. 'It's the name of the place where my parents were born in Ireland. Do you like it?'

'I love it - the name and the house. It feels like it's filled with love.'

'It is – my love for you. Now, come outside. I want to show you my favourite spot.'

She followed him to a low hill, overlooking the bay, where another brilliant red poinciana was just coming into bloom. Beneath it was a flat block of marble, resting on two stones.

'This is where I used to sit looking out to sea, thinking about you; dreaming about the day when we would be sitting here together as we are now.'

'You always knew it would happen, even though I asked you not to try to find out where I was?'

'Yes. And I got this marble from a place called Chillagoe. They mine it there. Do you know why I bought it?'

'To make a bench, by the look of it.'

'Yes; but also to become our headstones when we die.'

She looked at him softly. 'Oh, Michael; that's lovely! But may it be many years before it's needed for that.'

'But that's not all I have for you.' He led her to a small writing desk standing under a window that looked down on the bay. He unlocked the top drawer and ran his finger knowingly to a hidden lever deep in its recesses. Another tiny compartment sprang open, and Michael reached inside and pulled out a small satin bag.

'What is it?' she said, wonderingly.

He undid the drawstring, and a pearl necklace fell into his hand.

'Are these the pearls you found in Maaso's hut?'

'Yes. You once told me they were tainted with the blood of his victims. But now they've been washed clean of all that.'

'Just like the pearl Jesus talked about in the Bible: the Pearl of Great Price!'

'Yes, and now they are going to adorn the neck of my Pearl of Great Price.'

Sele's eyes filled with tears of joy. It was not what she would have chosen to do, but she remembered that the philosopher Thomas Aquinas once said: "Man sees the deed, but God sees the intention." And, like God, she knew Michael's intention was only for good.

Epilogue

20 October 1890

Six weeks later, the Brisbane Courier Mail's society column reported the wedding at Cooktown of Captain Michael Burns, police magistrate and owner of one of North Queensland's most successful fleets of pearling luggers, to Miss Sele Saena, niece of the Supreme Chief of Samoa and a missionary of the South Seas Missionary Society.

'The bride,' it said, 'looked radiant in a wedding gown of white silk, loaned to her by Mrs. Amelia Glaston, wife of the Reverend Geoffrey Glaston, who officiated at the ceremony. She also wore a necklace of the most exquisite pearls, given to her by her husband.

'The wedding,' it added, 'was attended by scores of people, including dozens of Kanakas who lined the street outside the church singing gospel hymns in their own haunting, island harmony, as the happy couple left the church to return to Refuge Bay, where they will take up residence at *Athlone,* one of the finest houses on the Cape York Peninsula.'

The paper also reported that HMS *Seraph,* which had rescued several dozen members of the now defunct *Fly River Gold Prospecting Association,* stranded on the banks of a river in New Guinea, had found the remains of a ship, thought to be the *Hoylake,* on which the gold-seekers had left Sydney. 'The wreck was stuck on a coral reef near one of the islands in the Louisiade Archipelago,' it said. 'But there was no sign of its master or crew. They did, however, confiscate a number of artifacts from headhunters, who fled when a party of armed sailors approached their village. Amongst them were a number of shrunken heads, including one that was much larger than the others and contained two gold teeth.'

www.ingramcontent.com/pod-product-compliance
Lightning Source LLC
LaVergne TN
LVHW050930080826
845145LV00001B/291